Sometimes trust and love come with
JUST ONE TOUCH

Rogan Hunt would like to forget his disreputable history and rebuild his family's ruined estate in peace and solitude. But when a damsel in distress requires rescuing from highwaymen, he dares not turn away—especially when she is Lady Caroline Ware, the enchantress he has admired for years from afar. Yet when her father offers Rogan her hand in gratitude, the reformed rogue is taken aback, for he never believed this treasure could truly be his . . .

A marriage to the notorious Rogan Hunt? The handsome scoundrel puzzles her, *terrifies* her. But in the night, his words are kind and caring, his touch tender and patient, arousing a desire she never thought she could feel for any man. But there is danger in his seduction—for surrendering to Rogan's love could court a peril that waits in the shadows of her past . . . and destroy a remarkable passion before it takes wing.

"*Just One Touch* is passionate and intense . . . don't miss this book."
Samantha James, *USA Today* bestselling author

By Debra Mullins

JUST ONE TOUCH
THREE NIGHTS . . .
A NECESSARY BRIDE
A NECESSARY HUSBAND
THE LAWMAN'S SURRENDER
DONOVAN'S BED
ONCE A MISTRESS

DEBRA MULLINS

JUST ONE TOUCH

An Avon Romantic Treasure

AVON BOOKS
An Imprint of HarperCollinsPublishers

This is a work of fiction. Names, characters, places, and incidents are products of the author's imagination or are used fictitiously and are not to be construed as real. Any resemblance to actual events, locales, organizations, or persons, living or dead, is entirely coincidental.

AVON BOOKS
An Imprint of HarperCollins*Publishers*
10 East 53rd Street
New York, New York 10022-5299

For my friends,
Rayna Vause
and
Jennifer Wagner

Chapter 1

Rage tore at him like a biting wind. He leaned over the horse's neck, the pounding of his mount's galloping hooves keeping rhythm with his thundering heart. Beneath the thin skin of civility, fury and frustration bubbled in a dangerous elixir that drowned out reason.

He *would* rebuild what had been stolen from him.

Moonlight lit the way as man and horse skimmed the boundaries of his neighbor's vast estate. Inside the elegant manor house, the duke slept peacefully, unaware that he held the key to a man's dreams—his very existence—in his hands.

The duke had no agenda; refusing Rogan's offer had been merely a matter of practicality, not a personal victory, and Rogan would not blame him for it. But the beast inside him howled for justice.

Leashing the beast was never easy. Deliberately, Rogan opened his senses to the land around him, sucking the fresh, cool air into his lungs, letting it serve as a calming balm to his boiling temper. The shadows of the bushes and trees surrounded him like old friends, and the darkness enfolded him like a warm cloak. In the sky, the moon shone like a candle left burning, and the stars glittered.

The beast slunk back into the dark recesses of his mind, snarling and reluctant, but obedient.

And beneath him, the stallion stretched its legs, eager to chase away the whispering of Rogan Hunt's demons.

Lady Caroline Ware tucked her cloak more closely about her and watched through the coach's window as the moonlit countryside rushed past. The urgent *heyah* of Denton the coachman and the crack of his whip told her he was doing his best to honor her request that they arrive home with all possible speed.

She glanced around the dark, empty coach and suppressed a shiver, wishing she hadn't sent the footman and her abigail and the guards home. But Mrs. Trenton's childbirth had taken hours longer than expected, and she hadn't wanted the servants to be away from their families for so long. All had gone home to their children while Caroline stayed at the Trenton home and kept her promise to widowed Mrs. Trenton that she would watch over the woman's other offspring during the birth.

She had expected to be home by dinner.

But Mrs. Trenton's ninth childbirth had developed complications, and so Caroline had stayed until nearly midnight to help Dr. Raines deliver the healthy baby girl.

The coach jolted, and she groaned as her sore back muscles protested. She huddled deeper into her cloak, hating the night, but hating far worse the fear that made her distrust every shadow. It had been five years, and still she could not shake the legacy her tormenters had left her.

Tired and achy from assisting with the birth, she sniffed back the tears that threatened, swallowed despair that she would never be able to have a normal life.

A husband.

Children.

A life of contentment where she would never have to be afraid again.

She wanted that, wanted it so much she was willing to climb mountains and swim the seas to have it. But the fear always stopped her. That craven, crippling dread of being touched. The panic that choked her and turned her into a whimpering, frantic animal.

How could she ever have children if she couldn't bear the simplest touch of a man?

The coach jerked to a stop. Unprepared, she slid to the floor in a tangle of skirts and cloak.

"Stand and deliver!"

Her blood froze. Highwaymen? Impossible!

Someone shouted. Denton's voice.

The crack of a pistol echoed around her,

vibrated through the coach. A soft thud sounded from outside.

Caroline cried out and scurried back into her seat, squeezing herself into the farthest corner of the coach. Her hair began to slip its anchorings, and she impatiently plucked out the hairpins, clutching them with white-knuckled fingers.

Footsteps. She huddled in her cloak, tried to make herself as small as possible. Then the door jerked open, and a brigand grinned at her, his uneven teeth a dull white in the moonlight. "Well, well. Good evenin', milady."

He reached for her and grabbed a piece of her skirt, dragging her toward him. Laughing.

He was laughing at her, amused by her helplessness.

Rage exploded out of nowhere.

She jabbed his hand with her hairpins. He howled as blood spurted, and he dropped her skirt. She scurried across the seat to the other door. He grabbed for her ankle, but she kicked him as hard as she could in the chest. He fell backward with a yell of surprise.

She managed to open the door, still clutching some of the pins in her hand. She slid from the coach, hesitated when she realized her only option for escape was the dark woods at the side of the road. A scuffling sound from the other side of the coach decided her, and she sprinted toward the woods.

An arm hooked around her waist.

"Just a moment now." The highwayman yanked her back against him, his breath ripe with ale and poor dental habits. "You're to come with us, milady."

Terror stopped her breath at the words. *Please God, not again!*

The brigand hauled her toward the coach like a sack of meal, her feet dragging on the ground.

Not again. Fury rose behind the words. *Never again.*

She jabbed upward. A yowl of pain rewarded her as the hairpins found a target in the villain's eye. He dropped her and clutched at his wound, blood seeping from between his fingers. She scrambled away from him on her hands and knees, then stumbled to her feet and raced for the woods.

Cries of alarm sounded behind her. She didn't look back, just ran as hard and as fast as she could. Then something hit her across the back, a huge weight that flattened her to the ground and knocked the breath from her lungs.

"Now then, Milady Bitch," a voice snarled in her ear, "let's get on with things, eh?"

Trapped on her stomach, she could do nothing as he rubbed against her, lewdly rocking his hips against her bottom. A whimper threatened to escape her lips, but she bit it back. She would not give him the satisfaction of showing her fear. But inside her mind, she screamed in horror as memories of the past rained down on her.

"We need ye alive for the ransom," he said, then licked her neck. "No one said we couldn't have fun with ye first."

A shudder rocked her, and he laughed. Then he rose. She pushed herself up on her hands and knees and managed to suck one breath of air into her starving lungs before he grabbed her by her long hair and hauled her to her feet. She looked up into his face; it was the first man, the one she'd stabbed in the hand.

"Let's get rid of those claws, shall we?" He grabbed her hand and gave it a cruel twist. She cried out and opened her fingers. The hairpins fell into the grass. "That's more like it," he sneered.

She fought as he tugged her back toward the coach. She dragged her feet, twisted in his grasp, but he had a good hold on her hair. She stumbled over the edge of her cloak, falling into him. He gave a snarl and jerked her upright again. Then he yanked the cloak from around her and threw it aside. She batted his hands away, but one of them curled into the bodice of her dress and ripped. Buttons and bows flew everywhere. He hauled the remnants of the dress off her arms, leaving her clad only in her chemise.

She threw back her head and screamed.

Her voice ripped through the night, piercing and long, until her captor's hand connected with her face. The scream cut off on a sob.

"Not so high an' mighty now, are ye?" he spat.

He towed her toward the coach. Denton lay in the road, a red stain splashed across his shirt. She whimpered at the sight. Her captor gave the body a kick, then laughed and continued on to the open door of the conveyance.

"You've got to drive," his cohort said, stumbling toward them, one hand clasped to his injured eye. "I can't bloody see!"

"You've got one good eye," the other man replied. "You can drive while the lady and I get better acquainted."

"I said I can't see! You can wait to take your pleasure until we get there."

"Ye'll not have her first!"

"I'm bloody bleeding!" the man with the wounded eye shouted.

"You'll live."

Caroline hung on to her sanity by the barest threads. The one brigand had her hair so tightly wound around his hand that she had no chance of breaking free. She hung from his grasp like a broken doll, memories of five years ago slamming through her brain and jumbling with the events of tonight.

Breathe. In. Out. As long as you're breathing, you're still alive. You can still escape.

She hung on to that basic truth with all her resolve. She had to stay alive. As long as she stayed alive, there was always the promise of escape. She stared longingly at the dark stretch of road that led home.

Something moved. She squinted, thinking it a trick of the moonlight but unable to ignore the spark of hope. Patches of darkness washed over

the road, shifting with the breeze. A soft, rhyth-
mic thudding reached her ears over the increas-
ingly loud argument of her captors. As she
watched, a shadow broke away from the rest, a
savior in a flowing cloak riding a powerful black
stallion.

"What the . . . ?" The villain yanked her closer
by her hair, making her wince. "Who the bloody
hell is that?"

"Go! Get in the coach!" One Eye screamed, running for the driver's seat. "Get in!"

The stranger withdrew a pistol, aimed, and
fired as he galloped past. One Eye let out a gurgle
and flew backward. Blood bloomed on his chest.
He didn't move again.

The stranger wheeled his horse in a tight turn
and charged back toward them. Her captor let go
of her hair and gave her a hard shove in the back,
sending her stumbling into the path of the stam-
peding stallion.

He was too close, couldn't stop.

"Get down!" the stranger shouted. Caroline
dropped into a crouch and covered her head with
her hands, waiting for the deadly hooves to strike
her. A rush of motion stirred the air above her, followed by the musky scent of horse. Then the
sound of hooves striking the ground beyond her.

Dear God, he'd jumped over her!

She rose, trembling, to her feet. The highwayman gave a shout of alarm as horse and rider
rushed the man. He raised his pistol. The stranger

kicked the weapon away with a booted foot, and
the brigand screamed. Cradling his injured arm
to his chest, he began to run.

Toward *her*.

Caroline darted toward the coach, the highwayman hot on her heels. She kept her gaze fixed on
the door to the conveyance, the promise of safety.
A movement out of the corner of her eye warned
her, and she dived beneath the coach just as her
would-be abductor tried to hook an arm around
her throat. His curse of frustration nearly made
her smile. He dropped to his knees and swept a
searching hand beneath the carriage. She shuffled
beyond his reach.

The thunder of approaching hoofbeats made
him curse. He jumped to his feet and ran. She
could see only the inky black legs of the stallion
pass by her as the stranger gave pursuit.

Edging herself closer to the ground, she was
able to view the scene down the road. Her rescuer
easily caught up with the fleeing villain. He
leaped off his horse, his flowing black cape and
extended arms making him appear like Death
striking. The two men hit the ground in a tangle
of arms and legs. Fists crunched into flesh. They
rolled, kicked.

The brigand stumbled to his feet. Still on the
ground, the stranger rolled to his side and sent a
fierce kick at the back of his opponent's knee. The
villain howled and dropped like a stone. Her rescuer rolled to his hands and knees and pushed to

his feet. The highwayman fumbled at his boot and then staggered up. Moonlight gleamed on the knife he held.

The stranger shrugged off his cloak and wrapped it around his arm, dropping into the fighting stance of a man who had clearly faced a knife before. The villain sneered and swiped. The stranger sidestepped. Both men circled each other. The knife wielder slashed again, and her rescuer evaded, bending backward as the blade skimmed where his throat would have been. He came back in the same movement, grabbing the brigand's knife hand and twisting. The knife fell to the ground even as the thief swung around with his other hand and struck a blow to her rescuer's jaw.

The stranger's head whipped to the side, and for an instant Caroline caught a glimpse of his face.

Rogan Hunt.

She knew him, had seen him at Belvingham several times. Had watched him . . .

His handsome features twisted into a snarl, and he came back around and slammed his knee into the brigand's stomach. The villain dropped to his knees, gasping for breath. Rogan kneed him again, this time in the chin.

Her assailant fell backward and did not move again.

Rogan stood there for a moment, chest heaving like that of a stallion who'd been given its head, and looked down on the defeated highwayman.

After a moment he seemed to decide that the ruffian posed no more danger, and he turned toward the coach.

Caroline stayed where she was. Her heart pounded like thunder in her ears, and her fingers clawed into the dirt of the road. She knew that it was safe to come out, that she was acquainted with her rescuer. Yet she still couldn't seem to move.

She began to tremble as she heard his footsteps, yet he didn't come near the coach. She could hear the soft shuffling as he moved somewhere nearby. What was he doing? Was he searching for a weapon? Robbing the bodies? Her imagination exploded with frantic possibilities.

The noises drifted closer. His booted feet came into her line of sight, then stopped with a soft scrape. "Come out, Lady Caroline."

He knew who she was. Panic threatened, and a whimper escaped her throat. He would . . . he would . . .

"Lady Caroline," he said again, his voice gentle and soft with a hint of Ireland, "your man is injured."

"Denton?" She barely whispered the word.

"Aye, Denton. I suggest we take him to Dr. Raines in the village if we are to save his life, but I fear we cannot do that as long as you remain underneath our transportation."

She rested her forehead on the ground. Denton was alive and needed a physician, and here she cowered like a child beneath the coach that would

get him there. She took a deep breath. And
another. The ghosts of the past drifted away, and
she slowly became grounded in the here and now.

"I'm coming out."

She edged out from beneath the coach. Strong
male fingers closed around her arm and nearly
sent her back into terror. But no, he was just helping her to her feet. He released her the instant she
had her balance.

"Are you injured?" He swept her tangled dark
hair out of her face, then immediately dropped
his hand to his side and searched her expression
for a clue to her state. His eyes looked dark in the
moonlight, but she knew they were gray. Storm-
cloud gray.

"No . . . no, they didn't hurt me."

"Are you certain?" He cast a quick glance down
her body, and she suddenly realized that she was
standing in front of him in nothing more than her
chemise—and that he had taken great care to look
only at her face until this moment. "If they hurt
you—in *any* way—" he began, his expression
darkening.

"No." Face flooding with heat, she averted her
gaze. "They were just . . . well, it doesn't matter.
Denton needs help."

His mouth tightened. "It matters."

He peeled off the cloak wrapped around his
arm and shook it out. As he settled it around her
shoulders, she realized it was still warm from his
body.

"Now we shall see to your man."

Clutching the cloak closed with clenched fingers, she nodded.

They made their way to Denton. Rogan dropped to his knees and tore open the man's bloody clothing. The bullet had ripped a hole near his heart, and blood oozed from the wound.

"How bad is it?" she whispered, bile rising in her throat.

"Bad enough." He leaned his ear close to Denton's lips and gave a short nod. " 'Tis a miracle he didn't die of it. Help me carry him to the coach."

He rose and went to the coachman's head, and Caroline moved to his feet. Rogan slid his hands beneath Denton's arms and lifted. The injured man groaned, and Rogan sent her a devastating grin that made her heart splutter even under such grim circumstances. "Still alive to complain about it, isn't he? Take his feet now and help me."

At her rescuer's instruction, Caroline curled her arms around Denton's legs as if he were an armful of firewood. The cloak slid off her shoulders, but she ignored it. Denton's life was at stake. This was no time for modesty.

Together they shuffled toward the coach.

The woman tempted him beyond all reason.

Rogan looked down at the bloody chest of the man he carried so as to keep his mind off his companion. He could have easily carried the smaller man by himself. He had only asked for Caroline's help to keep her attention focused on something besides her ordeal. His strategy seemed to be working; she hadn't succumbed to vapors and had set her mind to the task at hand.

But had he known the strain her scantily clad presence would put on his willpower, he would have wrapped her up in his cloak and tucked her into the coach from the first. Lady Caroline in her shift was a vision that would keep a man warm and smiling on a winter's night. How many times had he fantasized about her looking this way?

She stumbled, and Denton lurched in his arms. He stopped. "Are you all right?"

"Yes." She met his gaze, and though he saw fear in her lovely dark eyes, she wasn't giving in to it. She shifted her grip on Denton's legs, pulling them more tightly against her body and inadvertently plumping her small, firm breasts in a tantalizing display. "I'm ready."

He swallowed hard and looked away. "Let's move along then."

Together they managed to get Denton to the coach. Rogan frowned at the narrow doorway.

"Perhaps I could go in through the other side," she suggested. "I could pull him in, and you can push him from this side."

"Good idea."

She set down the coachman's feet and scurried to the other side of the coach. The equipage creaked as she climbed inside. Then she was there in the doorway, pressing against his back as she reached around him to grab Denton's shoulders. Rogan eased to the side, wrapping his arms around the injured man and pushing as she pulled until the coachman's head and shoulders rested inside the coach.

"Do you have him? I need to get his legs."

She nodded, breathing hard as she strained to keep her hold on a man twice her size. Rogan shifted his grip to Denton's legs and shoved, sending Caroline tumbling backward with the coachman on top of her. But he was in.

Rogan squeezed into the coach and rolled Denton aside; with a hand on her arm, he helped Caroline to slide out from under the dead weight. "We need to get him on the seat."

She nodded and moved to Denton's feet. Rogan crouched and took the upper body. With a great heave, they hauled the man onto the seat. The task complete, Caroline fell back onto the opposite bench with a sigh of relief. Rogan bent over Denton and checked his wound. "He's begun to bleed again."

"What do we do?"

He glanced at her and began to untie his neck cloth. "You're going to have to keep pressure on the wound while I drive us to the village."

"All right."

He yanked the cravat from around his neck and folded it several times, then laid it over Denton's wound. "Come here and hold this. I'm afraid you'll have to sit on the floor."

"That's all right." She came to kneel beside him. "Just show me what to do."

"Keep the pressure on. Like this." He took her hand and pressed her palm against the makeshift bandage. A red stain crept across the snowy material. "Blast it, he's bleeding too much. We'll need another bandage."

"My dress is outside," she said, her gaze focused on the sweat beading Denton's upper lip. "He tore it to pieces, so it's only useful for bandages now."

"I'll get it." He hopped from the coach and glanced back at her. "You've been very brave tonight, Lady Caroline."

"We survived, Mr. Hunt," she said quietly, startling him with the use of his name. "And if we hurry, Denton might survive as well."

He nodded and went to finish what must be done.

Chapter 2

Everything seemed almost normal.

A bizarre peace had settled over her, a quiet numbness that silenced the panic. The steady clop of the horses' hooves, the creaking of the coach as they rushed toward the village—why, it could have been just another day when she went about her charitable works.

Except, of course, for the fact that she wore only her chemise and her cloak, and that Denton's life bled out from beneath the torn piece of her dress that she pressed against his wound.

Rogan had fetched her cloak for her when he'd brought back the dress. He'd handed the garment to her without a word and as she'd hurried to cover herself, he'd proceeded to tear her favorite yellow muslin into bandages. Halfway into the journey she'd already gone through several strips of material, removing the old, blood-soaked pads every few minutes and replacing them with clean ones. Her coachman still breathed—though not steadily—and she worried about the paleness of his flesh and the fever that misted his face with sweat.

Rogan would get them to Dr. Raines before it was too late. She was sure of it. She dared not think otherwise.

Tossing aside a bloodied bandage, she folded another strip into a neat square and pressed it with her palm against Denton's wound. She didn't want to think about what might have happened to them had Rogan not found them. Denton would certainly have died, while she . . .

She swallowed hard, pushed back the painful memories. Best not to dwell on that. Denton needed her.

Deliberately she turned her thoughts to Rogan Hunt. She had formally made his acquaintance weeks before, when he'd come to offer to buy a mare from her father. *Her* mare, Destiny. But she had watched him before that, every time she'd seen him in the village. She'd nearly fainted the day he'd first visited Belvingham to offer to buy Destiny. Her father had refused that offer and the next two, but she had seen the determination in Rogan's face and knew he wouldn't give up.

Of course she knew why he wanted the mare. Destiny had been bred and raised by Rogan's family. By Rogan himself, in fact. And everyone knew the Hunts were the best horse breeders in England. Well, at least they had been.

Even cloistered away in the country as she was, she'd heard the gossip. Rogan's father and brother, both wastrels from the sound of it, had sold off all the valuable stock while Rogan had been away fighting Napoleon on the Peninsula. Not that he could have stopped the sale anyway, being the second son, but he had loved those horses, had made them his life. Everyone had thought he would pick up the hell-raising lifestyle of his prewar days and drown his sorrows in the bottle when he found out what his family had done.

But Rogan had surprised everyone by electing not to pick up the life of depravity he had once embraced. Instead he had shut himself away from people, causing even more talk with his brooding solitude. Eventually she learned that he planned to start his own stables, using a small estate he had inherited from his late aunt. And he wanted Destiny to be the foundation of his new breeding program.

Deep inside, she applauded his determination. It made her admire him even more. But, darn it, Destiny was *her* horse now.

The coach slowed, and she rose up on her knees as they swept past the shadowed outlines of the familiar village buildings. Most were dark, though down at the end of the street she could hear music and laughter coming from the taproom at the inn. Rogan drove on, passing the inn, and then turned, pulling up quietly behind the physician's house.

The coach lurched as he climbed down from the driver's seat. Then the door opened, and he stood there, a tall shadowy figure whose face she could barely make out with the moonlight behind him. "How is he?" he asked softly.

"Still bleeding," she whispered back.

He murmured what might have been a curse, then climbed into the coach. Keeping pressure on the bandage, she shuffled aside as he knelt by the coachman's head and checked his pulse with two fingers at the side of Denton's neck. "Not good."

He swung away to descend from the coach. She laid her free hand on his arm. "Mr. Hunt."

He froze, whipped his head around to stare at her, even as she realized what she had done. She was touching him. She never touched anyone, except her father. Her fingers began to tremble, but she left them resting on his coat sleeve. "Thank you."

He said nothing, and she couldn't make out his expression in the dark, so she stammered on. "I . . . once Dr. Raines sees me here, we won't be alone anymore, so I just wanted to express my gratitude now. You saved me from . . . well, you saved both of us, and I thank you."

Silence stretched between them, though her heartbeat pounded in her ears. Then he slowly lifted her hand from his sleeve and brought her fingers to his mouth. His lips were soft, his breath warm, and the kiss a mere brushing of his mouth against her knuckles. But the gentle squeeze of his hand around hers before he released her spoke volumes.

"I'll be fetching the doctor," he said, his voice rough and the faint Irish accent more pronounced than before. "I'm certain Mrs. Raines has a dress you can borrow."

"Yes." She lowered her hand to her side, cleared her throat. "I'm certain she does."

"Stay in the coach until I come for you." He climbed out and shut the door, then hurried toward the doctor's house.

In the darkness of the coach, Caroline flexed her tingling fingers. Then she closed her hand into a fist, holding on to the moment.

Rogan was never so grateful for the darkness as he strode up to the doctor's door and pounded on it. With one small touch, the girl had ripped his carefully maintained control to shreds.

Ever since the first day he'd seen her at her father's estate, he'd been drawn to Lady Caroline. He knew her history; everyone knew. Her kidnapping and rescue at the age of fifteen had fueled the gossips for weeks.

The ordeal had resulted in a young woman who'd tried to continue a normal life. A debutante who'd collapsed of the vapors at her come-out ball. A girl who sequestered herself away from society on her father's estate—an estate patrolled by guards and dogs.

The day he'd first seen her, her delicate looks had stopped his heart. She was so petite and slender, her heart-shaped face dominated by large brown eyes that made a man want to protect her. Shadows lurked in those eyes, horrible memories. He wanted to fold her into his arms, make that somber mouth smile, drive the fear away. But the same fragility that drew him to her was also the reason he had to keep his distance.

Lady Caroline was a dream he could never have, even if their difference in station had not forbidden the match.

He heard someone stir inside the house. Breathing deeply, he reined in his churning emotions. He hadn't been touched so gently, so tenderly, in a very long time. It had shattered him, had smashed down the walls he had so painstakingly constructed to hold back the beast in him.

He clenched his fist and pounded again, taking grim satisfaction in the thud of his hand against the wood. He'd managed to thwart the highwaymen with cold deliberation rather than insane fury, and yet five minutes in Lady Caroline's company had his carefully erected barriers crumbling. He had to forget about her; he knew what he was, and he didn't deserve such sweetness.

He glanced back at the carriage just as someone opened the door to the house. Light spilled out into the night, illuminating the well-sprung conveyance, glittering off the ducal crest mounted on the door.

A reminder of what could never be.

He turned back to see young Dr. Raines standing in the doorway, his brown hair mussed and spectacles hanging off his nose as he haphazardly shoved his shirttails into the waist of his trousers. "Yes, what is it?"

"I'm Rogan Hunt. A man's been shot."

"Rogan . . . Hunt?" The physician cleared his throat, clearly recognizing Rogan's name and the reputation that went with it, then nervously pushed the spectacles up with his finger and stepped outside. "Shot, you say? You didn't . . . ?" He shut his mouth with an audible click. "Where is he?"

Unfazed by the man's distrust, Rogan turned to indicate the carriage. "In there. It's a chest wound."

Immediately the doctor's uncertainty vanished, and he strode purposefully toward the coach. "Let's get him inside then." He reached for the carriage door. Rogan stayed his hand.

"I want to warn you that there's a lady in there as well," he said in a low voice. "She's been through an ordeal tonight."

"A lady?" The doctor glanced at the coat of arms on the door of the conveyance and blanched. "Good God, Lady Caroline!" He jerked open the door. "Lady Caroline, are you all right?"

Caroline knelt right where he'd left her, keeping pressure on Denton's wound. She'd pulled her cloak more snugly around her, and her long hair hung in tangles around her shoulders, giving her more the look of a madwoman than a duke's daughter. Yet she gave the physician a welcoming smile as if she were serving tea and not staunching the blood from a chest wound. "Good evening, Dr. Raines. I'm afraid my coachman has been shot by highwaymen."

"Are *you* injured?" The physician hopped into the carriage beside her, taking in her shocking state of undress. He glanced back at Rogan, suspicion flickering across his face.

"No, Mr. Hunt came along in the nick of time." Her eyes met Rogan's in an instant of warm communication before she sent a concerned glance at her coachman. "But I fear for Denton."

The doctor bent over the man and lifted the bloody bandages. "How long ago was he shot?"

"Less than half an hour." Rogan stepped forward. "I can help you carry him."

"Absolutely. We must get him inside at once. Lady Caroline, if I may—" The doctor pushed past her to take Denton's feet as Rogan squeezed his broad-shouldered frame into the doorway to grab his arms. Caroline sat back in the opposite seat and tried to make herself as small as possible so the two men had room to move.

"One . . . two . . . *three*!" The physician gave a soft grunt as they lifted the coachman and maneuvered him out of the coach. Caroline climbed out and hastened after them.

"To your left," Dr. Raines directed as they entered his home. "Now lie him on the table. And if you would please remove his clothing, Mr. Hunt?"

Caroline peered into the doctor's examining room. Rogan had begun to strip off Denton's garments, and Dr. Raines stood at a basin, scrubbing his hands. The sound of footsteps drew her attention as Mrs. Raines hurried down the stairs.

"Wesley, do you need me?" the pretty blond called. She had thrown on a serviceable gray dress and was tying her long hair back with a ribbon as she hurried toward the examining room. Her gaze fell on Caroline, and she stopped short in the hallway.

Dr. Raines appeared in the doorway, drying his hands off with a towel. "Amanda, please see to Lady Caroline. Her coach was attacked by highwaymen."

"Good heavens!" The doctor's wife came forward, taking one of Caroline's hands in both of hers. "Are you hurt?"

"No." She fingered her cloak, suddenly embarrassed. "Though if you have something I could wear . . ."

"Of course. Come upstairs with me."

As Caroline followed Mrs. Raines, Rogan stepped out of the examining room, fastening his cloak. "I've got one of the highwaymen tied to my horse outside," he said over his shoulder to the doctor. "I'll take him to the magistrate. Will you see to it that Lady Caroline gets home safely?"

A murmur of assent came from the examining room.

He was leaving? Caroline halted with one foot on the first step. "Mr. Hunt."

Rogan looked up, clearly startled to see her there. "Yes, Lady Caroline?"

She turned away from the stairs and walked over to him. He watched her warily, not moving a muscle as she stopped before him. She wanted to touch him again, to calm the tension she felt coming off him, but they weren't alone now. "I would appreciate it if you would return," Caroline said softly. "I would feel safer if you accompanied me home."

A muscle tightened in his jaw. "If you wish."

"I do wish it, and I'm certain my father will want to thank you."

He gave a jerky nod, then turned away with a swirl of his cloak and stalked from the house.

The Duke of Belvingham was being murdered.

Some would say he imagined it. Others might speculate that recent events had driven him to see enemies behind every bush and tree. But he knew it was the truth, even as his cold-blooded killer sat miles away in Somerset, smiling and drinking with his cronies, acting completely oblivious to the slow, inexorable demise of his victim.

Alone in his private library, the duke shook off the lassitude brought on by the late-night darkness. He hefted himself out of the chair where he awaited his daughter's return and shuffled to the window. His joints ached with the exertion, his heart screaming in protest as his lungs worked to suck in air. Clutching the window frame, he looked out at the night, at the fields and shadows of his estate, and wondered how long he had left to live.

"Bastard." The word wheezed through parched lips, an epithet spat at his distant, clever killer. At Randall Althorpe, his own flesh and blood, whose greed for the Belvingham title had driven him to murder—now, and eight years before.

His knees weakened at the memory, at the horror of discovering Randall's perfidy only weeks ago in the deathbed confession of one of the villain's former colleagues. Gripping the windowsill with shaking fingers, he somehow managed to remain on his feet, even as the face of his son flashed through his mind.

Stephen, drowned eight years ago in the estate pond in what had seemed to be a tragic turn of youthful folly.

But now he knew the truth, knew that Randall, a distant cousin who had stood second in the line of succession, had taken drastic measures to assure that he would move into position as Belvingham's only heir.

He shouldn't have confronted him. The duke's mouth twisted in a grimace at his own stupidity. Only sheer shock had driven him to visit Randall and challenge him with the truth. He'd seen the change in Randall's demeanor, how the amiable light had faded from his eyes, to be replaced by a sinister gleam. The agreeable boy he had always known had disappeared, to be replaced by a sneering, cocky weasel of a man who not only admitted to Stephen's murder but bragged about it as well. Because there was no evidence. There was nothing the duke could do to punish him. Heartsick, Belvingham had left in disgust.

Not long afterward, he'd slowly started to sicken.

He was being poisoned. He didn't know how Randall accomplished this; the duke took food and drink only from the hands of his cook, who'd been employed by him for some twenty years. Still he grew weaker and weaker, and the only thing keeping him alive was the determination to not let Randall win.

He gazed outside and shuddered to think what Randall would do to the estate if he inherited, to the tenants, to his stables.

To Caroline.

Beautiful, fragile Caroline. His daughter had been through enough horror in her young life. What would happen to her should Randall succeed in killing him?

Someone knocked on the door. He frowned, turned to face the portal. "Come in."

"I beg your pardon, Your Grace." Kerns, the butler, stepped into the darkened study, still properly dressed despite the lateness of the hour. "The magistrate is here. He wishes to speak with you on a matter of great urgency."

"Dear God. Caroline." The duke swayed, but managed to right himself by gripping the windowsill. "Show him in, Kerns. Immediately."

Kenton Docket entered the study with his usual

briskness. He sketched a bow, his balding head gleaming in the candlelight. "Good evening, Your Grace."

Belvingham shuffled toward his chair. "Mr. Docket, what's happened? Is it Caroline?"

Docket gave a deep sigh. "You've heard then."

"I've heard nothing." The duke slowly lowered himself into the chair. "But my daughter has not yet returned from her errand of mercy, and the magistrate stands before me. Just tell me she's unharmed," he beseeched.

"She's unharmed," Docket reassured him. "But there *was* an incident."

Belvingham took in a shaky breath. "Tell me all."

"Lady Caroline's carriage was overtaken by highwaymen. Your coachman was shot, but he lives. He's with Dr. Raines."

"And my daughter?"

"She was rescued by a passing rider. He heard her cries for help and incapacitated the villains before they could harm her."

"Thank God." The duke rubbed trembling hands over his face. "To whom do I owe my gratitude?"

"To Mr. Rogan Hunt. He killed one of the highwaymen, captured the other, and brought both Lady Caroline and her driver to safety at the home of Dr. Raines."

"And where is my daughter now?"

"The coach is but minutes behind me, Your

Grace. I felt I should ride ahead and advise you of the situation."

"You were right to do so." He signaled to a footman, who helped him to rise. "Come, we will meet them at the door."

Candles blazed in the windows of Belvingham Manor as the carriage made its way up the long winding drive. And the closer they got to the house, the more Rogan felt as if a noose tightened around his neck.

He was a man more comfortable with animals than people. He hated social situations and tried to avoid them as much as possible. He didn't like to attract attention. Yet here he was, riding beside Caroline's coach like some knight errant, about to face the gratitude of the Duke of Belvingham after having saved his daughter's life.

Clearly attention-attracting behavior.

He clenched his jaw as he noticed the group of people spilling out of the palatial home's doorway. The duke. Docket, the magistrate. Footmen and maids and the butler. Bloody hell, why hadn't he escaped when he'd had the chance? Why had he come?

Because she'd asked him to.

Like a splinter beneath the skin, Lady Caroline had slipped past his formidable defenses and taken his unworthy heart in her hand. He could no more refuse her than he could stop breathing. Cursing his own weakness, he dismounted as the carriage stopped before the manor. At least this would be the end of it. Then he could go back to his farm and his horses. Away from people.

Away from Caroline.

A footman scrambled forward to open the carriage door and drop the steps. Then he backed away as Caroline appeared in the doorway.

Rogan frowned. Did no one have the courtesy to assist her in descending?

The hem of Caroline's dress, borrowed from the taller Mrs. Raines, dragged along behind her as she took her first step out of the carriage. She glanced at Rogan, her dark eyes huge in her delicate face, her lips curving with a hint of intimacy, a secret that only they shared. Before he realized what he was doing, he stepped over and extended a hand.

With a whispered "Thank you," she wrapped her slender fingers around his and allowed him to help her down from the carriage. Her touch lingered for half an instant longer than necessary, just enough to make his heart stumble, and then Rogan turned to afford the chaperoning Mrs. Raines the same courtesy he had shown Caroline.

Watching the interplay from the doorway, Belvingham could barely believe his eyes. For the first time in five years, Caroline hadn't flinched away from a man. His throat clogged with emotion.

He noted the manner in which she smiled at Hunt before she turned away, at the protective way he leaned toward her, his expression for one instant betraying a longing that Belvingham was certain he didn't want anyone to see.

And just like that, the solution to his problem came to him, and the duke smiled at the newcomers in genuine welcome.

Chapter 3

When the sun rose the next morn, Rogan was up to his ankles in manure. Dressed in a shirt and his oldest trousers, he worked in the stables beside the two ex-soldiers, Grafton and Tallow, as they mucked out the stalls and mixed the feed.

The day had begun just like every other day, as if the events of last night had not happened.

But last night *had* happened. He could still smell the scent of Caroline's perfume, still feel the touch of her hand on his. Her father had been effusive in his gratitude, and Mrs. Raines had taken the role of chaperone most seriously, sweeping Caroline away into the care of her devoted servants, as if afraid Rogan might devour her charge.

She wasn't far off the mark.

He knew his reputation. His years as a hell-raising scoundrel still followed him, even after all this time. People still whispered about what had happened right before he'd been given his commission. And they talked about what had happened since. About Isabel. About his imprisonment on the Continent. The stories had made their way to England, adding chapters to his roguish history.

He hadn't taken it amiss when Mrs. Raines had insisted on chaperoning Caroline. Even he knew he was not the sort of man to be left alone with an innocent lady, and the more distance between them, the better. Once Caroline had retired to the bowels of the house, he had accepted Belvingham's thanks and then taken his leave, uncomfortable with the social niceties.

He had no business shaking a duke's hand or dreaming of a nobleman's pretty daughter. He looked around the stables, the way the sun shone through the chinks in the walls. He could smell manure and horses and the sweet scent of fresh straw.

This was where he belonged, sweating amid the sounds of shuffling horses.

A black stallion whinnied and stuck his head out over the door to nudge at Rogan's shoulder. "Easy, Hephaestus," he said with a chuckle, scratching the velvety black nose stretched toward him. "Your turn is coming, though I'm certain you just want to get out in the sunshine to see those pretty ladies."

The horse nudged his arm again, and Rogan stroked a hand down the satiny neck. Hephaestus was the only horse in the stable that truly belonged to him, a randy stud of sixteen hands that had cost him a good chunk of his modest inheritance. The rest of the animals were temporary residents, sent to him for training. The fees he charged helped run his small farm, as well as pay a small wage to the two placeless soldiers who had come to him seeking employment.

His mouth tightened. During the war, he had made an open offer of employment to any soldier in his company who might find himself unemployed when he returned home to England. At the time he had expected to be able to provide decent jobs to these good men at the lucrative Hunt stables. He had never imagined that he would be scraping a living out of his late aunt's estate, trying to recreate a dream that might well be lost to him.

For generations, the Hunt family had been known across England as the best horse breeders in the country. The Hunt line had been legendary, up until Rogan had returned from the Peninsula to find every last steed gone, sold by his father and brother to fund their drinking and gaming.

But he *would* rebuild the line. All Rogan's hopes for restoring his family's legacy lay with the stallion and this tiny patch of land. All he needed was a mare worthy of Hephaestus.

"And I know just where to find her," he murmured, resting his forehead against the horse's neck. "Now all I have to do is convince her owner to sell her to me for a pittance . . ."

"This one's full."

Rogan glanced up as Tallow dropped a few more pieces of soiled straw onto the pile that filled the wheelbarrow. "I'll dump this," Rogan said, stepping forward to grasp the handles. "Then I'll be back to move Hephaestus outside so you can do his stall."

"Better you than me." Tallow cast a nervous glance at the stallion.

"He won't eat you, Tallow."

"But does *he* know that? Captain, that black devil loves two things—you and his oats. And I'm not getting in his way of either." Pitchfork in hand, Tallow turned back to picking soiled straw out of the empty stall. Chuckling, Rogan hefted the wheelbarrow and easily steered his heavy load toward the stable doors.

The sun shone warmly on his face as he wheeled his burden away. The clear blue sky and mild morning air made him feel almost cheerful, despite how far away his goal appeared. Then the sound of hoofbeats on the drive carried to him, and he paused halfway to the manure pile, setting down his load and shading his eyes to see who approached.

Pray God it was not yet another recently returned soldier looking for work. Then again, a jobless soldier would hardly be able to afford the

fine mount that approached. Squinting, Rogan
made out the black and gold livery of the Duke of
Belvingham.

Well, well.

He waited as the rider stopped before him.

"You there." The servant cast a disdainful
glance over Rogan, then at the load of manure, his
lips twisting with distaste. "Where is Mr. Hunt?"

Rogan folded his arms and glowered at the
impertinent messenger. "I am he."

The man's eyes bugged with surprise. "Apologies, sir. I have a message for you from the Duke
of Belvingham." He slid off his horse and handed
over a crisp, folded piece of heavy paper.

Rogan took the missive and broke open the
seal, scanning the contents. A triumphant smile
tugged at his lips, but he wiped it away before he
looked at the messenger.

"Tell the duke I'll be there."

The stables were Caroline's world. Comfort-
ably clad in an old riding habit, she worked
alongside the grooms and trainers and personally
saw to certain horses herself. The horses had been
her salvation five years ago after her terrible
ordeal; it had been these gentle creatures that had
given Caroline a reason to live again.

Humming softly, she carried a bucket of hot
mash to Destiny, her favorite, and dumped it into
her trough. As the mare eagerly slurped up the
food, Caroline stroked her pretty bay-colored

neck and whispered compliments. The horse's
ears flickered as if she understood.

Caroline often suspected that she did.

Suddenly Destiny gave a whinny of welcome
and jerked forward, nearly knocking the empty
bucket out of her hands. Closing her eyes, Caroline took a deep breath and turned around,
already knowing whom she would see.

Rogan Hunt leaned in the doorway of the stables. The sun shone behind his tall frame, creating
a nimbus of light around his head and casting his
rough, masculine features into shadow.

"Good morning, Lady Caroline." He stepped
out of the sunlight into the building, arching a
brow as he noted her shabby attire.

She stiffened. Last night Rogan Hunt had
appeared the dark and daring savior, and she had
gravitated toward him because he made her feel
safe in a time of terror. In the bright light of day,
however, and with that intolerable glint of amusement in his storm-gray eyes, he didn't seem quite
so romantic.

Or quite so safe.

She gave him a polite nod. "Mr. Hunt."

He took another step closer, and she swept out
of the way, the bucket making a noisy clank that
ruined any chance for subtlety. Flashing her a
knowing look, he reached past her to stroke Destiny's nose. Her heart pounded. It was still there,
then, his curious ability to cloud her thoughts
with his nearness. She'd felt it last night and had

dismissed it as a symptom of her adventure. Yet it remained, disturbing in the light of day.

"I assume you've come here to offer to buy *my* horse again?" Irritated at her confusing emotions, she gathered her resolve and edged over to pet the opposite side of Destiny's neck.

"She was mine first, Lady Caroline." He leaned an elbow on the stall door and regarded her from his greater height. A lock of ink-black hair curled stubbornly at his temple. "And with luck, she will be again."

She forced herself not to back away from the determination in his voice. "Are you a lucky man then, Mr. Hunt?"

"Perhaps." He held her gaze for a moment, and she felt it again, the tension, the heat that seemed to rise whenever they were together. Her body quivered in reaction, and it was everything she could do not to run from the stables. Those sharp, smoky eyes missed nothing, and his glance fell on the frantic pulse pounding in her throat, lingered there.

She jerked back, her heartbeat skipping crazily. "Don't."

"Don't what?"

"Don't . . . look at me like that."

He gave her a gentle smile, but amusement flickered in his eyes. "Do I make you nervous, Lady Caroline?"

"No. It's just . . ." She laid a hand over her thundering heart and sucked in a breath. "Yes."

He studied her for a moment, then turned away to stroke his hand down Destiny's neck again. "How is Denton today?"

She blinked, thrown by the change in topic. "Better. You saved his life."

He flashed her a smile. "No, you did by keeping the bleeding under control."

She flushed and dropped her gaze, undone by the admiration in his voice. "I did what needed to be done."

"You kept your wits together, Lady Caroline, and walked away from your enemies, victorious."

"Thank you," she whispered. Torn between pleasure and apprehension, she couldn't look at him.

Suddenly Destiny leaned out of her stall and playfully shoved Rogan's shoulder with her nose, bumping him into Caroline. Caroline squeaked with alarm, stumbling back a step. Rogan grabbed her arm and steadied her, his fingers firm and strong near her elbow.

His flesh was warm where it touched hers. A fluttering sensation rippled across her skin, and she couldn't move. She glanced up into his face, torn between running away or leaning closer.

"It goes away, you know," he said quietly.

"What does?"

"The fear. It does fade after a while."

She jerked as if he'd shot her, yanking her arm from his grasp. "Who are you?" she whispered. "How could you know—"

"I've been to war, Lady Caroline. I've witnessed what happens to a man—or a woman—who's been through hell. And as for who I am . . ." He pulled a worn watch from his waistcoat and flicked it open. "I'm the fellow who has an appointment with your father to discuss purchasing this beautiful mare."

"An appointment!"

"*He* summoned *me*. Sent me a message early this morning. Bodes well, don't you think?" With a roguish wink, he strolled out of the stables.

Her father had summoned him? Did that mean . . .

"One moment!" She raced after him, silently cursing his long-legged stride. "Mr. Hunt, I pray you—wait!"

Rogan slowed, but not because of her plea. He seemed fascinated by something happening in the paddock. Just as she caught up with him, a piercing scream sliced through the peaceful morning, jerking her attention to the yard.

Mercury Mist, her father's new stallion, reared and pawed at the air. Stable hands swarmed around him, trying to catch the lead rope trailing from the horse's bridle. The huge gray shrieked again, sending the stable hands scrambling backward. The crumpled figure of a stableboy lay still in the mud, entirely too close to the beast's stomping hooves.

Rogan sprinted toward the scene, Caroline at his heels.

"Get back!" he snapped as he reached the paddock fence. "All of you, back away from him!"

"We've got to get Will!" one of the hands protested.

"You're just making it worse." The stable hands responded to the authority in his voice and melted away from the animal. Rogan shrugged out of his coat and tossed it over the fence post. Mercury snorted and pranced in place, tossing his head as he scented the new arrivals.

Caroline came up beside him. "What are you doing? You'll be killed!"

Rogan barely spared her a glance. "Trust me." He climbed up onto the fence. Caroline scrambled up beside him and grabbed his arm.

"You're not listening to me!"

He shook off her hold. "Lady Caroline, I've been around horses ever since I could walk. I know what I'm doing." He hopped down into the paddock.

"Mr. Hunt . . ."

Ignoring her, he slowly moved toward Mercury Mist.

Caroline gripped the fence so tightly that her nails bit into the wood. Rogan slowly approached the stallion, his entire demeanor calm and non-threatening. The horse pawed at the dirt beside Will's head, his gaze fixed on Rogan. The animal snorted, shook its head. Still Rogan approached, raising his hands in a reassuring gesture. Dimly she could hear him speaking, singing some sort of soft, lyrical words that made no sense to her.

Mercury's ears flickered, and he watched

Rogan, his tail swishing with impatience, his nostrils glistening as he took in the man's scent.

Rogan stopped just in front of the horse, still murmuring the strange language in a singsong voice. Mercury gave a kind of quiver, pawed at the ground once, ears perked forward, then back, then forward again. Then the horse lowered its head, and Rogan went forward, lifted his hand to gently stroke the animal's neck. With his other hand, he caught the lead rope.

Feeling the tug on his bridle, the horse tossed his head with a whinny of protest. But Rogan kept chanting, kept whispering in that musical language, and the animal calmed again. Then he led the horse away from the fallen boy, step by quivering step.

The stable hands raced forward and spirited the boy from the paddock. Rogan stood at the far side of the enclosure, both man and horse facing away from the activity, and he kept the animal calm until the injured lad had been safely removed from the yard. For long moments he stood there until the horse settled. Then he looked over and signaled for one of the grooms to take Mercury's lead.

"Amazing." The stable hand standing near Caroline shook his head and glanced at his mistress. "I heard stories that the Hunt family were wizards with horses, and now I've seen it for myself." He hopped over the fence and went to help the other stable hands.

Caroline couldn't take her eyes from Rogan as he walked back toward her. The breeze teased his black curling hair and molded his shirt to the contours of his chest and arms. As he moved, she couldn't help but notice he had the well-muscled thighs of a dedicated horseman. Color flooded her cheeks as she recognized the indecency of her thoughts.

He climbed over the fence to land lightly beside her, then took his coat from the fence post without a word.

She took a breath to calm her galloping pulse. "That was well done of you, Mr. Hunt."

"It wouldn't have been necessary if those bloody stable hands of yours knew what they were about." He shrugged into his coat, his face grim with foul temper.

Stunned by both his profanity and his brusque tone, she took a step back. "I beg your pardon?"

He noticed her movement and narrowed his eyes at her. "I won't hurt you, for God's sake. Didn't you learn that last night?"

Hot embarrassment flooded her cheeks. "Your manners are lacking today, Mr. Hunt."

"Is that so?" He cast a fierce, male glance over her that left her knees all but shaking. "Then allow me to alleviate the problem. I believe I'm late for my appointment with your father."

He gave a sarcastic little bow, and she watched him walk away. Despite her annoyance with his boorish manner, she couldn't resist sliding her gaze over him in appreciation of such a fine male form. If only . . .

With a sound of distress she turned away, grabbing the fence. What was it about this man? In all these years, she had felt nothing more than passing admiration on the rare occasion she had encountered a handsome man. Yet Rogan Hunt was different.

He had touched her.

She had touched him.

There had been no fear, no black memories crowding her mind. And now . . . good Lord, she *lusted* after his handsome form like some wanton! Despite his foul temper and lack of consideration for a lady's sensibilities.

She turned her head and took one last look at him, feeling as mesmerized as Mercury Mist and just as confused.

"Come in, Hunt." From the chair behind his desk, the duke signaled for Rogan to enter his study, then waved to the decanters on the sideboard. "Would you care for some brandy?"

"No, thank you."

"Wine, then? Whiskey?"

"No." Rogan managed a polite smile. "I make it a policy only to drink alone."

"Suit yourself." The duke gestured toward a chair. "Sit down then."

Wary, Rogan sat. The Duke of Belvingham looked older in the light of day, worn and weary.

He had clearly once been an intimidating-looking man, with thick brows and deep-set eyes and a great blade of a nose. Now his hair held more gray than brown, and his sunken cheeks and the tightness around his mouth betrayed his lack of vitality. He slouched in his seat, giving the impression that the furniture held him upright rather than his own muscles and bones.

Yet no matter his health, Belvingham was one of the most powerful men in England, and he wore that power with the ease of long familiarity. "First of all, Hunt, I'd like to thank you again for what you did for Caroline last night."

Uncomfortable, Rogan merely nodded. "I'm glad your daughter is unharmed."

"It could have been far worse, as we both know. You have done me a great service, and I am grateful." He regarded Rogan with steady dark eyes that seemed to size up everything about him in one hard stare. "I've reconsidered your offer."

Elation surged through him, but Rogan forced himself to show no emotion. "I'm pleased to hear it."

The duke gave a dry chuckle. "You might not be, once you've heard the terms."

Ah, yes. The money. Rogan's fingers tightened imperceptibly on the arms of the chair. "What are the terms?"

"I know your financial situation, Hunt." A cough shook the duke's fragile frame, and he reached for a glass of water on his desk. "Before last night, there was no way you'd have been able

to pull together enough blunt to buy that mare."
He sipped at the water, closed his eyes. After a
moment he opened them again and carefully
replaced the glass on the desk with a shaking
hand. His lips parted in a bitter smile. "But as you
can see with your own eyes, circumstances have
changed."

"You're ill?"

"I'm dying."

Rogan couldn't hide his shock. "But . . . a couple of weeks ago you were as hearty as a man ten
years your junior."

"Quite so, Hunt." Belvingham clenched his
trembling fists. "I'm being poisoned, to tell the
truth. Poisoned by that greedy bastard, Randall
Althorpe. And that's why you're here."

Rogan frowned. "I'm not acquainted with Mr.
Althorpe."

"He's my heir, a distant cousin." The duke
sneered. "Apparently I was not dying fast enough
for him."

Rogan digested this new information. "I
believe I'll take that whiskey now."

"Help yourself."

He rose and poured himself a generous portion
from the decanter. "Have you alerted the magistrate, Your Grace?"

"Wouldn't do a demmed bit of good," Belvingham snorted. "Althorpe's a clever bastard. I
haven't yet figured out how he's doing it."

Rogan paused with his drink at his lips, wondering suddenly if whatever ailment the duke had

contracted had also weakened his grasp of reality. "Are you certain it's Althorpe?"

The duke cast him a look of irritation as Rogan sat down again. "I'm not a madman, Hunt. I know how preposterous it sounds. I would never have suspected the boy myself except that I found out he's responsible for the death of my son."

Rogan put down his drink with a clink. "He killed your son?"

"So I was told by an associate of his. It was a deathbed confession, so he had no cause to lie. Quite the opposite, actually. And when I confronted Randall, he . . ." His voice trailed off as his gaze settled on a portrait of his son that hung on the far wall.

"Your Grace?"

"He laughed," the duke continued. "Never denied it, just laughed. And not long after, I began to sicken."

The utter certainty in the duke's voice shook Rogan. True or not, Belvingham clearly believed the tale. "And I take it there is no evidence linking Althorpe to your son's death?"

The duke gave a bitter smile. "Nothing. He killed my son, and he is killing me. The title will pass to him unless we discover an antidote. The best physicians in London haven't been able to help. And that's why I summoned you, Hunt." He gestured with a hand that trembled. "You were my daughter's hero last night, and I have need of a hero now."

"Forgive me, Your Grace, but I am at a loss."

"I am dying, Hunt, and the jackal who's killing me will inherit my lands and title. And my daughter will be at his mercy. I want you to protect her."

Surprised, Rogan reached for his whiskey. "What would you have me do?"

"I will give you the mare, Destiny," the duke said, watching him with canny dark eyes. "And I will include twenty-five thousand pounds . . . if you marry Caroline."

Rogan choked on his swallow of whiskey. "You want me to wed your daughter?"

"How else can you protect her but as her husband?" Pain threaded the duke's voice. "If I die—and it looks more than likely that I will indeed pass from this world if Randall has his way—then I need to know Caroline is safe. I will award you the twenty-five thousand pounds the day you marry her, as well as ownership of Destiny. Think of it, Hunt! Your problems will be solved. Not only will you be able to recreate your family's superior breed of horses, but by marrying the daughter of a duke you will also gain an entrée into society."

Impossible. Rogan finished his whiskey in one swallow. He wanted the money. He needed Destiny. But he had sworn never to marry, never to subject an innocent girl to the beast that was Rogan Hunt.

Especially not Caroline.

Her face rose up in his mind, fragile and beautiful, her dark eyes shadowed. Her touch last night had unraveled him, had filled him with longing for something he could never have. And yet the duke offered her. Through a quirk of circumstance, he could have Caroline. As his wife. In his bed.

For an instant he could imagine it. Passion. Trust. Knowing there was someone to take care of. Someone who would take care of him in turn. Caroline's small hands on his flesh as he taught her the ways of men and women, her cries of pleasure as he introduced her to the secrets of the bedchamber.

The beast inside him stirred. Stretched.

Ruthlessly, he shut the door on his impossible fantasies. It could never be. Caroline deserved more than a killer as a husband.

The duke's eyes glittered with hope. "Well? Answer me, boy!"

Rogan took a calming breath. "Your Grace, I am overwhelmed."

"And I haven't finished." Belvingham gave a hoarse chuckle. "When I die, my fortune—all of it—will go to Caroline. To her husband."

Staggered, Rogan managed, "But . . . it's not entailed?"

"The estates are entailed, but the wealth is mine, accumulated by me through private investments over the years, and I'll be hell's own jester before I see that murdering knave inherit it! It's going to Caroline, but if she isn't already married by the time I die, then I wouldn't put it past that schemer to wed her himself to get the money."

"I don't doubt it." Rogan rolled the empty glass in his hand. Part of him demanded that he take the money and the mare, which would enable him to reach his goal years sooner than he'd expected. But he knew he had to refuse the duke. For Caroline's sake.

Belvingham cleared his throat. "You've no doubt heard some rumors about Caroline."

"Some," Rogan acknowledged cautiously. "Vague references mostly."

"Most of the gossip is rubbish." Belvingham gave a harumph of frustration. "The truth is, five years ago my daughter was abducted. Her governess was killed before her eyes, and Caroline was taken for ransom." He met Rogan's gaze and held it, a wealth of meaning in his expression. "These men had her for four days before Bow Street found her."

"Four days?" Rogan clenched his fingers around his whiskey glass. "Was she . . . ?"

The duke let out a weary sigh. "The physician confirmed that she is yet . . . innocent, but apparently the villains frightened her enough that Caroline is now afraid of men."

"She was fortunate," Rogan murmured.

"Aye, fortunate!" Belvingham sneered. "The bastards only left her alone because they intended to sell her to a brothel. Apparently a virgin is worth a fortune!"

Rogan could think of nothing to say that would not sound cold or callous to the old man. He'd seen the results of brutal rape during wartime and knew that while Caroline had surely faced an ordeal, the outcome could have been worse.

Much worse.

But still . . . dear God. Caroline. How had she endured such an assault on her innocent sensibilities? No wonder she flinched from being touched. Knowing the truth, having watched her actions the previous night, he felt his respect for her grow. She would get past it eventually. She would marry, have children.

Just not with him.

He looked down at his empty glass and wished for more whiskey. Despite his feelings for her, he knew he couldn't agree to the old man's offer. He had vowed never to wed, never to expose an innocent to the curse of the Hunt men. And that vow superseded his desire for Destiny, his need for the money, his longing to have Caroline as his own. He would not endanger the lady to satisfy his ambition.

"I'll protect your daughter," he said, "but I can't marry her."

"You *must* marry her," Belvingham insisted. "Without the protection of marriage, Caroline will be vulnerable to the worst kind of fortune hunter, including that murderous heir of mine!" The duke leaned forward. "Damn it, man, you *must* help me. I know I can trust you with Caroline, to treat her with gentleness and respect. If you treat her with half the care you do your horses, she will certainly live a life of happiness and comfort. Come now, Hunt. All your problems will be solved with the simple uttering of the vows."

To control the restlessness that seized him, Rogan stood and ignored good manners by helping himself to a second glass of whiskey. "Your Grace, there are things you don't know about me. Things that would make me an unsuitable husband for Lady Caroline."

"I know more about you than you think, young man. It's true that in the normal way of things, a man of your social station would never be considered a suitable match for a duke's daughter, and you know it. But I need a man I can trust. Given your actions last night, I believe you are that man."

Rogan took a deep swallow of the whiskey before turning to face the duke again. "You honor me with such an offer, Your Grace, but I cannot accept."

The duke sighed, suddenly looking older and more weary than before. "Very well then."

Relieved, Rogan finished the whiskey in one shot and placed the glass beside the decanter. "I promise I will watch over your daughter. I will make it my mission to be certain no harm comes to her."

"You give me no choice, Hunt." The old man gave him a look that still intimidated, even with age and illness. "I had not wanted to bring this up, but you have forced me to do so."

"Sir?"

"Sit down, Hunt. We're not finished."

Rogan slowly returned to his chair, puzzled by the abrupt change in Belvingham's demeanor. At this moment the sick old man had vanished, and he appeared every inch the rich and powerful duke.

"I think you are unaware that your aunt Alice and I were good friends," Belvingham began. "Once your father inherited her late husband's estate, she often came to me with her troubles. Clearly, she didn't feel she could go to your father."

Rogan simply nodded.

"She was worried about you," Belvingham continued. "Your brother, Colin—he was too far gone when the lot of you came over from Ireland to claim the inheritance. Already following in your father's footsteps, wasn't he? I believe he's somewhat older than you."

"Eight years," Rogan answered, expressionless. The mention of his father only brought more clearly into focus all the reasons a man like him could never aspire to have a woman like Caroline.

"But you, Rogan. Alice said you had 'the gift' of the Hunts, a way with horses that had made your family the premiere horse breeders and trainers in England. And when you started showing signs of following the lifestyle of your father and brother, she wanted to intervene."

"She did intervene," Rogan whispered.

"Yes, that brawl at the Merry Maid. The night

you nearly killed Effingham's son in a drunken rage."

"Aunt Alice bought me a commission. Gave me a direction."

"And you went to the Peninsula to fight against Napoleon. But you ended up in an enemy prison."

"Yes." For an instant he saw Isabel's face again, pale and beautiful, and very dead. He closed his eyes and willed the vision away.

"You weren't ransomed when the rest of the noble sons were."

"No."

"You were ransomed later." The duke locked gazes with him. "*I* ransomed you, when your aunt Alice asked it of me."

Rogan sat frozen, unable to move, unable to utter a single syllable. He could barely comprehend the words the duke had just spoken, yet at the same time, everything inside him howled in denial.

"Did you hear me, Hunt?"

Honor. It bound him like chains.

"I will marry your daughter," he said, his lips barely moving.

"Excellent." The duke sagged back in his chair, relief sweeping over his face. "I will make the arrangements."

"Fine." Anger bubbled up beneath the surface, but Rogan reined it in with sheer will and allowed nothing to show on his face. He rose and bowed to the duke. "Summon me when it's time to sign the settlement papers."

Belvingham forced himself to his feet, his arms trembling as he used the chair for balance. "It would be best if you married quickly. I can procure a special license."

Rogan nodded stiffly. "I will await your messenger." Without another word, he turned and opened the door to the study.

On the other side of it, Caroline stumbled backward, having clearly attempted to eavesdrop. Rogan reached out and grabbed her arm, steadying her. She gave a soft gasp and glanced from his fingers banded around her forearm to his face. Her lovely brown eyes widened, and she tugged at her arm.

He released her, and she took a step back. She smoothed her disheveled dark hair with a trembling hand, tugging loose curls back into the knot at her nape. The stubborn locks merely fell back into tangled disarray. Beneath the shabby green velvet riding habit, he could see her chest rising and falling with anxious breaths.

"Mr. Hunt." She drew herself up and smoothed a hand over the skirt of her habit. "Am I to assume you've purchased a mare today?"

"In a matter of speaking."

Frustration flickered across her face. "Sir, please answer my question."

He bent closer to her. "Actually, Lady Caroline, I seem to have purchased *you*."

Chapter 4

Caroline took only a moment to watch Rogan walk down the hall, then she turned and hurried into her father's study. "Papa, what did he mean?"

The duke still stood, but then one arm gave way, and Caroline hurried forward to help her father ease back into his chair. He gave her a smile and patted her arm fondly. "Good news, daughter; I've just arranged your marriage. I hope you are pleased."

"You—" Her knees went weak, and she sagged into a nearby chair. "Marriage? To Mr. Hunt?"

Concern rippled across the duke's face. "He'll make you a good husband."

"But—"

"You need a husband." He held up a hand when she opened her mouth to protest. "Caroline, we cannot pretend anymore. We both know that I am dying."

"No," she whispered.

"Yes," he corrected gently. "And when I am gone, who will take care of you? The estate is entailed. Once Randall inherits—" He took a wheezing breath as if he choked on something distasteful. "Once he inherits, you will have nowhere to live."

A spike of fear pierced her heart. For so long she had lived, safe and protected, on her father's estate. The thought of being alone was nearly as frightening as the idea of marriage. She clenched her hands in her lap. "I don't want anything to change."

"Nonetheless, things do." Her father leaned forward and took one of her clenched fists in his hand, tenderly prying open her fingers. "Daughter, you're twenty years old. Many girls your age are already married. I believe Rogan Hunt will be a good husband to you."

"But what about—" She fluttered her hand, then dropped it, and her gaze, to her lap.

"He knows," her father said. "He's a good man, a strong man. I see kindness and patience in him—just look at how he treats his horses. How he came to your rescue last night. I feel certain the two of you will come to some kind of accord."

"I hope so."

"Perhaps if you got to know each other better. We could have him to dinner."

"Perhaps." She tried to smile for him, fighting back the panic.

"Caroline." The sternness in her father's voice had her meeting his gaze. "Daughter, I ask you to do this for me. Let me go to my grave without worry, knowing you are cared for."

She couldn't refuse the plea in his eyes. "Very well, Papa. Invite Mr. Hunt to dinner."

Rogan stood before the mirror and carefully scraped the razor along his jaw, flicking the suds into the basin in front of him. Tonight he was to dine with the duke . . . and his future bride.

He scowled, but then wiped the expression away since it interfered with the smooth sweep of the razor. How had he ended up in such a position? He had vowed never to marry, yet here he was, turning out his best appearance for the woman he had agreed to wed.

He dropped the razor beside the basin and grabbed a towel. As he wiped traces of soap from his face, he wondered how he was going to make this work. Tossing down the towel, he grabbed either side of the bureau, leaning close to the mirror. He searched his reflection for some hint of the beast that lurked within him. It was there, in the sharp features of his Irish ancestors, in the shadows in his eyes. Damn the Hunt curse anyway!

He spun away from the mirror and reached for his shirt. The curse went back in his family for generations. The Hunts were known for two

things: horses and a nasty temper. Most of the
Hunts were hotheaded, but when the gift for
horses manifested in a Hunt male, it was usually
accompanied by the blackest temperament of all.
Twice in his life Rogan had lost his sanity to the
kind of berserker rage that had endangered the
people around him. They had managed to save
Effingham's son; Isabel had not been so lucky.

Grief and guilt swept over him, leaving the bitter taste of regret in his mouth. He could still see
her slim form stretched out on the floor of her tiny
cottage, beautiful dark eyes staring sightlessly at
the ceiling as a pool of red gathered beneath her
head. He'd loved her, and yet she'd died at his
hands.

He swallowed back the emotions and tucked
the ends of his shirt into his trousers. From that
moment on, he'd sworn never to put another
innocent at risk. When he'd been released from
prison, he'd come home expecting to throw himself into working with the horses. But his father
and brother had sold every stick and pillow of the
estate to fund their life of debauchery, and the
valuable mares and stallions had been the first to
go.

Lost, he'd refused to join his relatives on their
path of depravity—that way only lay more death
for some other unsuspecting innocent. But then
Aunt Alice had died, and though he grieved for
this woman who had been more a mother to him
than his own, he'd also felt pitifully grateful that

she had left him her small estate. Without it, he truly would have gone mad by now.

Alice had always watched over him like a guardian angel from the very first moment he'd come over from Ireland as a lad of ten. She'd stood by helplessly as his father and brother destroyed everything her husband had loved, but when Rogan showed signs of following in his sire's footsteps, she had stepped in and bought him a commission. To make a man of him, she'd said.

And now he discovered that she'd bought him his freedom as well.

Obligation hung like a yoke on his shoulders. He took a cravat out of the drawer and slipped it around his neck, then began tying it in an elegant yet simple knot. He met his own gaze in the mirror and smiled grimly as an image of tying a noose around his neck was briefly superimposed on his reflection in the glass. Despite the money, despite Destiny, he would have avoided this course of action if he'd had a choice.

But he had no choice. He'd been able to stand firm against the offer of money and the mare, against the paranoid rantings of the duke about his heir. Even against his undeniable attraction to Caroline. But the duke had trapped him neatly with the slippery net of honor.

He only hoped Caroline would not regret it.

Panic washed over him, and he pushed it back. How was he going to do this? It was madness to wed a woman who feared men to a husband with a filthy temper like his. Would she cry the first time he went into a rage?

Just the idea of Caroline shedding tears made him want to shove the bureau out the window. This was insanity. It would never work.

But it had to. He had no choice.

With a snarl at his reflection, he turned to find his coat.

Never before had she dressed for a man.

Stopping before a mirror in the hall, Caroline stared at the stranger reflected back at her. She wore a dinner dress of pale rose with a hint of lace tucked discreetly into the uncomfortably low neckline. The dress had been a gift from her father, as Caroline possessed nothing in the latest style that might be suitable for a woman dining with her betrothed.

Her maid, Marie, had wound her hair into a fashionable confection of upswept curls, artfully threading a rose-colored ribbon through the coiffure, which somehow anchored it in place while making it look like the dark locks might come tumbling down at any moment. Pearls graced her neck and ears, and a cloud of attar of roses accompanied her every movement. The effect was one of innocent seduction.

Taking a deep breath, she stepped into the drawing room.

Rogan was already there, looking darkly handsome in his basic black evening clothes. He chatted with her father as she slipped into the room, but then he turned and looked at her, as if sensing her presence. The instant his eyes met hers, the breath left her lungs with a soft *whoosh*.

"Caroline, you are a vision!" her father said. From his chair, he signaled her to come closer.

She obeyed, bending to kiss her father's cheek. When she straightened, she saw that Rogan still watched her, a hungry ferocity in his expression that made her heart stutter. "Good evening, Mr. Hunt," she whispered.

He gave her a nod. "Lady Caroline. You look lovely."

Her tongue refused to form a reply. His very presence made her feel like a schoolgirl. For the first time, she wished she'd had the opportunity to socialize like the other girls of her age group, to learn to flirt and tease her interested suitors. Instead she'd spent those years sequestered away from society, haunted by memories of the dark side of men.

But ever since the highwaymen had attacked her carriage, it was as if she had awakened from a long sleep. She had become more aware of what she had been missing, more aware of the life that was passing her by. She hadn't wanted to wed in such a manner, but since her father had already arranged everything, and since the groom he'd chosen was a man she would have chosen herself, she had decided to accept the inevitable. To even enjoy it.

"I believe dinner is served," her father said.

"Hunt, do escort Caroline into the dining room. John Footman will assist me."

Rogan's mouth tightened, but he nodded in acquiescence and then extended his arm to her. Though his face gave nothing away, as she rested her fingers on his forearm, she got the feeling that there was more going on inside Rogan than his inscrutable demeanor would have her believe.

No doubt dinner would prove quite interesting.

Dinner dragged on with interminable slowness. The duke talked of the wedding plans—plans Rogan had had no part in making. Caroline barely said a word. Barely looked at him. She focused on her meal, cutting her pheasant into tiny, bite-sized pieces that she delicately chewed without raising her eyes from her plate.

His future father-in-law had arranged and paid for *his* wedding, and his bride couldn't even look at him. With every moment that passed, Rogan felt more and more superfluous. Manipulated. Used.

He hated feeling used.

Irritation grew. His replies became monosyllabic. Caroline cast him fleeting, fearful looks from across the table. A frown furrowed the duke's brow. The conversation eventually faded to uncomfortable silence.

Rogan ate his pheasant with methodical precision, each slice of the knife biting deeper until the metal scraped harshly against the plate. He put down his knife and fork, tried to breathe. His clothing suddenly fit too tight, his neck cloth all but choking him. The room felt too warm, too stuffy.

Caroline sent him another of those worried looks, biting her bottom lip with her small white teeth. The movement caught his attention, held it. He couldn't take his eyes away from her mouth.

He knew the instant she sensed his interest. Her dark eyes widened with alarm, and she pressed her lips closed. Still he watched her. His bride. She looked so beautiful in the light of the candles, the flattering rose-colored dress bringing out the lovely shade of her dark brown hair and emphasizing her creamy skin.

What would she look like wearing nothing but the candlelight?

Lust grabbed him with hot talons, twisting his loins into throbbing discomfort. For an instant he could imagine it, the two of them tangled in the sheets of his bed, her body trembling with pleasure as he introduced her to the world of sex. Was she the type to make that breathless keening sound in the back of her throat, the one that sounded like a crying kitten and drove a man wild? Or perhaps she was a screamer. Would she scream his name as she took her pleasure?

She met his gaze again. He gave her a slow smile, pleasantly aroused by his fantasy. Crimson swept into her cheeks as she read his expression, and her lips parted as if in protest. Then he read the gleam of interest in her eyes.

Followed immediately by fear.

The terror that flashed across her face doused his hunger like a bucket of icy water. What was he doing? He knew about Caroline. Yes, they were to be married, but with the way things currently stood, he knew he would be seeking his bed alone come their wedding night.

He focused on breathing, took a sip of wine to calm his overheated libido. He was no monster to be devouring his innocent bride. Wooing Caroline would take extreme patience and delicacy. He didn't want to scare her. He wanted her to come willingly to his bed.

Even if it killed him.

Caroline breathed a sigh of relief when dinner ended. Rogan's heated stare had left her edgy and uncomfortable. She thought to politely excuse herself and retire to her room, there to contemplate the strange events of the evening. But when they had all retired to the drawing room (the men eschewing their nightly cigars and port since Caroline was the only woman present), her father spoke before she could escape.

"I'm weary and would seek my bed," he said, remaining in the doorway with John Footman supporting him. "The betrothal agreement has been signed, and it would do the two of you good to become acquainted before the wedding on Friday. I'll trust you to conduct yourself as a gentleman, Hunt."

Rogan stiffened where he sat in the chair across from her, but merely nodded.

The duke turned his gaze to Caroline, who sat on the settee. "And should you need assistance, daughter, the footmen are outside the door."

Caroline flushed with embarrassment, because of both her father's lack of subtlety and her own relief at hearing that help was close at hand. "Good night, Papa."

Belvingham quit the room, leaving the door ajar.

She was alone with Rogan Hunt. Her fiancé.

She searched her mind for clever conversation, but found only flutterings of fear and nerves.

"Lady Caroline." His deep voice rumbled like a cannon in the silent room. "Should you continue to twist your fingers like that, I fear you will do yourself harm."

She glanced down, saw she was indeed clenching her fingers together like a brainless ninny. Deliberately she opened her hands, smoothed her palms over her skirt, and met his gaze with far more composure than she felt. "The situation is awkward, Mr. Hunt. I am not given to fretting and vapors, I assure you."

A smile quirked one side of his mouth. "I'm aware of that, Lady Caroline. Remember, I've seen you under difficult circumstances, and I've yet to meet a woman less likely to succumb to the vapors."

His sincere admiration washed over her like warm sunshine. "Thank you. But these circumstances . . . our betrothal . . ." She dropped her gaze. "It is . . . difficult."

"True." He sat back in his chair, stretched one leg out before him. "Everything happened rather suddenly."

"It's Papa." She sighed. "He's convinced he's dying, and he wants to see me settled."

"So he mentioned." He looked as if he would elaborate, then shrugged, apparently dismissing the idea. "It's done now. I suggest we both make the best of it."

"You don't sound very happy."

"Happy? No. Not happy." His lip curled. "Manipulated, maybe."

She frowned. "Manipulated?"

"I had no intention of taking a bride. All I wanted was a horse."

His comment stung. "Then why did you offer for me?"

"Offer for you?" He chuckled, but the sound had no humor to it. "I told you, I wanted the horse. But your father is a persuasive man, so I got both of you."

"He's . . . forcing you to marry me?" Appalled, she rose from the settee. "Then we can't . . . Tell him I've jilted you." She headed for the door, tears of mortification stinging her eyes.

"Damn it." He gave a growl of frustration, then caught up with her just before she reached the door, blocking her path with his big body. "I didn't mean it like that."

She wouldn't look at him, just stood there, tears welling in her eyes.

"Caroline . . ."

"No." She took a shaky step back from him. "Leave me some dignity."

"I didn't mean it." He held out a hand in supplication. "Please," he murmured.

She hesitated, poised to flee.

"Caroline." Watching her warily, he reached out and gently took her hand in his.

She looked down at their entwined fingers and tensed as if she would yank her hand away. One second. Two. But her hand remained in his.

"You can't know how humiliating it is to discover that your father has bought you a husband— for the price of a horse."

Rogan stared down at her bent head, unsure how to undo the damage of his hurtful words. "Caroline, I—" He stuttered to a halt, words failing him. "Curse my foul temper," he muttered. "I'm no good with people."

She glanced up at him, sympathy in her dark eyes. "Only horses?"

He gave a bitter laugh. "Indeed."

Her lips curved in a wry smile. "And I've been so long out of society that I'm not much better."

"Quite the pair."

"We are, aren't we?" She sighed and slipped her hand from his, moving back to the settee. "I don't want you to feel trapped by this, Mr. Hunt. You mustn't feel obligated, no matter what my father said."

He sat beside her, his knee brushing her skirt, and she scooted over to the far corner of the settee. "You are no obligation, Caroline."

"I certainly do not intend to be." She sighed and turned to face him more directly. "May I speak candidly, Mr. Hunt?"

"Rogan," he corrected.

A wrinkle appeared between her brows, giving her an adorable look of confusion. "Pardon?"

"My name is Rogan. If we're to be married, I think you should use it."

"Rogan." She tested the saying of it, as if it were a new kind of chocolate or a glass of fine wine. As if she were trying to decide if it was to her liking or not.

He found himself watching her mouth, waiting for his name to pass those soft pink lips again.

"Well." She clasped her hands in her lap and sat up straight as if she were going to recite her lessons. "I would like to talk about our marriage." She bit her lower lip. "If there is to be a marriage, that is."

"Do you still intend to jilt me then?"

He meant the remark to be teasing, but rather than stammer and blush, she surprised him by giving him a direct—and most serious—look. "After you hear what I have to say, you may want me to."

"I doubt it."

She took a calming breath. "I'm certain my father must have told you about certain events in my past. I want you to know that despite what happened to me, I have every intention of making you a good wife."

"Most comforting," he murmured.

She shot him a look of annoyance. "I'm serious, sir. These are things that need to be discussed between us—important things that will determine whether or not we will suit."

Chastised, he muttered, "Sorry."

"Mr. . . . Rogan, please don't make this any harder than it is."

The strain in her voice sobered him. "I'm listening."

She gave him a suspicious look, but then continued. "I have . . . problems that will affect our marriage. We need to discuss them now, before there's no turning back."

Pain etched her words, dissolving his amusement, his earlier bitterness. She was right; they were going to be bound together for the rest of their lives. Better to set the ground rules now.

But he couldn't sit by and watch her struggle to utter each word of a history that clearly brought her such grief. He stood so abruptly that she gave a little squeak of surprise, then he stalked over to the mantel. "Will it help if I tell you what I already know?" he asked, staring into the fire.

When she didn't answer, he turned to look at her. She was staring at him, her beautiful dark eyes alight with hope and relief. "Caroline?"

"Yes," she whispered, dropping her gaze to her hands. "Please."

Since she was clearly uncomfortable, he began to prowl the room, putting distance between them. "I know you were kidnapped when you were fifteen. I know it . . . affected you . . . to the point that you felt incapable of having a London Season. You came home to Belvingham and have stayed here all these years under your father's protection."

"Yes," she murmured.

"Your father has told me some of what happened to you." He took a chance and glanced over at her. She sat with her elbows resting on her knees, her face buried in her hands. "You and I will have to talk about it at some point."

"No!" Her head jerked up, her expression panicked.

"Not this moment," he reassured her. "But eventually."

The alarm faded from her expression to be replaced by resignation.

"We have time, Caroline. All our lives."

She didn't say anything for a long moment. When she did speak, her voice was so low he had to strain to hear it.

"I do need time, Rogan. If you can . . . if we can get to know each other better . . . maybe then we can have a . . . a normal marriage." She stumbled over the last words, a maidenly blush sweeping across her cheeks.

Desire stirred, awakening his hunger with a roar. The thought of sharing a bed with her ensnared his senses, seducing him. "Is that what you want?"

She looked at him, her dark eyes shimmering with longing. "Yes."

He took a step toward her.

She held up a hand. "But not yet. I need—"

"Time," he finished, halting. He curled his hands into fists. "I understand."

"I know it's not fair," she began.

"No. It's fine." He walked to the other side of the room, perused a painting of one of her ancestors without really seeing it. "We're strangers."

"Yes. But—"

He turned back to face her. "But?"

She stood up. "You saved my life."

He gave a chuckle. "You did some damage yourself."

She flashed him a self-conscious smile and took a step toward him, her hands clasped. "We went through adversity together. We have a bond."

"We do."

She approached him slowly, looking for all the world as if she would run screaming if he so much as flinched. He didn't move an inch, though with every step she took toward him, his body tensed even more.

She stopped in front of him, twisting her fingers again. She had her lower lip between her teeth, and apprehension filled her eyes as she looked up at him. Maintaining the eye contact, he slowly reached out and pulled her hands apart, leaving one of them resting harmlessly in his.

She made a little sound, of surprise, of alarm, of desire—he couldn't tell. She looked as if his slightest movement would send her running.

"Caroline," he murmured, "what do you want?"

She let out a slow, shuddering breath. "I want to stop being afraid."

"That won't be easy." Inch by inch, he turned his hand until it lined up with hers, palm to palm, their fingers entwined.

She glanced down at their joined hands. "I know. You're just holding my hand, and I want to run and hide."

"We can stay just like this." He crooked a smile at her. "No need to summon John Footman."

She cast a startled glance at the door. "I'd forgotten he was out there."

"I hadn't."

His wry tone startled a giggle out of her. She covered her mouth with her free hand, her soft brown eyes dancing with mischief.

Unable to resist, he stroked a finger down her cheek. "You should laugh more often," he murmured. She froze like a doe scenting danger, and he dropped his hand back to his side. "Sorry."

"No, it's all right." She cleared her throat. "You just surprised me."

"I like to touch you." He glanced down at their hands, then met her gaze with a warm smile. "You're beautiful."

"I'm not . . . I . . . oh, bother!" She took a deep breath, then looked him right in the eye. "I would like you to promise me that you will stand completely still."

He raised his brows. "All right."

She bit her lip again. "I mean it. Please don't move, or this won't work."

His blood stirred to life again. "You intrigue me, sweetheart."

"Goodness." She blinked, flustered, a delicate pink flushing her cheeks. "Please, Rogan."

"Very well. I'll behave."

She sent him a sidelong glance that made him want to carry her to the nearest flat surface, but he kept his word and remained still. Keeping a wary eye on him, she took a step forward—a step that nearly brought her flush against his body. His fingers tightened on hers.

She gave a squeak of alarm and stepped back again.

"No, don't go away." He relaxed his grip on her fingers. "I didn't move, did I?"

"No." She looked down, let out a weary sigh. "You didn't."

"You surprised me." He tugged on her hand so that she'd look at him. "I'm not moving, Caroline."

Still she hesitated.

"Come, sweetheart," he murmured. "You have me curious now."

"All right. But please stay still."

"Now that I know what to expect, I can do that."

She stepped close to him again, but this time he maintained control. Then she stretched up on tip-

toe and brushed a kiss over his cheek. "Thank you for saving my life, Rogan."

His heart pounded with the urge to pull her closer, to taste that sweet mouth. But then she jerked her hand from his and fled the room, leaving him hungry for more.

Chapter 5

She had kissed a man.

Caroline watched the countryside race by as her carriage—accompanied by three armed outriders—sped toward the village. She was on her way to visit with Mrs. Trenton and also to check on Denton, but her mind was far from her charitable works.

She pressed her fingers to her lips. She had kissed a man and then run away like a schoolgirl. What must he think of her? Did he realize it was the first time she had voluntarily done such a thing? Did he understand the significance of it? She thought that he did, but Rogan Hunt was a hard man to read.

There was a hunger inside him, something almost predatory in the way he watched her when he thought she wasn't looking. It frightened her.

And excited her.

She closed her eyes and slumped back in the carriage seat. Whenever Rogan was around, her emotions swirled and churned until she couldn't tell one from the other. Everything female in her jumped to attention whenever he entered the room. He was so handsome, so male. Strong, powerful, a man who lived by his own rules.

Yet there was a wildness about him. Something untamed that rode him like he rode that black stallion of his across the countryside. Passion, certainly. She'd seen—and felt the evidence of—his passions last night. He'd kept it under control so as not to frighten her, but part of her longed to see that uncivilized side of him, to experience the unleashed ardor of a fully aroused Rogan.

Anxiety rose up, quickened her breathing, yet the visions of her imagination continued to tantalize. Ever since her cousin Regina had gotten married last month, her cravings for a normal life had increased. There were obstacles, yes. But the longing remained.

Even beyond the fear.

She was tired of hiding, tired of being afraid. She felt like one of those sparrows who periodically flew blindly into the glass window of her father's study and ended up dazed or dead on the ground below. She had no intention of rushing forward, of knocking herself senseless, even metaphorically. Rogan was right; they had all the time in the world to learn each other.

And if last night was any indication, there was reason to hope that with his help, she'd find that open window and fly right through.

"What are you talking about?" Rogan frowned at Zachary Wiggins, the merchant from whom he bought his household supplies. Once more he tried to hand the man the money. "How can the account be settled? I have the money right here."

The little man smiled, giving him the look of an ingratiating weasel. "Not to worry, Mr. Hunt. Your future father-in-law settled the account yesterday. May I offer you congratulations on your upcoming marriage?"

"My future—" Rogan bit back an expletive and forced a polite smile. "Thank you, Mr. Wiggins."

"Always liked Lady Caroline," Wiggins commented.

"I am the luckiest of men." Folding his money, he shoved the wad of bills into his pocket. "Good day to you, Mr. Wiggins."

"Good day, Mr. Hunt."

Rogan made his way through the village, visiting every tradesman to whom he owed money. The story was the same everywhere. The duke had taken it upon himself to pay all of Rogan's debts.

And when he reached the tailor, he discovered that not only had Belvingham settled his account, but he'd purchased a new set of clothes for Rogan to wear at the wedding.

"I have your measurements, of course," jolly Mr. Fitzhugh said. "The suit will be ready in time for your marriage to Lady Caroline."

"Thanks," Rogan muttered and left the shop.

He strode down the street, nodding as people called out congratulations to him. Blast it all, had Belvingham hired a town crier to announce the news?

It was bad enough that he had been forced into marriage through obligation, irritating enough that Belvingham had insisted on arranging and paying for everything to do with the wedding without so much as consulting Rogan. But for Caroline's father to take it upon himself to handle Rogan's personal financial matters—that was outside of enough.

A man had pride, and Rogan's was rapidly being worn away by the force of the duke's arrogant interference.

"I say there, Hunt!"

Rogan stopped just outside the Hound and Horn as a foppishly dressed gentleman descended from a carriage in front of the bustling inn. Bloody hell, but this day just got better and better. "Beardsley," he acknowledged through gritted teeth.

Lord Beardsley brushed some road dust from the sleeve of his coat and sent Rogan a coolly arrogant look. "I heard you're marrying Belvingham's daughter."

"I am."

"Congratulations. Lady Caroline is far above the touch of a man of your social station."

Rogan bared his teeth in a smile. "It's a love match."

"Indeed? No wonder the duke arranged for a special license then."

Rogan stiffened. "Her father is ill, Beardsley."

"Ah." Beardsley gave a superior smile. "That certainly explains the haste. You wouldn't want the gossips to believe it was for some *other* reason."

Rogan leaned closer. "No. I wouldn't."

Beardsley didn't flinch, merely stood there with that patronizing smile on his face. "Would you care to join me for a drink, Hunt? I'd like to discuss that hunter of mine with you."

Surprised, Rogan backed down. "I thought you sent that horse to Hadley."

"I did. Now I want to send him to you. Let's discuss it inside."

"All right." Curious despite himself, Rogan followed him into the taproom.

It was amazing, Rogan thought later, how much a man's consequence could change when he was marrying the right woman.

Sitting by himself at the table Beardsley had vacated an hour ago, Rogan stared into his latest tankard of ale and contemplated the unusual turn of events.

Beardsley wanted him to train the spirited

hunter he'd purchased at Tattersalls some months ago, a horse he'd sent to William Hadley, another local breeder who, unlike Rogan, had no unpleasant family history to detract from his reputation as a fine horse trainer. The horse Beardsley had sworn Rogan would never work with—ever.

All that had changed, but not because Rogan had proven himself the better horseman. No, it had changed simply because in three days' time, he would be related by marriage to the Duke of Belvingham.

He swallowed some ale, hoping to wash away the bitterness that suddenly lingered. He should be a happy man. Not only was he marrying an heiress, but her family connections would help to better his business dealings. Any other fellow would be buying rounds for his friends at such news.

But the situation irritated him like a rock wedged in a horse's shoe.

He had not changed. He was still the same man with the same skills. Only because he would soon be wedding Caroline did his neighbors and business connections look at him differently. Not because he excelled at what he did. Not because he attempted to rebuild the famous Hunt line from nothing. Not even because he had left his life of drinking and brawling behind him.

Suddenly, because he was marrying a duke's daughter, he was good enough to do business with, whereas he had not been considered so before.

He lifted his tankard again, only to have it knocked out of his hands. The cup hit the wall with a clang and splattered ale all over the occupants of the next table.

"You bastard!" Hadley stood over him, his lean face taut with rage.

"New travels quickly." Rogan swiped a dribble of ale from his face. "Beardsley only left here an hour ago."

"He wasted no time. His men are even now moving King Charles to your pitiful establishment." He slapped his hands flat on the table and leaned forward, nearly nose-to-nose with Rogan. "How much did it cost your new father-in-law to steal Beardsley's business from me?"

Rogan stilled. "Belvingham has nothing to do with this."

"Doesn't he?" A resentful smirk swept Hadley's face. "It seems you're suddenly the golden boy, while the rest of us, who've worked long and hard, are left in the dust. How many more horses are going to disappear from my stables, Hunt? Who else will your new papa-in-law pay to change trainers?"

Rogan shoved to his feet, the chair screeching backward to slam into the wall behind him. Silence descended on the taproom.

Hadley straightened, but he didn't back away. "What's the matter, Hunt? Don't like the truth?"

"I prefer the truth. I'm still waiting for you to tell it."

Hadley gave a harsh laugh. "Pretending that

the duke has nothing to do with this, Hunt? Come now. We both know that your reputation is what's prevented people from bringing you their business. It's clear to me that your new relatives are smoothing your way to success with gold."

"I'm a Hunt. That's enough of a reputation for most people."

"A drinking, whoring Hunt? A wastrel of the first order?"

Rogan clenched his fist at his side. "A Hunt of Hunt Chase, Hadley. My family's reputation with horses goes back to the Conqueror."

"Yes, your family history is impressive," Hadley sneered. "Of course, that was before the Irish branch of the family inherited."

Rage simmered, awakening the beast. He tamped it back. "I'm sorry you lost the business, Hadley. Now do us both a favor and leave."

"Or what?" Hadley stepped closer to him, deliberately crowding him. The other man's eyes burned with hot emotion.

Rogan gave him a hard stare. His own temper had begun to boil, but the last thing he wanted was a fight in a public establishment. "You're making a fool of yourself."

"Me? *I'm* making a fool of myself?" Hadley laughed. "I'm not the one marrying soiled goods."

Rogan grabbed the other man by the lapels of his coat. "Apologize, Hadley. Now."

Hadley smirked. "Everyone knows the truth,

Hunt. Why else would Belvingham marry the girl to a nobody like you? Because no one else would have her, that's why."

Rogan shoved the man into the next table, sending patrons scattering. "I shall have to demand satisfaction, Hadley, unless you apologize at once."

"Pistols at dawn?" Hadley chuckled as he regained his footing. "Come now, Hunt. That's not our style."

"Your apology," Rogan ground out.

Hadley glanced around at their interested audience. "Very well. I apologize for calling your future bride a whore."

Gasps rose up from the crowd. Rogan fought back the urge to beat the sneering bastard to a pulp. He turned away.

"Thought you wanted the truth," Hadley called after him.

Rogan swung around and smashed his fist straight into Hadley's lying mouth.

The other man flew backward and shattered a table to bits as he landed, unconscious. Blood trickled from his mouth, but he lay still.

Rogan rubbed his knuckles, temper still simmering, and looked around the taproom. "Would anyone else like to make a derogatory comment about my future wife?"

Silence met his challenge.

Without another word, he strode away, the crowd parting before him. He paused to hand the innkeeper a wad of bills. "For the damage."

Jenson nodded, his eyes wide. With one last warning look at the patrons, Rogan left the inn.

Having discharged her duties to both her coachman and Mrs. Trenton, Caroline sat back in her carriage. Her last errand had involved visiting the local modiste to be measured for her wedding dress. Mrs. Denworthy had her measurements, but she had wanted Caroline to try on the basted garment so as to make sure it fit perfectly for the most important day of her life.

As she had stood there in the white and silver wedding dress, the magnitude of it all had finally hit her. Come Friday, she would be a married woman. Her life would change forever.

She didn't know if she was ready for the change.

She glanced out the window, then sat up straight as she noticed Rogan storming down the street. He looked neither right nor left, merely forged ahead with the intense concentration of the soldier he had once been.

And his hand was bleeding.

"Dear God," she murmured. Her first instinct was to duck inside the carriage and pretend she hadn't seen him. In what wickedness could he have indulged to cause such an injury? But then she remembered her resolve to take back control of her life. This man was going to be her husband. She would face him no matter what his mood or state.

"What is it, my lady?" her maid, Marie, asked.

"I see my fiancé." Caroline stuck her head out the window and signaled to one of the outriders to stop the carriage. The equipage jerked to a halt a moment later, and Caroline leaned forward and opened the door. "Mr. Hunt!"

At first she thought he hadn't heard her, but then he stopped and looked over at her, surprise flickering across his stern features. He didn't move for a long moment, then slowly he began to approach the carriage.

"May I offer you a ride, Mr. Hunt?" she asked as he reached her.

"My horse is at the livery."

"I can send one of my men to retrieve it." He didn't say anything, just watched her with that implacable expression. "Your hand is bleeding," she said finally, keeping her voice low.

He glanced down and flexed his hand, as if surprised to find it still attached to his body. Then he reached into his coat for his handkerchief and slowly wrapped it around the split knuckles.

"Rogan." He glanced up, and the ferocity in his eyes startled her. "Come into the carriage." She gave him a little smile. "I feel safer when you're with me, especially after my last trip to the village."

He gave a jerky nod, and she sat back in her seat as he climbed into the carriage. Marie scurried to sit next to her mistress, leaving the entire second bench free for Rogan. He settled into it,

stretching out his long legs, his face expressionless except for his blazing eyes.

The carriage seemed much smaller suddenly,
the intensity of the emotions emanating from
Rogan filling the small space with heat. Goose-
flesh rippled along her arms.

"Marie," she said, "please ride with Billings.
And send one of the outriders to the livery to
reclaim my betrothed's horse."

"Yes, my lady." Casting a wary glance at
Rogan, the maid scrambled from the carriage,
closing the door behind her with a snap. The
equipage rocked as she climbed up beside the
coachman, and then they were on their way.

Caroline studied her future husband. "Rogan,
what happened?"

He said nothing, just turned to watch the
scenery pass by.

"Rogan, please talk to me."

"What would you like me to say?"

"The truth."

"Ah." His lips quirked in a sardonic smile.
"The truth." He sent her a hot glance that pinned
her to her seat with its power and left her breathless. "Most people can't handle the truth, Caroline."

"I'm not most people," she managed.

"No, you're different, aren't you?" Speculation
swept across his face, but then he looked away
again. "Best not to start this conversation, love.
My control is thin today."

The endearment shook her on a deep, elemental level. Something had happened today, something that had brought out that untamed side of Rogan that she had sensed. He seemed . . . dangerous.

"I just want to be certain you're all right. How does your hand feel?"

"Don't worry, it's nothing." He looked down and unwrapped his hand, flexing his fingers and studying them. "I had worse than this as a boy."

"How did you hurt yourself?"

He flicked her a glance that was both amused and hungry. "Are you certain you want to know?"

"Yes." She held firm beneath that fierce stare. "Were you fighting?"

"Yes." He leaned back in the seat, challenge in every inch of him. "Are you shocked?"

"No." She bit her lip. "All right, yes."

He laughed, a deep, sensual sound that made her insides curl with unnamed pleasure. "Sorry you offered me a ride?"

"Not at all. You're going to be my husband. It seems to me I should become comfortable with you in all your moods."

His lips curved into a knowing smile. "Be careful what you wish for, love. Some of my moods are not that pleasant."

"Everyone gets cross sometimes. Even me."

"You? I can't envision that."

"Just wait," she warned, heart pounding from the predatory way he looked at her. "I can be the most shrewish of women."

"Indeed?" He shifted, bringing his knee up against hers. "Then it will be my job to tame you, won't it?"

"I . . ." She swallowed, suddenly out of her depth. "You didn't say why you had been fighting."

"No, I didn't."

"Are you going to tell me?"

"It was a matter of honor. Let's leave it at that."

She shifted her leg away from his. He said nothing, just kept watching her with that amused, adult gaze. "Stop looking at me like that," she said finally.

"Like what?"

"Like I'm a berry tart!" She crossed her arms. "I feel as if you're laughing at me, Rogan."

"Maybe a little." His gaze dropped to her lips. "Though I must say that I tend to take my berry tarts very seriously."

She honestly couldn't breathe. "Rogan . . ."

"Calm yourself, little one." He turned his head away, looking out the window again. "I won't pounce on you."

"Maybe . . . maybe I want you to."

His head whipped around, his eyes dark and hot. "What did you say?"

She pressed herself back into the seat, astounded by what she had said.

He smirked. "Change your mind?"

She didn't reply, words and feelings jumbling together in nervous confusion. She could only look at him, torn by the urge to get closer, yet held fast by the fear of what might happen if she did.

At her continued silence, he gave a brief laugh, worldly cynicism shadowing his features as he turned back to look out the window.

Fear. Once more it stood between her and a normal part of living.

She pulled a lacy handkerchief from her reticule and worried it between her fingers, casting a surreptitious glance at her fiancé. Finally she steeled her resolve and shifted across to sit beside him on the other bench.

His head whipped around in surprise. Her first instinct was to scoot away, but she made herself remain still, even when those dark gray eyes settled on her with piercing interest. Swallowing hard, she avoided his gaze and reached for his injured hand. His fingers flexed in hers, then settled as she dabbed at the blood with the feminine scrap of lace.

"Playing with fire, Caroline?" His deep voice vibrated between them, he was so close.

"Tending to my betrothed," she corrected.

"Very wifely of you."

This time she met his gaze. "I told you I intend to be a good wife."

"Shall we test your resolve?" Raising his other hand, he traced her cheek with his finger. "Or would you rather I allow you to escape back to your side of the coach?"

"That rather depends on what you have in mind."

His mouth quirked with amusement. "Don't worry, love, I have no intention of ravishing you in a coach."

"I . . . see." She crumpled the handkerchief in her hand, suddenly wondering at the wisdom of her boldness.

"A kiss," he said. "Perfectly acceptable for an engaged couple." He slid his hand behind her neck.

"Just one?" she whispered as he bent closer.

"One," he agreed. "For now."

His warm, ale-scented breath brushed her cheek as he lowered his mouth to hers. Her heart skipped a beat, then settled as their lips touched.

Soft. Skilled. After that first impression, coherent thought swirled away on a wave of sensation, and her eyes slid closed.

He took his time about it, learning the curve of her mouth, teaching her how to respond with a patience she hadn't expected. His fingers massaged her nape, and when she leaned closer, a low growl rumbled from his throat. Encouraged, she lifted a hand to his chest and let it lie there, his heartbeat thundering beneath her palm.

The carriage hit a bump, jolting them apart. With a groan, he pulled her tightly against him, burying his face in her neck. He held her like that, his arms like iron bands around her, his breathing shaky.

"Rogan." She shifted, hoping he would release her. "Rogan, are you all right?"

He made a muffled sound, his breath hot against her throat. She wriggled again, more strongly this time, but he didn't release her. His teeth scraped her neck.

Panic exploded. Trapped. *No! Can't get away. Let-me-go-let-me-go-let-me-go!*

A whine ripped from her throat, and she clawed at his chest, wrenching from side to side to break his hold.

He jerked his head up, startled. "Caroline?"

"Let . . . me . . . go!" she panted. Her heart raced, her breath coming so fast, she thought it would choke her. Blackness crept into the edges of her vision, and she pounded a fist against his chest. "*Let me go!*"

He relaxed his arms. "Caroline, it's all right. It's Rogan."

She shoved, breaking free of his encircling arms, and threw herself across the coach to the other bench. There she pressed herself into the farthest corner and stared at him, lifting one trembling hand to cover her mouth.

He hadn't moved. "Caroline," he said quietly, "you're safe. I'm not going to touch you."

Mortification swept over her. She realized she was shaking, that tears stung her eyes. Five-year-old memories lingered in her mind like the scent of fresh blood at a fox hunt.

She squeezed her eyes shut, wanting to hide

from the world. She had thought she could do it, could get close to him and handle the attentions of an attractive male. But no, she had panicked like a lunatic, just as she had that night at her come-out ball. Everyone had looked at her like a bedlamite that night, and she couldn't bear it if she saw the same look in Rogan's eyes.

"Talk to me, Caroline."

She opened her eyes to see him looking at her with honest concern. She wanted to forget the last few minutes, pretend they never happened.

Except for the kiss. The kiss she wanted to remember.

Rogan leaned forward in his seat, his hands draped over his knees. "I need you to tell me what I did wrong, Caroline," he said quietly. "I need to know so I don't do it again."

His gentleness nearly undid her fragile control. "I can't . . . I can't talk about it."

"You have to." Slowly he extended a hand to her. "Hold my hand, Caroline. I promise I'll stay right here."

She shook her head. "I can't. Please, just forget what happened."

"I can't forget." He didn't move. "You held my hand the other night, and nothing bad happened."

"I know."

"I won't scare you again, I promise." He kept his gaze steady on hers, compassion in his eyes. "I was angry before you met me today and then

when we kissed . . ." He sighed, his mouth twisting with self-disgust. "When we kissed, all that
anger turned into something else. I lost control."

She glanced down at his extended hand, then
back to his face. "I thought I was the one who lost
control."

"Maybe we both did," he agreed, a gentle smile
curving his lips.

"They thought I was mad, you know."

"Who did?"

"Society. The people at my debut ball. When I
collapsed, they thought I had been driven mad."

"I don't think that."

She gave a disbelieving little laugh. "You
must."

"I think you've been hurt, and that something I
did scared you."

"You held me too tightly." The words tumbled
from her lips before she thought about it. She
pressed them together.

"Then I won't do that again."

She let out a long breath and rested her face in
her hands. "I thought I wouldn't be afraid. I
wasn't two nights ago."

"This isn't something that goes away overnight.
And I'm afraid that if you don't take my hand
right now, we'll be worse off than when we
started."

He was right. She stared at his hand, and he
didn't move a muscle. Slowly she reached out,
rested her palm against his. He curled his fingers

lightly around hers and left their hands entwined. She knew that with the slightest tug of her hand, he would release her instantly.

Her pulse slowed, the panic draining away. She was still wary but no longer felt the urge to flee.

"Caroline, I've been to war," Rogan said. "I've seen women who've been . . . hurt . . . by men. I understand that it will take time—maybe a lot of time—before you're completely comfortable with me."

She nodded, unable to speak.

He squeezed her hand, waited until she met his gaze. "I can wait," he said softly.

She looked down at their joined hands, grateful for his strength, willing to believe that miracles could happen.

Chapter 6

It poured rain on their wedding day.

Caroline and Rogan were married in the family chapel at Belvingham. It was a small, quiet ceremony witnessed by Caroline's father and the select members of local society who had been invited, followed by a lavish wedding breakfast at the manor house.

Rogan hadn't bothered to invite his own family.

He stood beside his bride, wearing the new clothes that had been ordered for him from the tailor, and accepted congratulations from the well-wishers. Caroline smiled politely to everyone who congratulated her, but he could feel the stiffness of her body, sense the strain she was under. While the number of people at the wedding was much smaller than the number of guests

at her debut ball, he could tell that the crowd still
made her uneasy.

During a break in the well-wishers he leaned
down and murmured, "Are you all right?"

"I'll be fine," she whispered back, smiling at a
passing guest. "I refuse to succumb to the vapors
at my own wedding!"

He chuckled. "That's my girl. After all, you
made it through the ceremony."

She glanced up at him, a vision in silver and
white with a wreath of white flowers in her dark
hair. "Now I just have to survive life as your bride,
sir, and all will be well."

The twinkle in her eye delighted him. "Why,
Lady Caroline, are you flirting with me?"

Her cheeks pinkened. "If a woman cannot flirt
with her own husband, who can she flirt with?"

Her teasing words brought forth a burst of possessiveness. "No one else."

Her eyes widened at his tone, and she glanced
away.

He frowned. "Caroline?"

She didn't look at him. "As if I could flirt with
anyone but you, Rogan. As if I could stand to *be*
with anyone but you."

Her words grabbed him by the throat.
"Caroline—"

"What's *he* doing here?" she groaned. "I had
hoped he had another engagement."

"Who?" Distracted, he followed her gaze to
where a good-looking young man had just
entered the room.

"Randall." She sighed. The humor was back in her eyes when she looked up at him. "My father's heir. I was hoping he wouldn't come. He has a tendency to treat me like a mad aunt who should be locked in the attic."

"That's Althorpe?" Rogan watched with interest as the fair-haired young man made his way through the crowd toward them, exchanging greetings with the other guests as he did so.

Althorpe's blond hair fell across his brow in the latest style, and his coat of Spanish blue denoted an excellent tailor. He acknowledged acquaintances with sophisticated charm, smoothly moving along after a moment or two of pleasantries. Yet upon closer scrutiny, his eyes never reflected the warmth of his smile, and he tended to glance about him as if measuring some sort of threat.

Rogan narrowed his eyes. Though not a tall man, Althorpe moved with the ease of someone who could handle himself in a fight, and this, coupled with the duke's suspicions, was enough to make Rogan's body tense in readiness as the fellow stopped before them with a charming smile.

"Cousin Caroline, you look radiant! May I offer my congratulations?" Althorpe didn't kiss Caroline's hand, clearly cognizant of the fact that Caroline did not like to be touched. Instead he sketched a polite bow. "And to the groom as well, of course. Hunt, isn't it? My felicitations, sir."

"Thank you."

"Husband, this is Mr. Randall Althorpe, my cousin," Caroline murmured.

"Ah, Belvingham's heir, is it?" Affecting a mien of conviviality that earned him a startled glance from Caroline, Rogan smiled broadly and shook the other man's hand.

"Quite." Althorpe glanced around the room. "And where is dear Uncle? I should like to greet him properly."

"Entertaining guests no doubt," Caroline said.

"If you will excuse me, I will seek him out." With a polite nod of his head, Althorpe disappeared into the crowd.

"Hopefully he won't stay long," Caroline remarked. "He and Papa don't get on that well."

"A man can't choose his family." Senses on alert, he watched over her head as Althorpe spoke to a servant, then slipped from the room.

Noting his distraction, Caroline followed his gaze. "What are you looking at?"

"Nothing." He smiled at his bride. "Tell me, why does Althorpe refer to your father as 'uncle' if they are actually cousins?"

"He's always called him that. And you will not distract me so easily, Rogan. Answer my question."

"Actually, I believe I should find your father."

She laid a hand on his arm, smiling in a way that didn't erase the suspicion in her eyes. "We can look for him together."

"Unnecessary." He lifted her hand to his lips. "The bride should stay here to greet the guests."

She narrowed her eyes at him. "Rogan, what's going on?"

"Business, that's all." He squeezed her hand. "I'll be back in a moment." Before she could say another word, he slipped away through the crowd.

"Good morning, Uncle."

The duke jerked with surprise at the sound of Randall's voice. With shaking hands, he shoved the settlement papers for Caroline's marriage into his desk drawer and slammed it shut. Given his heir's fairly calm demeanor at the moment, he didn't think the volatile young man knew about the money he had settled on her. "Althorpe. I don't recall your name on the guest list."

"A sad oversight, I'm sure." Still smiling that amiable smile, Randall sauntered into the room. "And how is your health, Uncle? Well, I hope."

Though his heir's tone remained solicitous, the duke caught the knowing gleam in Althorpe's eyes.

"I'm certain you would know better than I."

"I don't know what you mean." Prowling around the room, Althorpe ran a finger along the back of a chair, studied a painting. "You know, when I inherit I think I'll redecorate this room in a dark green. What do you think?"

"I'm not dead yet, you—"

"Temper, temper," Althorpe chided. "We wouldn't want your heart to give out now, would we?"

"Is that what comes next?" Despite the weakness of his limbs, Belvingham got to his feet. "Is that what will finally kill me, you hell spawn?"

Althorpe widened his eyes in apparent distress. "Uncle, how can I tell such a thing? Am I a sooth-sayer?"

Rogan stepped into the room. "Good question. Are you?"

Althorpe swung around, clearly surprised to see the bigger man in the doorway. "Ah, the happy bridegroom. I was simply trying to calm my uncle's fears. His illness addles him some-times. It's so very distressing."

Belvingham grabbed a small, heavy statue from the desk. "I'll show you addled!"

Rogan strode across the room and took hold of the statue, placing it on the desk. "Calm yourself, Your Grace."

"My thanks, Hunt." Althorpe touched the dia-mond stickpin at his throat. "I fear the duke is overset."

Rogan assisted Belvingham into his chair, then turned to face Althorpe. "It's not good for His Grace to overexert himself."

Randall's brows rose. "Certainly you don't blame me for my uncle's rantings."

"Did I say that?" Rogan gave a small, menacing smile that drew a startled look from the other man. "I was merely cautioning you not to upset the duke."

"Are you threatening me, sir?"

"That depends." Rogan placed his hand over

the statue he had just taken from Belvingham. "Is it working?"

Althorpe's eyes narrowed. "You assume much."

Rogan shrugged. "My bride would be displeased to know that her father was upset by your visit, Althorpe."

"And you must keep the lady happy, I suppose." Randall's mouth curved in a condescending smile. "As long as Uncle holds the purse strings, at any rate."

"You young whelp!" the duke snarled.

Rogan took a step closer to Althorpe, the desire to knock the supercilious smirk off his face nearly more than he could resist. "Leave my wife out of this."

They stared at each other for a long moment, neither giving an inch. Finally Althorpe broke the contact, reaching for his pocket watch and flicking it open with his thumb. "I do believe I am late for an appointment," he said, his tone heavy with ennui. "I only stopped by to extend my felicitations to the bride and groom. Good day, Uncle. Hunt."

Rogan gave a short nod but said nothing. He watched Randall saunter out of the room, then turned to look at Belvingham.

"Don't be fooled," the duke said, sagging back in his chair. "He appears charming, but he's a murdering bastard."

"I believe you." Rogan went to the doorway

and watched as Althorpe strode down the hall. "I admit, I wasn't certain before. But I believe you now."

"The ramblings of a sick old man?" Belvingham snorted. "I wouldn't have believed me, either."

Rogan swung away from the doorway and back toward the duke. "That man is dangerous."

"I suppose it takes one to know one." Belvingham shifted in his chair, winced. "You see then why I was concerned for Caroline."

"I do. Does she know . . . ?"

"No! And she never will. I won't have her frightened. Hopefully her marriage to you will be enough to keep her out of Althorpe's reach."

Rogan sat down in a chair by the duke's desk. "Do you think he means to harm her?"

"I don't know." Belvingham slouched back in his chair. "Questions were raised during the investigation into her kidnapping, questions that to this day remain unanswered."

"You believe Althorpe was behind that?"

"There is no proof. My heir is careful to keep his hands clean of such messes. But given recent events, I cannot help but wonder if that incident was Randall's doing as well."

"If he is capable of murder, the kidnapping of a young girl would be child's play." Rogan clenched his jaw. "But Caroline isn't a child any longer."

"With me out of the way and a clear path to the

title, I don't expect that he would have done any worse than to marry her off to some reprobate or, worse yet, wed her himself to get his hands on her fortune."

"He can't touch her now."

"No." Belvingham closed his eyes and let out a deep sigh of relief. "My daughter is safe."

"And she'll stay that way. That I promise."

It was her wedding night.

As the carriage stopped before the tiny manor house, Caroline studied her new home. It looked cozy and private, a far cry from the palatial estate she had called home these past twenty years. She would share this house with Rogan, live with him as his wife.

He opened the door to the carriage and hopped out, then turned and extended his hand to her. "Welcome home, Caroline."

She took his hand, and a jolt swept through her. His fingers were so warm, his smile intimate. Her stomach did a little flip-flop. He did understand, didn't he, that she wasn't yet ready to become his wife in truth? That she couldn't yet share his bed?

She stepped down from the carriage, and he tucked her hand into the crook of his arm. As he led her to the door of her new home, her heartbeat sped up, and her breathing grew shallow. What if he expected to consummate their marriage to-night? What would she do if he forced her?

She closed her eyes, swallowed hard. She had to

believe that he would give her time to work through her fears. They had talked about it, hadn't they? But she remembered that afternoon in the carriage, when he had seemed a different person, a dangerous man. When her fears had reared up and sent her scrambling from his arms.

How could this possibly work?

"Caroline." His soft voice drew her attention to his face. Suddenly she realized that they stood on the doorstep of his home and that her fingers clutched his arm with enough force that he could no doubt feel her nails digging into his flesh even through the material of his coat. Mortified, she loosened her hold.

"Don't be frightened, love." He gently placed his hand over hers before she could withdraw it. "I know you're not ready."

"Not yet," she whispered, her muscles relaxing in relief. "I wasn't certain if—"

"We talked about this, remember? I'm not going to force you. We have the rest of our lives to get used to each other."

"Thank you." She mustered up a smile, lost for a moment in the tenderness that softened his gray eyes.

He leaned close to her ear. "I'll be satisfied with a kiss good night."

His suggestive whisper sent a shiver of desire through her. Aroused and confused, she felt her face grow hot even as her flesh prickled with awareness.

He chuckled, clearly satisfied with her reaction to his flirting. "Come, my blushing bride. Welcome to your new home." He opened the door and gestured for her to enter first.

Caroline tentatively stepped inside, and Rogan couldn't suppress a surge of possessiveness. Though he had fought it, this lovely, dainty lady was now his wife, and he couldn't be sorry. He would protect her from Althorpe and anyone else who threatened her.

Even himself.

He closed the door behind them and hung up his hat as Caroline peered into the snug little parlor. Then she whirled around, eyes wide and face pale. "Rogan, there's a man in there!"

Rogan grabbed her by the wrist and pulled her behind him as he stepped into the parlor doorway. He recognized the intruder at once and bit back a curse that would certainly have blistered his new bride's tender ears. He'd hoped to avoid this for some time, but he should have known better. He narrowed his eyes as he noted the way the dark-haired intruder relaxed beside the fire, legs stretched out before him as he helped himself to Rogan's favorite whiskey.

The handsome fellow looked up as Rogan entered, then gave a charming smile and raised the glass in salute. "And here he is, the lucky bridegroom. Good evening to you, Rogan."

Rogan didn't move from his position in the doorway. "What are you doing here, Colin?"

"Can't a man stop by and wish his brother happy on his wedding day?" Colin got to his feet in one sleek move and tossed back the last of the whiskey, then set the empty glass on the mantel. "Of course I realize it's more appropriate to offer my felicitations at the wedding; however, I fear my invitation must have been misplaced."

"You might find it on the manure pile."

"Really, brother." Colin placed a hand over his heart and affected a tragic expression. "You wound me."

"Rogan?" Caroline's nervous whisper reached his ears even as she moved to stand at his side, slipping her tiny hand around his arm.

Colin's dark eyes lit with appreciation. "And you must be my new sister-in-law. My brother is indeed a lucky man."

"Caroline, this is my brother, Colin," Rogan said, seeing no way to avoid the introductions. "Colin, my wife, Lady Caroline Hunt."

"Charmed, dear lady." Colin gave a graceful bow, then slanted a glance toward Rogan. "If I attempt to kiss the bride, do you suppose yon bridegroom will plant me a facer?" Caroline shrunk back closer to Rogan, and Colin chuckled. "Shy, is she?"

"Very." Rogan turned to Caroline. "I apologize for my brother's outrageous behavior, my dear. He is an ass, and there is no cure for it."

Caroline gave a startled giggle, then glanced from Colin back to Rogan. He knew what she saw; the family resemblance was unmistakable.

Except for having dark eyes where Rogan had gray, and except for the definite age difference with Colin being eight years older, Colin and Rogan could be mistaken for twins.

"What a lovely smile your bride has," Colin said.

"You didn't come here to compliment my wife," Rogan said. "What do you want, Colin?"

"Again you wound me, brother." Colin sent Caroline a mournful look. "Can you believe his cruelty, dear sister-in-law?"

"Fine. We'll play it your way." Rogan turned to his wife and gently removed her hand from his arm. "Caroline, why don't you go upstairs while I talk to my brother? Your room is the second door on the left. I believe your father already sent Marie over to unpack."

"All right." She glanced at Colin. "Nice to meet you."

"The pleasure is mine." Colin watched the lady depart with a gleam of appreciation that raised Rogan's hackles.

"Get out." Rogan strode into the room, picked up his brother's hat off the table, and threw it at him.

Colin caught the hat with both hands, then placed it on the chair, clearly in no hurry to leave. "Now, Rogan—"

"I don't want to hear it." He grabbed Colin by the shoulder and shoved him toward the door. "This is my wedding night, you jackanapes. Be gone!"

Colin twisted from Rogan's hold. "I know it's your wedding night, despite the fact that you didn't invite your family to the ceremony."

"Is it any wonder?" Rogan picked up the hat and tossed it into the hallway. "There's the door. Don't let it hit you on the way out."

"Hey, that's my favorite hat!"

"Sorry." Rogan gave his brother a shove between the shoulder blades. "Out."

"*Stop pushing me!*" Colin spun around and shoved Rogan in the chest with both hands.

Rogan stumbled back a step, then surged forward, grabbing his brother's arm and twisting it up behind his back. "This is my house," he gritted out. "This is my wedding night. I want you gone."

"Your wedding night," Colin panted, struggling to free himself. "Why the devil don't you take the girl on a wedding trip then? I hear you have the blunt now."

"Her father's very ill." He dodged Colin's other elbow as he jabbed it backward. "I should have known you'd have heard about the money. Is that why you're here?"

"Of course not. I came to wish you happy." Colin threw his weight sideways, sending them both crashing to the floor. Freed of his brother's hold, he nimbly jumped to his feet. "*Then* I was going to ask you for money."

Rogan rolled and stood. Colin had taken on a fighting stance, fists at the ready. Rogan balanced himself on the balls of his feet, watching his brother's eyes. "I had hoped the lack of invitation to the wedding would have made you realize that you aren't welcome here."

"Now is that any way to talk to your older brother?" The two men circled, more than familiar with each other's styles after a lifetime of brawling.

"Be glad I didn't set the dogs on you."

"You don't have any dogs."

Rogan bared his teeth in a grim smile. "Then I guess you just have to worry about me."

"I'm shaking." Colin narrowed his eyes. "Come now, are you going to hit me, or shall we dance all night?"

"When I'm ready."

"You know, if I were you—" Colin let loose a punch.

Rogan dodged. "But you're not me."

"If I were you . . ." Colin fell back, and they circled again. ". . . I would be thinking about dancing with my pretty young wife and not about knocking out my brother's teeth."

"I have my priorities." Rogan came in with a fast one-two punch. The second one caught the edge of Colin's jaw. Not enough to knock him down, but enough to give Rogan a surge of satisfaction.

Colin regained his footing, working his jaw as if to check the damage. "My priority would be sweet Caroline in the marriage bed, dear brother.

I am amazed that you bother with me when such pleasure awaits you."

"Leave her out of this." Rogan feinted with his right and came up with a hard left.

Colin spun out of the way an instant before it connected and came up behind Rogan. He locked an elbow around his brother's throat. "You know, you didn't even hear me out. Yes, I came to ask for money, but it's for Hunt Chase."

Rogan wedged both hands around Colin's arm and pulled, sucking in air. "I'm sure."

"It is." Both men swayed as they fought for balance. "I want to make some improvements to the place."

"You and Father did enough." Rogan jabbed Colin hard in the midriff with his elbow, surprising him into loosening his hold. Colin fell back a pace, and Rogan darted away, spinning around to face his brother. "The two of you destroyed generations of our family's work. Your gaming and wenching was more important than your legacy."

"Will you continue to hold that over my head?" Colin folded an arm around his middle and sucked in air. "I came here sober, didn't I? The property is mortgaged to the gills, and if I can't find some way to pay the note, Hunt Chase will pass out of Hunt hands forever."

"You should have thought of that before you sold it off, piece by piece."

"It was Father's idea, not mine." Colin straightened, but he didn't raise his fists. "It wasn't my property yet, Rogan. I couldn't stop him."

"I know you were the one who sold Destiny. You knew she was my horse, what she meant to me."

Colin gave him a cocky smile. "Oh, yes. You're right, that *was* my idea."

Rogan let out a roar and leaped at his brother. The two men smashed into a table, sending a lovely vase crashing to the floor. They rolled, and Rogan came up on top, swinging a mighty right straight into Colin's face. Colin grabbed Rogan by the coat with both hands and flipped sideways, sending his brother tumbling. Colin rolled and came to his feet as Rogan scrambled to his. Rogan came right back swinging, landing blows to Colin's stomach and ribs.

Colin staggered backward, coming up against the mantel. He grabbed a Dresden shepherdess and smashed it over Rogan's head. Rogan stumbled back, shook his head like a wet dog. Colin grabbed the empty whiskey glass and hurled that as well. Rogan deflected the glass with a sweep of his hand, sending it smashing into the fireplace.

Colin darted behind one of the large, upholstered chairs beside the fire. "I take it this means you won't lend me the money?"

Rogan growled and grabbed a poker. Colin ducked behind the chair, then dropped to the floor and shoved the chair at Rogan with his legs. Rogan went down, and the poker skittered across the floor.

"Perhaps I should take my leave." Colin hopped to his feet and darted for the door.

Rogan caught up with him just as he reached the doorway. He grabbed Colin by the coat and slammed him up against the door, holding him there with a merciless hand at his throat. Colin made a croaking noise and clawed at Rogan's hand.

"I don't want to see you around here anymore," Rogan growled. "You destroyed our family's legacy, and I won't have you do the same to mine."

Colin gasped, his eyes watering in his reddening face. Working his fingers beneath Rogan's, he bent back Rogan's thumb.

With a howl of pain, Rogan yanked back his hand. Colin sagged, sucking in a breath. Then Rogan slammed him back against the door with his forearm against his throat. "That," he snarled, "was very stupid."

Real fear darkened Colin's eyes. Rogan smiled grimly, his blood thundering through his veins, his whole body alert for the slightest movement. He pressed just a tad harder against Colin's throat, reveling in the panic that flickered across his brother's face.

"Rogan?"

Caroline's soft, feminine voice reached him even though the fury pounding through his veins. He glanced up, saw her standing in the doorway, a look of horror on her face. He glanced back at his brother, at the way he held him pinned to the wall as if he would choke the life from him . . .

Rage dissipated in an instant. Horrified, he released Colin and stumbled back a step.

Slowly Colin slid down the wall as if his legs would no longer hold him and sat on the floor. "I'd forgotten about that black temper of yours," he croaked, fingering his throat.

"You shouldn't have come," Rogan snapped, then whipped his gaze back to his wife. "Caroline?" He reached out a hand, but she shrank back with a whimper, her eyes widening. "My God, I'm so sorry."

When he made to approach her, she shook her head violently, backing up a step. Rogan paused, wanting to touch her, to make certain she was all right. But he saw the way her hands shook, so he stayed where he was. "Caroline, are you all right? Please tell me."

She looked at him, her big, dark eyes full of such shock and fear that he felt as if she'd punched him. "You were hurting him."

He swallowed hard. "I know. I didn't mean to."

"Our Rogan has a nasty temper," Colin offered. "Famous for it, in fact."

"Shut up and leave while you still can," Rogan said with quiet menace, never taking his eyes from Caroline.

"Excellent notion." Colin hauled himself to his feet and lurched toward the door. Caroline shrank away as he passed her. "Felicitations again, sister-in-law. We shall meet again."

"Do you need a doctor?" she asked, stopping him in his tracks.

Colin turned back to her, surprise lighting his features. "No, thank you. Rogan and I have been at this for years. I do believe I'm used to it." He grinned, then flipped his brother a jaunty wave before taking his leave.

Caroline turned back to Rogan, her expression still troubled. "I don't understand this. Why were you fighting?"

He shrugged, uncomfortable. "We always do. Always have."

"But he's your brother."

"All the more reason." Rogan sighed. "Look, Colin and I have never seen eye to eye. He and my father . . . well, they were wastrels, the both of them. They destroyed our family's business. Now that my father has passed on, Colin has inherited what's left. He was just looking for money."

"I know about your family," she said. "Even sequestered in the country, one heard stories."

"Yes, well." He dropped his gaze, unable to look at her. "I hadn't planned for you to meet my family just yet. If at all."

"Is what he said true?"

He gave her a crooked smile but received none in reply. "Which part?"

"The part where you have a fierce temper."

"Yes." He met her gaze squarely. Better to admit his flaws now than to lie and have her find out the truth later. "Most of the time I can control myself, but under certain circumstances . . . well, you saw what happened."

"Yes." She glanced around the wreckage of the room. "Will this be a frequent occurrence?"

"Not if I can help it. My brother tends to bring out the worst in me."

"I see."

She continued to study the broken statuary, her eyes solemn and her mouth grim. She twisted her fingers together, a sure sign of anxiety.

"Caroline." He swallowed hard when she looked at him with those serious dark eyes, eyes that held a hint of disappointment. "I know this has . . . Damn it all," he muttered. "Please tell me you forgive me. I couldn't stand it if you didn't. Not after all the progress we've made."

She glanced again over the ruins from the fight. "I was afraid you were going to kill him," she whispered.

"So was I." Shaken by the fear lingering in her eyes, he held out a hand to her. "I don't want you to be afraid of me, Caroline."

She looked at his hand for a long moment, but didn't move from the doorway. "I don't, either." She gave him a small, sorrowful smile. "Good night, Rogan." Turning away, she left the room.

He watched her go, knowing the beast had won this night.

Chapter 7

Caroline dismissed her maid and climbed into bed, still unsettled by the side of her husband she had seen tonight.

Of course she had heard the stories of his temper, such as the night he had almost killed Lord Effingham's son. It had taken three men to pull him off the fellow and drag him from the tavern where the altercation had taken place. He'd gone to war soon after that, but after he returned, people had once more brought up all the old stories of his past, of the reckless drinking and fighting. Like father, like son, they'd said. And though he had turned his attention completely to his work once he'd returned, the villagers still looked at him askance, still crossed the street when they saw him coming.

No wonder he didn't deal well with people.

She sat up and hugged her knees to her chest. Since he'd returned from the war, Rogan had spent all his time at his estate, working to rebuild his family's legacy. He hadn't gone out carousing at the local inn or raising hell at various society functions. If anything, except for his occasional wild rides across the countryside in the dead of night, he'd become something of a hermit.

She knew the feeling.

She sighed, sweeping her long hair back from her face with both hands, then letting it fall around her shoulders again. This wasn't how she'd imagined her wedding night to be. As a young girl, she'd treasured the usual romantic fairy tales of a loving husband who would sweep her away to his estate and shower her with attention. After her kidnapping, the idea of a husband had nearly terrified her. How could she possibly allow herself to be so vulnerable to a man after what had happened to her?

Then she'd met Rogan. Rogan, who seemed to instinctively understand when she needed to be touched and when she needed to be left alone. She couldn't name another man who would have so calmly accepted her retreat this evening. Most bridegrooms would be banging down the door, demanding their rights. But not Rogan.

Oh, he wanted her. She'd seen the evidence of that, felt it. If she gave him the word, he'd happily share her bed and make a woman of her. For an instant she reveled in the delicious fluttering in her lower body as she imagined his kisses. But then as the fantasy continued, as she imagined him joining her in bed, removing her clothes, climbing on top of her, the terror rose like a shriek in her throat. She bit it back, but the aftertaste remained.

No, she wasn't ready yet to consummate her marriage. But neither had she intended that her wedding night would end in such contention. She had imagined some romantic moments—soft touches, a kiss good night. The spark of desire in Rogan's eyes, the feeling of safety his strong arms could bring. The knowledge that he understood her situation and would respect the boundaries.

Instead there had been arguing and a fistfight. What had possessed her to go downstairs when she'd heard the ruckus? Such foolishness from a normally intelligent woman! Would she have stepped between two stallions vying for supremacy in the herd? Of course not. Neither should she have gone anywhere near the two men.

She splayed a hand across her bosom as she remembered the scene that had met her eyes. Rogan had looked murderous as he held his brother in a chokehold. He was so strong, and he'd been so furious. She'd seen the light of battle in his eyes. But the instant he'd heard her voice, that gleam had faded. His concern had been for her, and she could tell by the agony in his voice that he'd been horrified by what had happened. He'd apologized over and over, tried to comfort her, but she'd been too upset to accept it.

And so they'd gone to their separate beds, she afraid and he hating himself.

Was this the memory she wanted when she thought of her wedding night years from now?

She flung aside the covers and slid from the bed. Her hands trembled as she slipped on her wrapper, but she was determined. Years from now, she would not look back on her wedding night with sadness. She would make a memory worthy of cherishing this night.

Rogan lay in bed, his hands folded behind his head as he stared at the ceiling and contemplated the evening. He couldn't have made a worse muck of things if he'd tried his hardest.

Then again, just being Rogan Hunt seemed to be enough to ruin most good things anyway.

He'd had some notion in his head of a quiet dinner with his wife—and maybe a kiss or two—before sending her to bed. Since the incident in the carriage, he'd recognized the importance of getting her used to his touch. She was like a mare that had been abused, skittish and distrustful. But as with a mare, kindness and tender care would eventually lead her to accept his touch. The trick was in allowing her to retreat when she felt she needed to and showering her with warm affection when she did venture into his arms. Eventually the pleasure she found with him would take precedence over the terrible memories of her kidnapping, and they would be able to have a true marriage.

If his bloody temper didn't chase her away before they reached that point.

What the hell had he been thinking, to start a fight with Colin with his bride in the house? Then again, to be honest, thinking rarely played a part in his interactions with his older brother. His instincts always told him to hit first and listen to explanations later. It had been that way ever since he could remember; his family communicated as much with fists as they did with voices—and usually raised voices at that.

There were times when he truly hated his family. His mother had gotten fed up with the lot of them and run off with a lover years ago. In the meantime, his father had proudly taught both his sons everything he knew—where the best ale was to be had, who was a Captain Sharp and who was a ripe pigeon for the plucking in a game of cards, and which brothels tended to provide disease-free and amenable companionship. Adoring his father and older brother, young Rogan had eagerly followed in their footsteps.

Sir Quentin had also taught his sons to fight and defend the family's pride, especially when their Irish heritage was insulted. Rogan had especially taken those lessons to heart.

Now his father was dead and there was only Colin. Aside from Caroline, Colin was his only family, and he wished him to the devil. He had managed to make a life for himself away from the chaos of his father's legacy, and he didn't need Colin stirring things up again.

A soft knock at the connecting door startled him. Before he could say a word, the door opened and Caroline slipped into the room.

Astonished, he pushed himself into a sitting position. "Caroline? Is something wrong?"

Closing the door behind her, she turned to face him, twisting her fingers in that way that told him she was nervous. She wore a modest white night-dress and wrapper, and her dark hair flowed loose over her slender shoulders to her waist. He itched to touch it, to bury his hands in the silky mass, to feel it sweep across his bare flesh. His body responded to the vivid image, and he bunched the covers in his lap.

"Caroline?" he prompted again. "Are you all right?"

"Yes." The word came out in a bit of a croak. Her eyes widened as she took in his bare chest. "I just wanted to . . . um . . . say good night."

"Didn't we say good night downstairs?"

Crimson swept into her cheeks. "You're right. We did. I'm sorry for . . ." She turned and fumbled for the doorknob.

"Caroline, no, wait." He wanted to go to her, but he knew the sight of a naked—and aroused—man would only send her running faster.

She paused, then took a deep breath. "You're right," she said, still facing the door. "We did say good night downstairs, but that's not good enough."

"It's not?" He glanced at his robe draped over the chair across the room and wondered if he could get to it without sending his wary bride into a fit of vapors.

"No." She bent her head as if gathering strength, then straightened up and turned back to him. "What happened downstairs is not how I would remember my wedding night."

Her bravery touched him even as her words sent hot lust straight to his loins. "I'm sorry for ruining it for you."

"No." She took a step toward him, then stopped. "No, that's not why I came."

"So you're not—" He stopped, searched for the right words. "Caroline, are you still afraid of me?"

"Yes. And no." She swept her hair back over her shoulder in an impatient gesture that for some reason struck him as both sweet and arousing. "I'm not upset about what happened downstairs anymore. But I am still the way I was . . . um . . . before."

"I see." He waited for her to elaborate, but she said nothing more. They simply looked at each other, the length of the bedroom—and the bed— between them.

Caroline began to fidget, switching from one foot to the other, and twisting her fingers again. Every movement shifted her clothing, granting him delicious glimpses of her delicate curves beneath the fine material. He clenched his fingers in the bedcovers. He wanted to explore her body, the softness of her skin, the elegant length of her neck, the subtle feminine secrets hidden beneath the nightdress. He imagined burying his face in her fragrant hair as he claimed her as his wife.

"Rogan?"

Her hesitant tone distracted him from his fantasy. "Hmm?"

She swallowed hard and dropped her gaze. "Do you . . . I mean, are you . . ." She waved a hand, words failing her. ". . . dressed . . . under the covers?"

His mouth twitched with amusement. "No, I'm not."

"Oh." Her blush deepened, and she looked everywhere but at him.

He shrugged. "I was in bed when you chose to visit me, love, and that's how I sleep."

"Of course. You sleep . . ." Her gaze touched on his chest again. "Anyway, I didn't want there to be bad feelings between us. So I'll just go back to my room." She reached behind her for the doorknob, never taking her eyes off him.

"Perhaps a kiss good night?"

She literally jumped with surprise. "Pardon?"

"A kiss. We're married now, Caroline. It's perfectly acceptable behavior."

"Of course it is." She shook her head and let go of the doorknob. "I'm acting like a ninny."

"You'll have to come over here." He couldn't resist a wicked grin as he added, "Or I could come over there."

"No." She took a step toward the bed. "No, you'd better stay there."

"Do you trust me, Caroline?"

"I think so."

He held out a hand. "Then come here and let me kiss my bride good night."

The way he said the words "my bride" sent a flush of heat through her body. He patiently held out his hand, summoning her with nothing more than that sinful smile, his dark hair rumpled from the pillows and his eyes gleaming with the light of temptation. Slowly she made her way across the room, becoming more and more aware of his large, male body sprawled beneath the bed-clothes. She stopped beside the bed, her gaze dropping despite herself to the bare expanse of muscular chest and shoulders only inches away.

"Caroline." The word wrapped around her like a caress as he took her wrist in his hand. "Come closer."

She did, enticed by the knowledge that he was naked beneath the sheets. That he was her husband and there was nothing wrong with them being together like this. Yet at the same time she didn't want to get too close. Didn't want things to get out of control. But then she found herself studying the line of dark hair that arrowed down the middle of his flat stomach, disappearing beneath the coverlet. She flexed her fingers, wishing she had the courage to touch.

"Caroline." His voice roughened as he said her name. He swallowed hard, then swept his thumb across the palm of her hand. "Do you want to touch me?"

She jerked her gaze to his, stunned by the unbridled hunger she found there. "I don't know if that would be a good idea."

He gave a dark chuckle. "I don't know, either, but I do know that I want you to. I promise not to move."

She considered the offer. Her palm itched to smooth along the rippling muscles of his chest and abdomen, and before she could think too much about it, she nodded. He guided her hand to his chest, the prickle of hair tickling her palm. His skin felt softer than she'd expected. And it was hot, so hot. Beneath her fingers, his heart beat strongly.

He flattened his hand over hers, holding her there. She accepted the invitation in his eyes and perched on the edge of the bed, incredibly conscious of his naked body only inches away. The bedclothes seemed like an insubstantial barrier; she could feel the heat of his flesh even through the material. Then he cupped his other hand behind her neck and pulled her into his kiss. Her eyes slid closed as she gave herself up to the pleasure of his mouth.

Her head spun when he kissed her. Beneath her hand, his heart thundered. With a little moan, she lost herself in the play of his lips on hers, her body flaring to life like a winter's fire. She wanted to move closer. Everything inside her screamed to climb into bed with him and let him take her places she'd never been. But she didn't dare. She couldn't.

But oh, how she wanted to.

He groaned and reached for her with both hands, cupping her face and deepening the kiss. She thought she'd be scared. But she wasn't. He wasn't holding her down or crushing her against him. He just held her face in his hands and kissed her with utter concentration.

She rested both hands flat on his chest and responded to him, driven by a sweet craving she'd never felt before. Her fingers curled into his muscles, raking through the silky pelt with an eagerness that surprised even her. His grunt of pleasure urged her on, and she slid her hands down his torso, glorying in his hard, masculine physique.

"You're driving me mad," he muttered. Taking her lower lip between his teeth, he opened his eyes and looked straight into hers, letting her see the desire that burned inside him. Her breath hitched. Before she could panic, he speared his hand through her hair and pulled her into a deeper, intimate, openmouthed kiss.

Her soft moan lodged in her throat as his tongue touched hers, gently probing. He wasn't demanding, wasn't trying to possess her. He was asking permission, and she granted it. Lost in the drugging pleasure of his mouth, blind from the delight of his flesh beneath her hands, she responded with all the passion that vibrated through her.

Then her hands slipped down too far, and she

encountered something hard and hot and all too familiar.

With a cry, she ripped herself from his arms, nearly fell off the bed as she clambered to her feet.

"Caroline." Sounding a bit breathless himself, Rogan calmly rearranged the covers with one hand while reaching for her with the other. "It's all right."

She shook her head frantically, covering her mouth with her hand as she fought off hysteria.

"Caroline, please." He swung his legs over the side of the bed, dragging the sheets with him as he sat up. "Don't let it get hold of you, love. Don't let the fear take you away from me."

"I don't want to, but I can't help it." She turned away from him and walked to the hearth. There was no fire burning, as it was early May and still pleasantly comfortable at night. She stared into the sooty emptiness of the cold fireplace, wondering if she would ever be able to live life as a normal woman.

"Maybe we should talk about it."

"About what? That I can't touch my own husband without becoming hysterical?" She gave a bitter laugh. "Perhaps you would have been better off with just the horse after all."

"I wanted you, Caroline," he admitted softly. "I just don't think I deserve you."

"You must be mad." She turned to face him, her lips trembling as she struggled to hold back her tears. "If anything, you deserve more."

He gave a deep sigh and raked both hands through his hair. "What a pair we are."

"Indeed." She twisted her fingers together, then caught herself doing it and dropped her hands to her sides. "What now?"

"I think we should talk about this. I think the more I know about what happened to you, the better I will be able to help you overcome it."

"You really think I can overcome this?" She sent him a look of disbelief. "Look at me. It's our wedding night, and I'm afraid to come near you."

"You weren't before." He gave her an intimate smile. "You like my kisses."

She looked at him, sin personified as he sat wrapped in nothing but the bedsheets, his muscular chest and shoulders bared for her enjoyment. His hair was tousled from the pillows and from his own impatient fingers, and pure wickedness gleamed in his eyes.

If ever there was a man to tempt a woman, it was he.

"I do like your kisses," she replied. "I always want more. But it is the 'more' that frightens me."

"Which is why I need to know what happened to you."

"What about you?" she threw back at him. "What was that about not deserving me? Apparently I am not the only one with something to tell."

His jaw tightened, but his voice remained gentle. "Caroline, you won't distract me. If we are to

make a go of this marriage, I need to know something of what happened to you. You don't have to
tell me everything right away. Just what you are
comfortable with."

He was right. She knew he was right, but . . .
"I'm afraid," she whispered.

"Of what?"

"If I talk about it . . . it brings it all back." She
took a deep breath. "And you may look at me differently. I don't think I could bear that."

"It's not your fault." He started to stand, then
was jerked back by the sheets still tucked into the
bed. "Blast it. Would you hand me my robe, love?
I think both of us will feel better if I'm not naked
while we have this conversation."

"Of course." She managed to control her blush
as she grabbed his robe from the chair and
brought it to him.

He took it from her, his eyes soft with compassion as he looked into her face. "Thank you."

She could feel the heat from his body even a
pace away, and while her mind urged her to back
away, her feminine instincts encouraged her to
move closer, to touch him. He seemed to sense her
thoughts. His gaze settled on her mouth, and his
fingers clenched around the thick material of the
robe.

"Turn around," he said hoarsely. "Unless . . ."

Now nothing could stop the surge of heat that
flooded her cheeks. Though he hadn't finished the
sentence, the unmistakable sexual heat between

them made words unnecessary. She spun around, presenting him with her back.

Material rustled as he shed the sheet and shrugged into his robe. She imagined him standing naked behind her, tall and muscled and absolutely one of the most attractive men she had ever seen in her life. Then she remembered what had frightened her, how aroused he'd been, and the delicious pleasure curling her stomach turned to churning anxiety. He was behind her. She couldn't see him. He was naked. He could . . .

"No!" She whirled to face him, poised to fight or flee.

Clad in his robe, he gave her a puzzled look. "Are you all right?"

Feeling foolish, she could only nod, the frantic emotion subsiding.

"I think we both need a drink." He moved to the other side of the room and poured two glasses of whiskey. He held one out to her. "Here, drink this——but slowly. It will settle your nerves."

She came over to accept the glass and took a tentative sip. The liquor burned her mouth and throat like fire. She choked, holding the glass out to him as her eyes teared. "I don't think I'll have any nerves left after that."

He chuckled and set the glass on the table, then tossed back his own drink without so much as a ripple of discomfort. "That's the point."

She swiped the moisture from her eyes and inhaled deeply. Her breath felt amazingly cool after the heat of the whiskey. "If I'm not calm, at least I'm numb."

"I know this is hard for you." He rested his hands gently on her shoulders. She tensed for an instant, but then realized that he left the touch light so that she knew she could move away if she wanted to. "But I can't avoid hurting you if I don't know what happened."

"I know." She rested her forehead against his broad chest, took comfort from the strong beat of his heart. He swept a soothing hand through her hair. "I'll tell you what I can."

Caroline began to pace the room, and Rogan sat down in a nearby chair. He leaned forward, elbows resting loosely on his knees, granting her his full attention.

His intent male focus unnerved her, especially since his current position made the neckline of his robe gap open, granting her a tantalizing view of his bare chest. She looked at the fireplace, at her feet—anything to avoid those shrewd gray eyes. "Where do you want me to start?"

He gave her question a moment's thought before he replied, "I know you were kidnapped. Tell me how it happened."

"I was out with my governess. She was escorting me to my friend's home when the men attacked our carriage."

"And where did this happen?"

"At Chiverton, one of my father's estates just outside London." She shivered, hugging herself as the dark memory swept through her. "Papa told me he would have sold the house after that if it hadn't been entailed."

"How many men were there?"

She shrugged, the image of that day still indelibly carved in her mind, bitterly flavored with a young girl's terror. "Two, three. I'm not certain. More than one." She took a shaky breath. "One of them shot Miss Sawgrass. Right in front of me."

"I'm sorry." He reached out a hand to her, but she shook her head and stepped away.

"I'm all right." She regained control and continued with her story, still not looking at him. "Someone put a sack over my head, and they tied me up. Then one of them put me on a horse and rode behind me. It seemed like we rode forever."

"And then what happened?"

She shrugged. "They tied me up and sent Papa a ransom note."

"Caroline." His chiding tone grated.

"What?" She spun to face him, knowing that he knew there was more to it. That it hadn't really been as simple as that. And she hated that he knew, that he would make her put words to what they had done to her. "That's what happened. They locked me in a closet, so now I'm afraid of the dark. They murdered my governess in front of my eyes, so I did whatever they told me. *Anything* they told me."

He stood, never taking his gaze from her face. "Anyone would have done the same. They were ruthless men, Caroline."

"Well then." For some reason her breath was coming in pants, and her heart pounded as if she'd run for miles. When he stepped toward her, she turned away, not wanting him to touch her. To look at her.

"There's more to the story," he said quietly.

Her muscles tensed. She crossed her arms tightly as if she would hold back the scream that threatened to burst from her chest. "Bow Street found me, and Papa came to get me. He saw to it that the men were sent to prison for their crime."

"Prison?" His eyes grew cold. "I would have killed the bastards with my own two hands."

She glanced back at him, startled that his thoughts so closely echoed hers. "I wish you had been there then."

He clenched his fists and moved away. "Tell me the rest."

Her throat closed up. "I can't."

He spun back, his eyes fierce. "You must."

"No." She swept both hands through her hair, clenched it tightly between her fingers before letting it fall around her shoulders again. "Don't ask it of me."

"Damn it, Caroline!" He hurled his whiskey glass into the empty grate. She flinched as it shattered. "Are you so much a coward? Are you going to let them win?"

"Coward?" She stared at him in stunned disbelief. "How can you call me that? I'm still alive, am I not? They didn't kill me. They didn't best me because I did everything they wanted, and that's why I'm still alive."

"Are you?" He raked a contemptuous gaze over her, his lip curling in a sneer. "You exist, Caroline, but you don't live."

His words struck like a blow to the chest. Her breathing hitched as raw emotion roared into a blazing inferno. "You know nothing about it."

He stepped closer, thrusting his face near hers. "Then tell me."

"What do you want me to tell you?" She shoved at his chest with both hands, sending him back a pace. "Shall I tell you how they touched me? The disgusting things they said?"

"Yes." Unfazed by her outburst, he watched her, the ferocity fading from his expression.

She took a deep, shuddering breath. "They gloated in detail about the things they wanted to do to me. Fondled themselves while they talked. One man even . . . he showed me his male part." Revulsion rippled through her.

"Caroline." He reached for her, his voice gentle, his eyes softening with compassion.

She slapped his hand away. "Don't touch me. Shall I tell you more? Would you like to hear the details?"

"That's enough for now."

The tenderness in his voice splintered her control. The words tumbled from her lips, shrill and defiant. "That one man, he used to do things to me when the others weren't looking. Grab my bottom, pinch my bosom. One day he held me down, touched me. Made me touch him . . . made me tell him how much I liked it. And I did it. He threatened to kill me if I didn't."

"Did he hurt you?"

"You mean did he force himself on me?" She gave a little laugh made harsh by hysteria. "They stopped him. But if you're keeping a list, Rogan, add 'Don't hold down Caroline' to it."

"Stop," he whispered. The distress in his eyes nearly made her knees buckle.

But she couldn't stop.

"You wanted to know, Rogan, and I'm telling you." She came closer to him, driven by some violent emotion that she couldn't even name. "In their sick little game, they told me how to please a man. Made me repeat the instructions until I was physically sick. It meant I got to live." She slid her hand beneath his robe and caressed his chest. "I can show you what I learned."

He closed his fingers around hers and gently moved her hand away. "Don't, Caroline. It's all right."

"It's not all right!" She jerked her hand from his. "Nothing they did was all right!"

"I know." He tried to gather her close, but she resisted.

"They broke me. They turned me into a whore." She curled her hand into a fist against his chest.

"You're not a whore."

"Why did they do that, Rogan?" Tears spilled down her cheeks, and she pounded her fist against his shoulder. "Why?"

"They were evil men." He tried again to gather her into his arms, but she shoved him away.

"You don't understand. You can't understand how helpless—" A deep wrenching sob shook her, and she clung to him, gripping his robe in her fists. "I don't want to remember," she whimpered.

Rogan squeezed his eyes shut, torn to pieces by her pain. He cuddled her close, keeping his hold loose enough that she knew she could walk away at any time, yet tight enough that she didn't crumple to the floor. He stroked her hair with a hand that trembled. "Shhh. It's all right."

Her only answer was another of those gut-ripping sobs.

He didn't know what to do for her. Yes, he'd been harsh in an effort to get her to face her fear. But he hadn't expected this. Never this.

He cradled her in his arms, torn between the need to console her and the rage that burned inside him. How could anyone have ever done such a thing to someone so pure of heart, so innocent? He wanted to track the men down and kill them all personally. Painfully.

Caroline made a soft sound of protest and shifted in his arms. He realized he was squeezing her too tightly and immediately loosened his hold. She settled against him again, limp as a dishrag, the emotional storm spent for the moment.

For both of them.

He glanced around the room, looking for some-place to sit. They couldn't just stand in the middle of the room indefinitely. His gaze settled on the bed, and he hesitated for a moment. Then he made the decision and scooped her into his arms.

She didn't protest. If anything, she cuddled closer to him, even when he sat on the bed and settled back against the pillows with her on his lap. He stroked her hair and murmured soothing nonsense in her ear, and she snuggled into him, one hand against his chest and the other curled beneath her cheek. He pressed a kiss to the top of her head, then leaned his head back and closed his eyes.

Sleep claimed them, bringing peace at last.

Chapter 8

Caroline came awake slowly, conscious of the toasty comfort of the bed and a feeling of being well rested and safe. She shifted, stretching her limbs lazily, and only then realizing that she wasn't alone in the bed.

She stilled, her senses coming instantly alert. A large, warm body lay snugly against her back, curved against hers as if they were two spoons in a drawer. The heavy weight of a male arm rested around her waist, and a large hand splayed over her abdomen. The spicy scent of a man's cologne tickled her nose even as she became aware of the steady rise and fall of his chest against her back.

She had slept in Rogan's arms the entire night.

She shifted, inch by inch, trying to slide out from underneath his arm. He grunted in his sleep, tightening his grip around her and pulling her back against him even more closely than before. His warm breath played across her neck, and his fingers flexed on her belly before he settled back into sleep.

Well, mostly.

There was one part of him that seemed to be very definitely awake, if the hard ridge pressing against her buttocks was any indication.

Panic rose, and she quivered like a rabbit caught in a snare. What if he awoke? What if he—

She jerked her thoughts to a halt, heart thundering, breathing shaky. She had spent the night in Rogan's arms, and he had not taken advantage of the fact. She needed to cling to that simple truth.

Once more she tried to slip out of his hold, but he groaned and buried his face in her neck even as his hand slid upward from her stomach. He cupped her breast through her nightgown, teasing her nipple with his thumb, sending an unexpected wave of pleasure through her.

Dear God, now what?

"Rogan." She tried to jab him with her elbow, but the dead weight of his arm made such a move impossible.

He pinched her nipple between his fingers, then gently squeezed her breast in his big hand and shifted his hips so his hard erection pressed into her bottom. Her breathing hitched. Her heart pounded in her ears. Need rose like a flame, burning through her limbs with undeniable demand.

Her reaction startled her. Scared her with its intensity.

"Rogan, stop." Flooded with mind-spinning desire, she struggled to pull away. "Please."

He muttered something in his sleep and nuzzled her neck, his fingers tracing her pliant flesh with experienced skill.

She closed her eyes as hot pleasure swept over her. What was happening to her? How could she feel so good and yet be so afraid? What kind of woman did that make her?

"No!" She grabbed his thumb, jerked it backward.

He gave a bellow and yanked his hand away. "What the— Bloody hell!" He rolled out of the bed and stood for a moment with his back to her as he adjusted his robe.

Slowly she sat up in the bed, clenching the covers around her. "You were asleep," she whispered.

He bowed his head, his shoulders tense. "I'm sorry. Did I scare you?"

"A little." Her heartbeat slowed. "You didn't know what you were doing."

He gave a hard laugh. "Part of me did."

She didn't know how to answer that, so she said nothing. He clasped his hands behind his head and took several deep breaths, clearly trying to get his unruly body under control. As she watched him struggle, she gathered her courage. "Does that happen a lot?" she asked quietly.

"Does what happen a lot?" He lowered his arms and shook them out.

"That." She could barely get the words out, and she knew her face burned with embarrassment. She knew much about horses but nothing about men. And she knew he would tell her the truth. "Your . . . er . . . male part."

He spun around to face her, astonishment plain on his face. "Did you just ask me what I think you asked me?"

"Dear Lord, don't make me say it again." She hid her flaming cheeks in the rumpled sheets.

"No, it's all right." She felt the bed dip as he sat on the edge of it; then he tugged the sheet away from her face. "Caroline, I don't mind your curiosity."

"Pretend I said nothing."

He stopped her when she would have ducked beneath the covers again. Taking her chin in his hand, he turned her head so their eyes met. "It's a natural condition for a man in the morning."

"Oh." Even as she took comfort in the fact that he hadn't been trying to take liberties, a curious sense of disappointment flickered through her. "Then it wasn't something I did."

"No." He smiled reassuringly.

She pulled away from him and slid off the opposite side of the bed. She kept her back to him for a moment and ran a hand through her tangled hair as she collected herself.

"Caroline, are you all right?"

"Of course." She turned and gave him a smile. "Thank you for answering my question."

He stood slowly, eyeing her with concern. "What's the matter?"

Afraid he would see the confusion in her eyes, she glanced toward the sunlight streaming through the window. "It's morning. Did you have plans today?"

"Never mind my social calendar. Something's bothering you." He came around to her side of the bed.

She turned away before he could reach her and headed for the door. "I think I'd like to ride this morning, so I'll just go see if Marie—"

His fingers closed over hers on the door latch. "Tell me what's wrong, love."

Her heart lurched. He'd used the endearment before, but after last night, it seemed to mean more. God help her, was she besotted?

"Nothing's wrong." Gathering her courage, she stood on tiptoe and gave him a wifely peck on the cheek. "I assume you have a suitable mount for me?"

He frowned at her but didn't push the matter. "Your father sent Destiny over last night."

"Lovely. I'll see to breakfast then." With a falsely cheerful smile, she darted into her room and closed the door, leaving him staring after her.

With the horse thundering beneath him and the wind whipping through his hair, Rogan finally felt somewhat normal as he rode across the fields with his new bride. He let Hephaestus have his head, the landscape whooshing by in a blur of green trees and grass. Destiny kept pace with Rogan's black stallion, and Caroline threw back her head and laughed with pure joy as they galloped hell-for-leather.

Rogan glanced over at the happy sound, entranced by the vitality of his young wife's face. Her brown eyes sparkled with happiness, her cheeks flushed from the vigorous exercise. A skilled horsewoman in her own right, she moved easily with the pace of the animal, unafraid of what lay ahead.

She'd never looked more beautiful. Or more desirable.

They galloped over the rise and headed for the main road that led to town. They had no particular destination in mind, just enjoyed being together. As their horses' hooves touched the road, an equine shriek split the air. Hephaestus tossed his head and lost his even gait for a moment, shuffling in agitation in response to the unknown horse's scream. Destiny reacted in similar fashion, prancing backward and forward in indecision, ears flickering, tossing her head in distress.

The high-pitched screech came again. Caroline glanced at him, and Rogan nodded his head. In unison, they both spurred their mounts forward in the direction of the unfortunate animal.

Minutes later they came upon a scene that horrified both of them. A fellow—gentry from the look of him—stood at the side of the road. He had tied his mount to a tree and was beating the animal with vicious cuts of his crop. The horse shrieked again, trying to free its head, which was trapped low to the ground so it couldn't see what its owner was doing. Blood flecked the horse's fine gray coat.

Caroline pulled up on Destiny, frozen by the torture the man inflicted on the animal. Rogan rode up practically on top of the man, then slid off Hephaestus before the horse had even come to a stop. As the black pranced out of the way, Rogan reached out and grabbed the abuser's wrist with one hand while wresting the crop away with the other.

"What the devil do you think you're doing?" the unknown man demanded, whirling to face Rogan. "Give me back my crop immediately!"

Rogan grabbed the man one-handed by the throat and slammed him against a tree, the crop clenched in his other hand. "Only if I use it on you first."

"Rogan!" Caroline cried.

"Are you mad?" the fellow croaked.

"You're the madman, beating a helpless animal like that." Rogan slapped the crop against the tree, inches from the man's face. "Give me one good reason why I shouldn't do the same to you."

"No! Stop!" Freed from her shock, Caroline quickly dismounted and rushed over. "Rogan, let him go!"

"Not until he answers my question." His eyes glittering with anger, he shoved his face close to the stranger's. "Come now, give me one good reason why I shouldn't take this crop"—he slapped it against the tree again, making the fellow flinch—"to *you*."

The man tried to answer, but apparently couldn't get the words past the fingers clenched around his throat. His face was turning an alarming shade of red, and he clawed fruitlessly at Rogan's hand.

Caroline slipped around so she could see her husband's face. The rage in his eyes scared her right down to her toes, and her heart pounded so loudly she thought he could hear it. "Rogan, please let him go."

"Did you see what he was doing to that animal?" he demanded, his voice low and feral.

"I see what you're doing to *him*." She reached out a shaking hand and stroked it down his sleeve, poised to flee should he turn his fury on her. "Please, Rogan. For me."

He flicked her a sidelong glance, then suddenly flung the man away from him. The fellow staggered away from the tree, coughing.

"I'll check on the mare." Rogan stalked toward the horse.

Caroline took a moment to breathe deeply, closing her eyes and willing her pulse to return to normal. Her heart thundered and her hands shook, and she was certain her knees would give out at any moment. But she'd managed to divert Rogan's attention, and that was all that mattered.

She would think about the consequences later.

A sound behind her reminded her they weren't alone. She turned to face the horse's abuser. "Are you all right?"

"He's insane." Still choking, the fellow thrust a finger in Rogan's direction. "I've half a mind to report him to the magistrate."

"Then report yourself as well," Caroline retorted. "Only a monster would beat a horse like that."

The fellow stiffened, his eyes narrowing. "Madame, you have cheek, I'll grant you! Your husband just assaulted me, and yet you call *me* a monster?"

"My husband doesn't abuse helpless animals."

"No, just his fellow man." The stranger gave her an arrogant look down his thin, pointy nose. "Might I inquire as to your name, madame?"

"I am Lady Caroline Hunt, daughter of the Duke of Belvingham," she replied in her haughtiest voice.

The fellow paled. "Belvingham's daughter?" he whispered.

"Not to mention my wife," Rogan growled, walking back toward them. "See that you keep a civil tongue in your head."

Caroline turned and placed herself between her husband and the stranger. "Calm down, Rogan. Raging is not going to settle this matter."

He flashed a lethal, white-toothed smile. "It

would settle it for me." He made to go around her, but Caroline stepped in front of him and planted her hands on his chest.

He stopped mid-stride and stared down at her fingers against his dark blue coat. "Caroline, get out of the way."

"No." She made herself look into his eyes, those beautiful gray eyes that were currently alight with a wild gleam that made her mouth go dry with anxiety. Her heart started pounding again. "I'm not moving."

He lowered his face so their gazes were even. "I don't want to hurt you."

The low tone made her stomach lurch with uncertainty, but she didn't dare relent. "Then don't hurt me. Tend to the mare, and let me deal with this gentleman."

"The mare won't let me near her." He sent a glare over her head. "The blackguard's trauma-tized her."

The lanky gentleman puffed himself up, but Caroline sent him a look that made him close his mouth before making things worse with an insult. "What do you mean, Rogan?"

"I mean she won't let me near her. I can't see to her injuries. She's in some kind of shock." He scowled at the man behind her.

"She won't let *you* near her?" Caroline pursed her lips. "That can't be good." She glanced at the stranger. "Mr.—I'm sorry, I don't believe you introduced yourself."

The mare's owner blinked his watery blue eyes at the change of subject. "I am Mr. Jerome Peterson."

"Jerome Peterson," Rogan repeated slowly, as if committing the name to memory.

"Did you hear what Rogan said, Mr. Peterson? You've so terrorized your mount that she won't let anyone near her."

Peterson's expression grew sulky. "The bloody animal won't listen. What else was I supposed to do?"

Rogan reached around Caroline and prodded the man in the ribs with the crop. "Watch your language in my wife's presence, Peterson."

"Apologies." Peterson withdrew a handkerchief and wiped his face. "I won this mare in a game of chance, but it's the worst horse I've ever had. It won't obey any of my commands, don't you see?"

"Beating a horse into submission never solved that particular problem," Rogan snarled. Caroline kept her hands firmly on his chest, and while he made no move to lunge, she could feel his powerful muscles flexing beneath her hands.

"Oh?" Peterson looked down his nose at Rogan. "And I suppose you are some sort of expert on horse training, sir?"

"I am Rogan Hunt of Hunt Chase," Rogan informed him through gritted teeth.

Peterson paled. "A Hunt of Hunt Chase?" he repeated weakly. "Ah . . . then you do know something of horses."

"Something," Rogan agreed, tapping the crop against his boot in an impatient rhythm.

"Now, Rogan." Caroline moved one hand to his arm, stilling it. "Mr. Peterson, perhaps we can make a bargain."

"A bargain?" Peterson repeated.

"What bargain?" Rogan asked, narrowing his eyes at his bride.

"Mr. Peterson won this mount in a game of chance, husband, and clearly he is unhappy with the animal. Perhaps we should offer to buy the horse from him. This way he gets his winnings in a form that is more palatable to him . . ." She sent Peterson a diplomatic smile. "And you and I get another mare for our stables."

Peterson's eyes lit up at the talk of money. "Indeed, I would be most pleased to sell you the animal."

Rogan said nothing for a long moment, just glared at Peterson.

Caroline stroked her hand down his arm, drawing his attention. She tried to smile at him, tried to reach the man she knew lurked behind the fury. "It's a good solution, Rogan. Please."

After a long moment of deliberation, Rogan gave a jerky nod. "I'll make you an offer, Peterson," he said with quiet menace. "And I advise that you take it and leave this area with all haste, lest I decide to see how you like the bite of the crop on your flesh."

"Come to our home this evening, and we shall settle the account," Caroline said, once the bargain had been struck. "We are at Riverside, just over the hill. My husband will write you a bank draft."

"Indeed," Rogan agreed, his smile more menacing than polite.

"Excellent. I'll be on my way then." Peterson made as if to approach the gray, but Rogan stepped between him and the wounded animal, Caroline's hand still on his arm.

"You'll not be riding this mount, Peterson." The gambler's gaze darted to Hephaestus and Destiny. "And you'll not be riding any of my horses, either. I would not want them damaged."

Outrage twisted the man's features. "Who are you to—"

Rogan stepped closer, shrugging off Caroline's calming hand, and shoved his face near Peterson's. "You will walk, Peterson. I assure you, you will get your funds. But you will have no further opportunities to harm any more helpless animals."

Peterson's mouth opened and closed, but he finally snapped it shut. Turning on his heel, he marched down the road, spine stiff, the very picture of indignation.

Rogan watched him leave, then spun back to face Caroline. "Why did you step between us? Have you no sense?"

Her mouth fell open. "I couldn't let you kill him!"

"I wouldn't have killed him, but he deserves a

thrashing for what he did to that horse."

Caroline swallowed hard, still shaken by the violence that lurked inside him. "There are other ways to deal with problems without resorting to fisticuffs."

"Should I have written him a polite note of protest?" Rogan sneered. "Is that how the duke would have handled it?"

"No, my father would have blistered the man's ears with a scalding set-down and then exercised his influence to make Mr. Peterson most uncomfortable in his business and social endeavors."

"I don't have any influence," he pointed out bitterly. "Without our horses, the Hunt name holds no meaning."

"Nonetheless, you can't go about getting into fistfights with everyone who displeases you. Children react, Rogan. Adults think matters through. You're no child."

He stiffened. "I'm aware of that."

"Then prove it." She shook her head, weary and frightened at what the future might hold. "I've been married to you for one day, Rogan, and already I wonder if I can live like this."

"We have no choice. The deed is done."

She met his eyes with a determination she hadn't felt in a long while. "There's always a choice." She turned away, unwilling to argue further. "Now, what were you saying about the mare not letting you near her?"

A sharp crack had her whirling back. Rogan

met her gaze, the crop in his hands snapped in two. Tension nearly choked her, and silence screamed between them. Finally he glanced down at the broken crop, and with a grimace of disgust, he flung the pieces into the woods.

Caroline dragged in a deep breath, feeling as if she had narrowly avoided some terrible catastrophe. "Rogan?"

"The mare's afraid of me." His attention focused on the animal now, his voice losing some of its angry edge. "She gets agitated when I come near her."

"Poor thing," Caroline murmured. With only a moment's hesitation, she turned her back on her husband and took a tentative step toward the gray. The horse lifted her head at the movement, flicking her ears as she regarded Caroline. "Rogan, look."

"Say something else," Rogan prompted. But at the sound of his voice, the mare shifted nervously.

"You poor baby," Caroline crooned. The gray seemed to calm down, and Caroline took another step forward. "I know you're scared, but we'll take care of you now."

Caroline maintained eye contact with the mare as she approached, pleased that the animal didn't back away from her.

"Blow in her nostrils," Rogan murmured. "See if she'll let you touch her."

The animal flicked her ears back and forth at the sound of Rogan's voice, but she didn't move. Caroline took up the horse's reins, then did as Rogan suggested and blew gently in the horse's nostrils. The animal gave a soft *whuff*, and Caroline reached out a tentative hand to stroke her neck.

"Well done," Rogan said, stepping forward.

The mare snorted and pranced. Only Caroline's hands on the reins prevented the horse from running off. "Stay where you are, Rogan."

Rogan froze in his tracks, and Caroline reached out and caressed the gray's nose. The animal flinched for an instant, but then she settled down and allowed Caroline to caress her. "It's all right," Caroline murmured. "He won't hurt you."

"Be careful," Rogan warned.

The horse flicked her gaze at Rogan but didn't move away from Caroline's caressing hand. "Perhaps she doesn't like men. That would explain her reluctance to obey Mr. Peterson and also how skittish she becomes when she hears you talking."

"Perhaps."

Caroline looked into the mare's big brown eyes, compassion flooding her heart. "If we can get her past her fear, she'll make a fine riding mount." She stroked the animal's velvety nose. "Yes, you're beautiful, aren't you?"

"How do you propose we get her past her fear?" Rogan murmured, careful to keep his tone low and even. "I can't get near her."

"I'll train her." She laid her cheek against the mare's neck and cast Rogan a smile. "I think she needs me. I understand her. Do you think I could?"

His lips curved. "I can't think of anyone better."

Chapter 9

Once they realized that the gray would respond only to Caroline, they had much more luck getting the horse home. Caroline rode ahead, leading the gray. Rogan trailed behind, his thoughts miles away, his pensive gaze on his wife's schoolroom-straight spine.

Curse his blasted temper! He'd seen the fear in Caroline's eyes when she'd positioned herself between him and Peterson. And that talk of choices. Was she thinking of leaving him?

He'd been resistant to the marriage at first, but now that Caroline was his, now that he had her in his house—if not in his bed—he intended to keep her. And apparently the only way to do that was to tame his thrice-damned temper.

Easier said than done. Restlessness still plagued his body. There was still something untamed lurking there, something barely civilized, whenever he thought about what Peterson had done to that horse.

He hadn't felt anything so intense since Spain.

God, Isabel. He closed his eyes in anguish as the memory of her dead body flashed through his mind. She'd made him crazy with her beauty and her lies. He understood some Spanish, especially the words that were never taught to young lads by qualified tutors, and so he'd recognized quickly enough what the locals had been talking about that night in the tavern.

Isabel, the woman he loved, the woman he'd considered marrying, was a whore.

Betrayal still stung, even years later. He'd gone to her house in a black rage, demanded the truth. She'd laughed at him, had taunted him with how she'd told him Banbury tales of love and devotion when her sympathies lay with the other side.

When *she'd* lain with the other side.

They'd quarreled. Her Spanish temper had clashed with his Irish one. She'd thrown crockery at his head.

And then she was dead, her neck broken as she stumbled back against the fireplace and landed too hard on the stones of the hearth.

What would he do if something like that happened to Caroline?

Damn it to hell, this was why he hadn't wanted a wife! He tangled his hands in his stallion's mane, tempted to rest his forehead against the animal's warm neck. When the rage was upon him, he became a beast, and those around him paid the price.

He didn't want Caroline to pay.

But he didn't want to lose her, either.

The familiar buildings of Riverside loomed ahead. Rogan stared at the gate, reluctant to enter while bad humor still nipped at him. He glanced back at the green fields that stretched as far as the eye could see. A wild race across the land would ease his temper, give him back some semblance of control. Then he could he be trusted around Caroline.

But then he looked back at his wife, at the wounded mare, and he knew he wasn't going anywhere. That horse needed him.

They both did.

The gray pranced skittishly as Tallow and Grafton came out of the stables to greet them.

"Stay back," Caroline said. The two men stopped short.

"What happened to her?" Grafton asked, clearly appalled.

"She was beaten," Rogan replied, dismounting from Hephaestus. "She doesn't seem to like men, so Caroline will tend to her."

Tallow scratched his head. "Are you certain that's wise? No disrespect intended, Lady Caroline, but that horse is a heck of a lot bigger than you."

"There's no other way." Caroline glanced down at the hand Rogan extended to her. For an instant she hesitated, still unsettled by his display of fury earlier. But his eyes were calm, if grim. She took his hand and let him help her from the horse. "Mr. Tallow, please see to Destiny. Mr. Grafton, do we have an empty stall?"

Grafton nodded. "This way." He headed into the stables.

Caroline untied the gray's reins from Destiny's saddle and walked the horse a few paces away so that Tallow could take Destiny. He led the mare into the stables, leaving Caroline alone with Rogan and the gray.

"Do you need help with her?"

Caroline shook her head. "No, but I'd like you to stay close by. She seems to be perfectly well behaved as long as you keep back."

Rogan gave a short nod and followed several paces behind as she led the gray into the stables.

Grafton waved her down to the end, where a stall door stood open. He backed away as they approached, and Caroline had no trouble getting the gray into the stall.

"Close the door, Mr. Grafton," she said. "Then please fetch some water and whatever you think would work best for these cuts."

Grafton closed the door and hurried to do her bidding.

"Is everything all right?" Rogan's voice seemed to come from the very walls.

She looked around, glanced out of the stall as far as she could without unsettling the horse. "Where are you?"

"In the next stall. I thought it would be better if she couldn't see me."

Caroline glanced at the horse, who stood placidly enough, though wearily, after her ordeal. "I think you're right."

"You said you wanted me close by."

The humor in his voice warmed her after the chaotic events of the morning. She grinned. "You're right. I know horses, but I've never healed wounds like these before. I need you to help me."

"You know I will."

The wall between them gave his voice a husky, seductive tone. Her body warmed in reaction, even though her new knowledge of his hair-trigger temper had sparked second thoughts about their relationship.

In the next stall, Rogan began to softly sing in Gaelic.

The gray's ears flickered, but otherwise she did not react. After a few moments, Caroline caught the tune, and she began to hum along with Rogan, stroking her hand down the gray's satiny neck.

The song had the cadence of a lullaby, and the words Rogan sang were beautiful. His voice wrapped around Caroline, calmed her, encouraged her to yield. She began stroking her hands through the gray's mane as her body softened, and her heartbeat slowed to a steady beat that kept pace with the song. With his voice Rogan wove a spell of intimacy and trust.

The gray's head came up, and her ears flickered

as if listening. Caroline continued to hum along, her hips gently swaying with the rhythm, her hands caressing the mare along her neck, where she hadn't been hurt. The gray nudged Caroline with her nose, and Caroline stroked that, too.

Grafton approached slowly with soft cloths, water, and salve. Still humming, Caroline took them from him without missing a beat of the song.

"Rogan," she said, "I need instructions."

"Keep humming," he said. "I'll tell you what to do."

So she kept humming the ancient Irish lullaby as Rogan softly walked her through the steps to correctly treat the mare's wounds. Though the gray flinched once or twice while Caroline was trying to clean some of the cuts, for the most part she appeared calm under the spell of the song.

Finally all the wounds had been tended. Caroline picked up the water, salve, and soiled cloths and let herself out of the stall. The mare gave a soft whinny and stuck her head out for one last caress on the nose. Then Rogan came out of the next stall, and the gray retreated back into her own.

Caroline gave Rogan a huge smile. "I did it! All her wounds are clean."

"Excellent." He smiled at her, touched her cheek. "I'm proud of you, love. You caught on quickly."

Caroline stepped back, uncertain. "Thank you."

He frowned. "What's the matter?"

She tried to retain her smile. "Nothing."

Eyeing her closely, he took the basin of water from her and set it aside, then took the cloths and salve. "Something is wrong. You flinched away from me."

With nothing to occupy her hands, it was all she could do not to twist her fingers. "It's been an exciting morning. Now if you will excuse me, I intend to visit Papa this afternoon."

She tried to dodge around him, but he caught her about the waist. She froze.

"Caroline?" Puzzlement shadowed his eyes. "Are you afraid of me?"

"Of course not." She willed her muscles to relax.

"You are." Abruptly he let her go.

Botheration! She'd hoped to come to terms with this herself before he noticed the difference in her. How could she explain her confusion?

He came around in front of her, tipped her chin up so she met his gaze. His gray eyes held concern and affection and not the slightest hint of anger. "What's happened, love?"

She sighed. Clearly he would persist until he'd wormed it out of her. "What happened last night—and this morning—made me uncomfortable."

He let out a slow, deep sigh. "I was afraid of that."

"I don't know what to think, Rogan." She gave

in to the urge and twisted her fingers. "Last night, I told you what had been done to me. And you were wonderful. So caring, so understanding. Then this morning you wanted to kill a man."

"I was angry about what he had done to the mare," Rogan said. "You saw her."

"I did. And I saw you." She shook her head. "Last night it was your brother. Today it was Mr. Peterson. Who will be next? Will it be me?"

"No." He took her face in his hands, his expression utterly sincere. "No, never."

"Can you promise me that? I don't think so." She pulled away from him. "You have no control over your temper, Rogan. Who's to say it won't be me who angers you next time? I'm afraid, and I don't want to be."

"I don't want you to be afraid of me."

"But I am. I need to think, Rogan." She hurried toward the stable doors.

"Think about what?" He started after her.

"About our marriage." She slipped through the doors, but before Rogan could follow, Tallow appeared in the doorway.

"Lord Chessington is here about his stallion," Tallow said. "He's in the study."

Caroline heard Rogan curse behind her and hurried her pace toward the house. Lord Chessington would keep him busy, at least long enough for her to change and slip off to see her father.

* * *

"You're not going back to him!" The duke ruined his imperious command by succumbing to a tremendous coughing fit.

Caroline sighed and crossed the parlor to bring her father a glass of water. "Papa, calm down. You're not helping matters."

The duke sipped at the water. As he got himself under control, he turned a narrow-eyed look on his daughter—a glare that might well have been intimidating had his eyes not been red and watery from coughing. "You came to me, daughter, and confided that you fear your husband's black temper. That twice—*twice*—since your wedding yesterday, you have seen him engage in brawling, once with his own brother! And now you ask me to calm down?"

"All I wanted was your advice, Papa. I didn't mean to upset you."

"Here's my advice—the marriage can be annulled. I can find you another husband."

"You will do no such thing!" Her cheeks flushed with frustration and a hint of embarrassment. "For heaven's sake, Papa, I don't need you to defend me. Rogan is my husband, not some villain."

"No need to stand up for the fellow, daughter. Everyone knows of his wild reputation. I made a mistake in picking him for you. I thought since he had saved your life that he had changed."

Caroline turned away from her father, fists clenching at her sides as she stared fixedly out the window at the sunny morning. "Please do not remind me how you manipulated the man into marrying me, Papa. The deed is done. *I* will decide whether or not I stay with Rogan."

"Nonsense! You're my daughter, and I can still protect you. If Hunt is not the man I thought him, I will take care of the problem. What is done can be undone. Unless . . ."

At his uncharacteristic hesitation, Caroline glanced at him. "Unless what, Papa?"

"Botheration," the duke muttered, red flags of embarrassment coloring his cheeks. He avoided her gaze.

Caroline realized what he meant. She pushed aside her own embarrassment and reminded herself that she was a married woman now. "Unless the marriage has been consummated?"

He jerked his gaze back to hers, his gnarled hands clenching on the arms of his chair. "Never tell me the blackguard has forced you! Did he hurt you? I swear, I shall kill him for this!"

"Papa, please." Caroline rolled her eyes as her father fell into another fit of coughing. "Now see what you've done." She took up the glass of water and held it so he could take a sip. "Rogan hasn't hurt me at all, and I will thank you to stop this talk of annulment."

"Then why are you here?" he wheezed. "Why aren't you at home with your bridegroom?"

"Because I was worried about you." She laid her hand on his cheek and smiled.

He covered her hand with his. "You flatter an old man, daughter. But you're really here because you had a falling out with your new husband."

She gave an exasperated sigh and stepped away. "It wasn't exactly a falling out. More like an unexpected complication. And I didn't know where else to go."

"This will always be your home, Caroline. At least as long as I breathe."

"Now I feel foolish." She took a seat on the settee near his chair. "Running home to Papa at the first sign of discord."

"And who else should you run to?" The duke gave her one of his rare grins, and for an instant she could forget that he was so ill, that she might lose him to his mysterious ailment. "Besides, your marriage was my doing, so if there's a problem, I am to blame."

"Indeed, it was your doing." She sent him a look of fond exasperation. "But now it's my problem. I'm not a child anymore, Papa."

"You're *my* child, and I want to be certain you are cared for should this illness get the best of me. I thought Rogan Hunt was the man to do that. I cannot live forever, Caroline."

"Don't say that." Distressed at this easy talk of death, she placed her hand over her father's where it rested on the arm of his chair. "You will get better, Papa. You have color in your cheeks today."

"Only because I'm embarrassed at having to

discuss the intimacies of married life with my daughter." His eyes widened. "Dear God, Caroline, your mother wasn't here to talk to you."

"Don't worry, Papa." She squeezed his hand and glanced away. "I already know what happens."

"No, you don't."

Her lips twisted in a bitter smile. "Of course I do, remember?"

"No." With effort, he sat up in his chair, reaching to hold her hand between both of his. "Daughter, you do have knowledge that I wish you didn't. But when it comes to the intimacies between a husband and wife, you are as innocent as any girl your age."

"Dear Lord, Papa," she whispered, mortified that such a subject had come up.

"This is not easy for me, either." He squeezed her hand, urging her gaze back to his. "Believe me when I tell you that you know nothing about being married, my dear. I am distressed that I sent you to your husband without arranging that another woman speak to you first."

"And yet I survived." Pushing aside her own bitterness, she managed a calm smile for her father. "You did not fail me, Papa."

"Caroline, you are my life. If I have made a mistake in marrying you to Rogan Hunt, please tell me so I can rectify it."

"Yes, do tell us, Caroline," came a voice from the doorway. Caroline jerked her head around and saw Rogan standing just inside the room, his gray eyes fierce with emotion. "Was our marriage a mistake?"

"Rogan." She stood. "What are you doing here?"

"I missed your fair company." He cast a glance at the remains of luncheon. "I assume, since none of the servants barred me from the door, that your father has yet to dispatch a letter to the archbishop to annul our marriage."

"Watch your tone, Hunt," the duke warned. "My daughter has every right to seek my counsel."

"She's your daughter, but she's my wife." Rogan slapped his riding gloves against the palm of one hand, never taking his gaze from Caroline. "And if she feels there is a problem, she should discuss it with me, not you."

Caroline twisted her fingers together. "You were busy with Lord Chessington."

"I'm never too busy for my bride." Rogan strode into the room, tossing his gloves on a nearby table.

She forced herself not to look away. "I simply came to check on my father."

"All well and good." He walked over to her, tucked a strand of hair behind her ear. "We need to talk, Caroline."

"I know." She stepped away from him, shaken by that simple touch. She studied his face, looking for some trace of the furious stranger from this morning. She could practically feel the annoyance coming off him in waves.

"She's not going back with you," the duke said. "Not if she doesn't want to. I can ruin you, Hunt."

"Papa, stop it!" Aghast, Caroline whirled to face her sire. "I told you, *I* will address the problems of my marriage."

Rogan ignored the older man's blustering. "Caroline, it's time to go home."

"I'm not ready." She stepped closer to her father's chair.

Rogan's eyes narrowed, and for an instant he looked every inch the dangerous stranger from that morning. "You can't hide here forever. You're going to have to talk to me sooner or later."

"Stop badgering my daughter," her father commanded. He took Caroline's hand and tugged her closer. "Or I'll have you removed."

"Papa!"

Rogan stiffened, his posture shifting into a fighting stance. "You can try."

Caroline jerked her hand from her father's. "Both of you stop this!"

The duke sat up straight in his chair, never taking his eyes from Rogan. "Are you challenging me, Hunt?"

"I've tolerated a lot of interference from you, Your Grace," Rogan replied, his voice low and gritty with irritation. "You arranged the entire wedding, obtained the special license, even purchased me a suit of clothes and paid off my debts.

Despite my resentment of your high-handedness, I said nothing. But now—don't think you can meddle in the private affairs between me and my wife. I won't tolerate it."

"You won't—" Caroline's father spluttered incoherently. "You young pup! Why, I could have you transported this very day if I had a mind to do so!"

"Go ahead." Rogan bared his teeth in a taunting smile.

"Give me one good reason why I shouldn't!"

"Will you both stop?" Caroline shouted.

"Hush, daughter."

"Don't fret, love."

Neither man looked at her. They were too busy posturing in some mystical male way that made no sense to Caroline.

"I can ruin you with but a few words," her father warned. "Step lightly, Hunt."

"If you ruin me, you ruin your daughter."

"I can protect Caroline."

"Like you did before?" Rogan gave a harsh laugh. "I don't know if you've done her a favor or a disservice by keeping her sheltered here all these years."

"You know nothing about the situation—"

"I won't tolerate your manipulations—"

The shattering of a small vase against the mantel brought complete and absolute silence to the room. Both men stared at Caroline, astonished.

She took a deep breath. "Now that I have your

attention, I must insist you stop arguing immediately."

"Daughter, did you *throw* that vase?"

"I did." Caroline lifted her chin in defiance, though having two such powerful males staring at her did tend to make her feel rather uncertain.

"When did you develop a temper, love?" Rogan asked softly. Dangerously.

"I don't know." With effort, she kept her voice even. "However, now that I have your attention, I demand that you listen to me."

Rogan blinked in surprise, then folded his arms and set his feet in a way that indicated he was listening, but not happy about it. He clenched his jaw, clearly holding back some sort of blistering set-down.

The duke beetled his brows at her in that way that meant he was extremely displeased with her. When she had been eight years old, that look had been enough to reduce her to tears.

But she wasn't eight years old anymore.

"Papa, I would like to speak to my husband alone." The duke opened his mouth to reply, and Caroline raised a hand, silencing him. "This is a private matter between a husband and wife, and I shouldn't have come here looking for answers. You can't help me with this."

"But—"

Caroline turned to her husband, ignoring her father's spluttering protests. "You're right, we do need to discuss matters; however, this will be a civilized discussion between two educated and refined individuals. If you are incapable of such a conversation, please tell me now."

A glint of humor flickered across Rogan's face. "I think I can manage to participate without too much trouble."

"Very well. Let's go to the conservatory." She glanced at her father. "Papa, I trust you will not send anyone to spy on us?"

The flash of guilt in her father's eyes told Caroline that was exactly what he had planned. Frustrated with her sire, she nonetheless went to him and kissed his cheek. "No spies, Papa," she whispered near his ear. "Else I shall never forgive you."

He scowled and sank back in his chair, reminding her of a petulant child.

Shaking her head, she led the way out of the parlor and toward the conservatory, all too aware of Rogan right behind her. She smiled at the familiar servants they passed, but when they reached the door to their destination, she grabbed Rogan's hand and made an abrupt turn, skirting the conservatory and darting through a set of French doors at the opposite side of the hallway. She pulled him outside into the rose garden, then quickly shut the doors behind them.

"What—?"

"Shhh." Caroline waved him to silence and cracked open the door, peering through it at the hallway. She had to wait only a few minutes before she saw Gregson, her father's trusted assistant, head toward the conservatory. "I knew it!" she whispered.

"Knew what?" Rogan murmured.

"He sent Gregson to spy on us." Caroline shut the door with a quiet click and grinned up at Rogan. "But we've outsmarted him. Come with me. I know a place no one will find us."

He arched his brows, his eyes lighting with interest. "Lead on, wife."

Chapter 10

Entranced, Rogan followed Caroline through the maze of hedges and rose bushes. He didn't think he'd ever seen her so full of mischief as she led him willy-nilly through the gardens. Finally she darted behind a large lilac bush. He followed, only to find himself in a clearing just big enough for two people and a small stone bench.

"No one will look for us here," Caroline said, peering back through the bushes.

"I find it encouraging that you allow yourself to be alone with me," Rogan said.

She stiffened and glanced at him over her shoulder. "I can assure you, Rogan, that I can scream very loudly."

That quickly, the feeling of camaraderie vanished.

"Damn it all," he muttered. "Of course you're safe with me, Caroline."

"Before this morning I would have believed that."

"I assure you," he said with a bitter twist of his lips, "I am in full control of all my impulses."

"Good." She turned to face him completely. "Because that is what we need to talk about."

"I don't blame you for feeling uncertain."

"Uncertain?" Her expression took on a cynical cast that no girl her age should ever wear. "I've seen behavior like that before. I just didn't expect it from you."

He swiped a hand over his face. "Caroline, I once told you that I can be very bad-tempered."

"Yes, you did."

"It's worse than that. Much worse."

"Worse, how?" She edged toward the perimeter of the clearing, wariness flickering in her eyes.

"Caroline, stop shuffling away from me. I won't hurt you. Blast it!" He moved away from the bench, toward the far end of the clearing two paces away. "Sit down and listen to what I have to tell you."

The suspicion that still lurked in her eyes sliced his heart to pieces. Only last night he had held her in his arms all night as they slept, and this morning she feared him.

He swept a hand toward the bench and gave her a wry smile. "As you said, you can scream very loudly. I'm certain your father's man would hear you."

Still she hesitated, and every second that passed felt like agony.

"Caroline, you led me out here so we could talk about what happened."

She sighed, the distrust fading from her expression. "You're right." She slipped past him and took a seat on the bench, folding her hands in her lap and looking at him expectantly. "You were saying something about your temper."

"I was." He took a moment to collect his thoughts. "Short tempers run in my family. Any one of us can blow into a rage at a moment's notice and over the smallest trivialities."

"Such as when your brother paid us a call on our wedding night?"

"Exactly." He grimaced. "What you witnessed is not uncommon for my family. We tend to hit first and discuss later."

"And that explains what happened with Mr. Peterson."

"Yes." He pulled a leaf from the lilac bush and began to shred it. "My family has always had a gift for horses. Not everyone gets it. Some of us are born with a kind of inner sense that allows us to communicate with the horse on an instinctive level."

Her dark eyes reflected her disbelief. "Are you trying to tell me you're some sort of mind reader for horses?"

"No, not minds." He threw the leaf aside. "It's like I can sense what they're feeling and soothe away anything that is upsetting them."

"The way you did with Mercury Mist."

"Exactly. Not everyone in my family is born with the gift, but usually there's at least one in every generation. My father didn't have it, but his cousin, the man he inherited the title from, did."

"And you have it."

"Yes."

She said nothing for a long moment, considering what he'd told her. "How does this gift relate to your tendency to fly into a rage at the slightest provocation?"

"Every gift has its price. Usually the one born with the gift also inherits the fiercest temper."

"And because you are the gifted one, your temper is worse than your brother's."

"Yes."

She shook her head. "It sounds like a fairy story, Rogan."

"I know, but it's something that goes back in my family for generations." He plucked another leaf and met her eyes as he tore it into pieces. "What happened this morning . . . I'm sorry for that."

"I know you are."

"Peterson enraged me. What he was doing to the horse enraged me. I lost my temper."

"Yes, you did."

"I'd like to tell you it would never happen again, but I don't know if I can," he said bluntly.

"You're not reassuring me, Rogan."

"Damn it, Caroline, I don't know what else to say!"

She raised her brows at his language, but didn't chastise him.

"This is why I didn't want a wife," he grumbled, tossing aside more shredded leaves. "I didn't want anyone I cared about to get in the way of my bloody rages. Especially you."

"Especially me?" She gripped the edges of the bench. "What do you mean, especially me?"

He closed his eyes, silently cursing himself for revealing too much. "I'm fond of you, Caroline," he finally said quietly. He opened his eyes, had to see her face when he told her. "More than fond, actually. I rushed over here as soon as Chessington left because I was afraid you wanted to end our marriage."

Her eyes were as wide as saucers. "Oh."

"Oh," he repeated with a hard chuckle. " 'Oh' indeed. I'm the last man on earth a woman like you should be shackled to, yet here we are, husband and wife."

"What do you mean, a woman like me? You mean a duke's daughter?"

"That, and other things." He spun away, needing to pace, but there was little room in the clearing for such activity. He clenched his hands at his sides and faced her again. The morning breeze stirred the wispy curls around her ears and forehead and teased the hem of her soft pink morning dress. She watched him so earnestly. In a way she was yet innocent, despite her kidnapping. He didn't deserve her.

"Rogan? What did you mean?"

Her soft voice washed over him like a soothing balm, offering to heal the wounds of his battered heart. But he didn't dare accept it. Didn't want to become even more tangled in the intricacies of married life, only to hurt the last person on earth he wanted to harm.

"Oh, no, you don't." She stood and marched over to him, laid her hand on his arm. "You will not retreat into silence now, husband. I forbid it."

He looked down on her, his mouth quirking with amusement as he noted that the top of her head only reached his chest. "So fierce, love." He skimmed his thumb along her smooth cheek. "You have me quaking in fear of your wrath."

She thudded her small fist against his chest. "Stop teasing me, you lout. Is all this because I am a duke's daughter? Is that why you didn't feel we would suit?"

"That's the practical part of it." He closed his hand over the fist that still rested against his heart. "Caroline, you're beautiful and loving and your heart is so tender." He brought her hand to his lips. "After all you've been through in your life, the last thing you need is a foul-tempered beast for a husband."

She narrowed her eyes. "Are you saying I'm too fragile to be your wife?"

"Of course you are."

"Bollocks!" she snorted and yanked her hand from his gasp.

He stared, torn between humor and shock. "Where did you hear that particular phrase, gentle wife?"

"I practically lived in the stables. After a while the grooms forgot I was there and weren't so careful with their language. But do not change the subject."

He folded his arms across his chest. "I wouldn't dream of it."

"I am more than a duke's daughter," she said, her body stiff with indignation. "I may be a small woman, and I may have been raised to be a lady, but I have seen things and survived things other women of my acquaintance would swoon to even think about."

"I know," he agreed quietly.

"But for some reason, both you and my father seem to think I am sensitive and delicate, that I can't get on in real life." She held up a hand when he would have spoken. "Yes, I do have fears. Annoying, frustrating fears that keep me from doing many of the things I would like to do in this life. And I'm sick to death of it."

"It's not unnatural, given what you've been through."

"Indeed. When they rescued me, I barely recognized myself in the mirror." She turned away, stared at the softly blowing leaves of the lilac bushes around them, clearly lost in the past. "I didn't fare well those first few months. My mother died soon after I was rescued. Papa and I were in mourning, living at Belvingham. I seemed to get better.

"When I was seventeen, Papa arranged for my debut. Only after I saw the masses of people did we realize that I wasn't well, that I hadn't recovered from my ordeal. I fainted," she told him with a wry smile. "I fainted in front of the cream of London society, and when they revived me, I became hysterical. Belvingham's mad daughter."

"It was too soon," Rogan murmured.

"Too soon," she agreed, "and I had gotten used to the peace of living at Belvingham. My father had armed guards around the estate. I knew I was safe there, and so we went back. Weeks turned into months, and months turned into years. I could lick my wounds in relative obscurity, secure in the knowledge that Papa would take care of me."

"Maybe that's what you needed at the time."

"It was, but it went on too long, I think." She flashed him a sad smile. "Really, Rogan, essentially I have been hiding for five years. My friends all married and produced children while I rode my horse and read books and slept at night with the candle burning."

"Don't be so hard on yourself. You were a little more than a child yourself."

"I don't like feeling helpless, Rogan." She plucked a rose from a bush and sniffed it. "Those men made me feel helpless, made me lose myself. I stayed alive, but so did the memories."

"I know how it feels. When the rage takes me, I am lost."

She bobbed her head in acknowledgment. "My father protected me, Rogan, but I'm beginning to think he protected me too much. When those brigands tried to take my coach last week, I had just been thinking that I was tired of hiding, tired of being afraid of shadows. That I wanted a normal life. I wanted to get married to a man I could have some affection for. I wanted to have children, to live the life of a normal woman."

"Instead you got me," he said with a humorless laugh.

"I got you," she agreed. "But, Rogan, you must understand that you are the first man I have ever met who has understood me. You give me time, you proceed gently. You don't let me flee back into the shadows."

"Unless I lose control, in which case I become a raging lunatic."

She sighed. "That is a problem, yes, but I do believe it is a matter of control. Did your cousin tell you anything about these rages? If he had the gift as you say, he must have been prone to them as well. Maybe he knew how to cope, how to control them."

"I never met him. He died, and my father inherited. I spent my first ten years in Ireland."

"No assistance from that quarter, then."

"I met his widow, though. We called her Aunt Alice. She was a friend of your father's."

"Alice Hunt. Yes, I remember her. She was a lovely woman."

"She's the one who bought me my commission." His lips twisted. "Else I would have followed my father and brother to hell in a whiskey bottle."

"And she left you her estate when she died."

"Our house was her dower estate," he confirmed. "She owned it outright and left it to me after my father destroyed what was left of Hunt Chase."

She sighed and gazed at him, her beautiful dark eyes troubled. "You're going to have to learn to control your temper, husband. I cannot live with a madman."

"I take it that means you are coming home with me."

"Of course." Her tentative smile warmed him like the sun after a soaking rain. "I never intended to leave you, Rogan. I just wanted to talk to someone, and Papa is all I have."

"You have me."

"Unless you're busy pummeling someone."

His own smile faltered. "Caroline, I wouldn't be able to live with myself if I did something to hurt you."

"We can only deal with these things as they occur," she said with a sigh. "At least promise me you will *try* to control your anger."

"I promise. We've made some progress, especially regarding your fear of being touched. I'd hate to think we need to start all over."

"I don't think we do." She came over to him, a secretive, feminine smile curving her lips. "Stand still, Rogan."

He didn't move a muscle, fascinated by the flirtatious light in her eyes. She slid her hand up his chest to his shoulder, tilting back her head, her lips slightly parted.

"Are you seducing me, wife?" he murmured as her other hand curled around his neck, tugging his head down.

"Yes." Her coquettish smile unleashed a hot wave of desire. "Kiss me, Rogan."

He slipped his arms around her, lifting her gently into his embrace as he bent down to touch his mouth to hers.

She made a soft mewl of pleasure, spearing her fingers into his hair as she kissed him with an abandon he hadn't felt from her before. Hunger simmered in his veins, but he kept it under control, not wanting to frighten her. He let her set the pace of the kiss, accepting the sweet surrender of her mouth, the arousing feel of her small, feminine body against his.

He broke the kiss and looked down at her, nearly undone by the desire that clouded her dark eyes. The breeze came up, stirring the flora around them and releasing a sweet fragrance into the air that blended with her delicate perfume. The sun shone down on the little clearing, warm and bright, bringing out threads of gold and red in Caroline's dark hair. "Are you all right?"

She smiled. "I'm fine."

"Good. Then open your mouth."

"What—" Her words disappeared in a soft groan as he kissed her again, gliding his tongue along her lips before darting it into her mouth. She made a squeak of surprise, and he pulled back.

"You don't like it?" he murmured, pressing a tiny kiss to the corner of her mouth.

"I-I'm not sure."

He nipped her lower lip. "Shall we try again?"

She nodded.

He took her mouth again, and she stretched up to meet him with arousing eagerness, parting her lips obediently at his urging. He swept his tongue into her mouth, the taste of her clouding his senses like fine whiskey. Silently he taught her how to kiss him, and she was an apt pupil, learning quickly what he liked.

When they finally broke apart, both of them were panting.

She touched a finger to his damp mouth. "Oh my."

He licked her fingertip. "Indeed."

She glanced up at him from beneath her lashes, a seductive curve to her lips. "I didn't panic."

"Progress," he said with a grin.

Her gaze dropped to his mouth. "Kiss me again, Rogan. Make my head spin."

He sucked in a breath. "Are you certain you want to continue this in your father's garden?"

"Why not?" She traced her fingertip along his lip. "Perhaps that's why I'm so relaxed."

"You think yourself safe?"

"I suppose so."

He chuckled. "My darling wife, if you only knew how many passionate assignations occurred in gardens."

Her eyes widened. "You're teasing me."

"I assure you, I'm not. Many an illicit affair has started with an innocent walk in the garden."

She bit her lip and pulled back a step, wariness flickering across her face.

"No, it's all right." He gave an impatient sigh. "I shouldn't have told you that. Now you'll think I intend to have you on that stone bench over there."

"What?" she yelped, casting a panicked glance at the bench.

He laughed despite his state of frustrated arousal. "Calm yourself, love. I have no intention of consummating our marriage in such a manner. Come back into my arms and let me hold you."

She cast one last, disbelieving look at the bench and then stepped back into his embrace. He folded his arms loosely around her so that she knew she could walk away, and rested his chin on top of her head. "Thank you for trusting me."

"Aside from my father, there's no one else I trust at all." She snuggled against his chest, wrapping her arms around his waist. "There are times you make me feel like a normal woman, Rogan."

"At first I thought we were completely wrong for one another," Rogan said. "But now I wonder if we could ever be right for anyone else."

She made a soft noise of agreement, then said, "Rogan?"

"Yes, love?"

"Do you really think we'll be able to consummate this marriage?"

He hugged her to him. "I do. When you're ready."

"I'm scared," she whispered. "And I hate being scared."

"You have more reason than most brides to be afraid. It's all right." He tipped her face up to his with a finger beneath her chin. "I want you to want me, Caroline."

"Part of me does already. But the other part—"

"Shhh. I know." He pressed a soft kiss to her lips. "Don't fret about it. You'll tell me when you are ready."

"I'm so glad I married you," she murmured. "We'll make it work."

He pulled her close to his heart, where she belonged. "We will."

Chapter 11

"I want to be a good wife to you," Caroline said. Her hand lay tucked within her husband's much larger one as he led out of the clearing and through the maze of her father's garden. The sensation of his warm, strong fingers encircling hers gave her a feeling of security—and made her feel very feminine. "While I will take over the running of the house, I thought perhaps I might also manage your ledgers. I'm quite good with numbers."

"I have no objection." Rogan glanced back over his shoulder and smiled. "I have no love for those books."

She found herself smiling back as warmth swept through her. Dear Lord, he was handsome. "I'm more than happy to help you make your business a rousing success."

Before he could reply, they heard a cry of alarm, followed by the sound of something large crashing through the shrubbery. Instantly Rogan settled into a fighting stance, shoving Caroline behind him with a sweep of his arm. She didn't argue, gladly seeking the shelter of his big body and bracing herself with a hand on his back as she peered around him.

"Who's there?" Rogan demanded. "Show yourself!"

There was silence for a long moment, then the slow crackling of something moving through the flora. A moment later, Gregson broke through the hedge, twigs stuck to his hair and coat.

Caroline came out from behind Rogan. "Gregson!"

The secretary straightened his spectacles, a sheepish expression on his thin, handsome face. "Good afternoon, Lady Caroline."

"Good afternoon indeed!" Caroline planted her hands on hips. "Gregson, I know you must obey Papa's orders, but . . . skulking about in the bushes?"

Gregson flushed and glanced at Rogan, who folded his arms and glowered. The secretary cringed. "I heard you coming and didn't want you to see me. I knew you'd be displeased."

"Quite so." Caroline shook her head. "Papa really must learn to leave things be. You may tell my father, Gregson, that my husband and I have resolved our quarrel."

"Yes, Lady Caroline." The young man bobbed

his head in acquiescence, then cast an uncertain look at Rogan.

Rogan curled a lip in disgust. Gregson blanched, and Caroline nearly giggled.

"I'd best not catch you following us again," Rogan warned. "I don't care what the duke told you."

"O-of course not, Mr. Hunt." The secretary gave a quick bow and scurried off down the path.

"Rogan, I do believe you have intimidated Mr. Gregson," Caroline mused, laying a hand on her husband's arm.

He made a noise that might have been a grunt or a chuckle and tucked her hand more firmly into the crook of his arm. "Your father is a martinet, Caroline."

She sighed. "I know. He means well."

"He doesn't trust me to take care of you."

She smiled up at him. "I do."

The annoyance faded from his gray eyes. "I'm glad." He began to walk, escorting her down the path as gracefully as any courtier. "When did you want to look at the accounts?"

"Tonight perhaps," Caroline replied, sweeping her skirt out of the way of a prickly rose bush. "Right now I'd like to stop in the village to see Mrs. Trenton and her new baby on my way back home. My father tells me she's been asking to see me. Then I'll return home and check on the gray. I've decided to name her Melody. What do you think?"

"I think I don't want you going to the village alone."

"Aren't you coming home?"

"I need to have a few words with your father. Business. I'll be along soon."

"In that case, my father can send a number of men to accompany me."

"Hmph. I'm not certain your father's men can be trusted to bring you home to me."

She squeezed his arm, casting him a glance of warm affection. "But you can trust me. I'll come home to you, Rogan."

A slow smile curved his mouth. "You'd better."

Rogan saw Caroline on her way, tucked into his coach with her maid and three armed escorts riding alongside. As soon as she was gone, he turned and went back inside the manor house.

He wanted a word with Belvingham.

He found the duke in the study where he'd left him. Belvingham ignored him when he strode through the doorway, as he was intent on giving instructions to Gregson.

"Give this to Roberts," the duke said, handing the young man a note. "He's the steward there. Tell him he's to do nothing with the sheep until you examine the flock."

Gregson slowly tucked the letter away in his coat pocket. "But Your Grace, I know nothing about sheep!"

The duke chuckled. "But he doesn't know that.

And if Roberts is cheating me, he'll be intimidated by the fact that I sent a sheep expert like you to handle this matter in my stead." He clapped a hand on Gregson's shoulder. "I have faith in you, Gregson. I expect you back in two days' time."

The young assistant looked vaguely ill as he turned away, and his pallor increased as he noticed Rogan standing just inside the room.

"Ah, Hunt," the duke said. "Do come in. Gregson was just leaving."

The secretary hurried out of the room, and Rogan sent a hard stare after him.

"A problem with one of my other estates." The duke sat back in his chair and produced a handkerchief, which he used to dab at his perspiring face. "One of my stewards thinks that because I am ill, I am also stupid. He's trying to cheat me. And no man cheats Belvingham."

"So you sent your assistant to sort it out." Rogan took a chair across from the desk, folding his hands across his stomach. "The way you sent him to spy on Caroline."

Belvingham shrugged without a hint of remorse. "I look after my daughter, Hunt, no matter that she is a married woman now. I will do anything to keep her safe."

"In that we agree, Your Grace." Rogan's lips twitched in a reluctant grin. "I pity your poor steward. He should be lucky it is only Gregson you are sending to handle the matter."

"I can't travel, or I would go myself. I would so

enjoy confronting the cheating bastard myself." The duke shook his head. "This illness is draining the life from me, Hunt. I fear I'm not long for this world."

"Unless we can stop Althorpe."

Belvingham gave a sigh and rested his head against the back of the chair. "The greedy snake is clever, I'll grant you that. He manages to never be around when trouble is brewing, so suspicion never falls on him."

Rogan raised his brows. "I'm suspicious of him."

The duke laughed, a rusty sound that sent him into a fit of coughing. Rogan got up and poured a glass of water from the pitcher on the sideboard, then handed it to him. The duke nodded a thank-you and sipped at the water, getting his cough under control.

Rogan didn't bother to sit again. "Where does Althorpe live? What does he do with his time? Who are his friends? I need to know more about this man if I am to protect you and Caroline from him."

"Caroline must be your priority," Belvingham commanded. "I'm an old man, and I'm sick. I may die, but Caroline will surely suffer if Althorpe gets his hands on her."

Rogan's mouth thinned. "He won't."

"He's a ruthless bastard," the duke insisted. "I would do anything to keep her from his clutches."

"Perhaps you should tell me everything you know about him." Restless, Rogan began to wander about the room.

"He's a distant cousin and my heir now that Stephen is gone." Belvingham clenched his hands on the arms of his chair. "Curse his black soul!"

"Stephen." Rogan looked up at a painting of the duke's son. "Tell me how he died."

"It was eight years ago." The duke crushed his handkerchief in his hand. "Before Caroline's abduction. Stephen was home from school. Althorpe had offered to take my son and his friend fishing." His mouth trembled, and he pressed his lips together in a thin line. "We were told it was an accident, that he had slipped on the bank and struck his head on a rock when he fell into the water."

"What about Stephen's friend?" Rogan turned back to the duke.

"Albert Westing, my neighbor's son, witnessed the accident. I'm told Stephen died instantly."

"Where is Albert now?"

"Dead." The duke reached for his water again. "The lad got shot in a duel. It was his deathbed confession that made me aware of Randall's perfidy. Apparently Albert had witnessed the bastard hitting Stephen over the head and pushing him into the pond. He owed Althorpe money and was too afraid to speak up."

"Too bad. His testimony might have stopped Althorpe and prevented our current difficulties."

"Don't I know it," the duke muttered bitterly.

"And that was eight years ago." Rogan prowled around the room again, his mind working through the intricacies of the past. "What about Caroline's kidnapping?"

"As I said before, Althorpe had to have been behind it. Damn him!"

"I wouldn't be a bit surprised. And one wonders if he tried again, more recently. I believe Mr. Docket still holds the surviving kidnapper, James Black, in custody. Perhaps I should have another word with the blackguard."

"Yes," Belvingham agreed. "Maybe he'll be more forthcoming this time and tell you who sent him. If not, make him."

"Be certain I will. Back to Althorpe for a moment. Who were his parents? Where was he educated? Any and all details about this rogue will only help in stopping him."

"His father was a vicar, and his mother was the daughter of a respectable merchant. While his parents weren't wealthy, they weren't poor, either. Both of them are dead now." The duke stared at the ceiling as if trying to organize his thoughts. "These days he spends much of his time at the fringes of the fashionable set, and he's enamored of horses and gaming. He's had his greedy eyes on Belvingham for a long while now."

"Who are his friends?"

"Some of the young bloods from respectable families. Oh, he's a smart one. Never steps a toe out of line. No one would ever suspect him of any wrongdoing."

"Everyone has secrets. I will discover his."

Belvingham laughed. "Good luck to you, Hunt. Don't you think I've tried to dig up some juicy morsel with which to blackmail him? But there's nothing."

"There's always something." Rogan glanced at his father-in-law, a grim smile on his face. "And I'll find it."

"I just told you there was nothing. Unless you can convince Caroline's kidnapper to confess that Althorpe sent him, my heir will continue to get away with his villainy."

"No, he won't. I've hired an investigator by the name of Gabriel Archer. If anyone can discover the truth about Althorpe, it's him."

"No!" Belvingham objected. "No one else can know about Althorpe. I fear for Caroline's safety if he discovers we're investigating him."

"He won't. Archer is the best. I've already sent word to London, and he's accepted the job."

The duke thrust a finger at him. "You'd do better to concentrate on protecting Caroline instead of chasing the impossible."

"I fully intend to protect my wife." Rogan folded his arms across his chest. "And I don't need your interference to do it."

"My interference!" The duke sat straight up in his chair, outrage firing in his dark eyes. "You young pup, you have no idea the kind of influence I have, sickbed or no!"

"I know that you try to manipulate people. You manipulated me and our entire wedding until things went along to your satisfaction. But now Caroline is *my* wife, Belvingham, and I will protect her."

"And who will protect her from you?" His frail hands clenched the arms of the chair. "She came flying back home in tears because you had quarreled. She's a fragile young woman, Hunt. I thought you knew that."

Rogan clenched his jaw. "There were no tears, and married couples quarrel. It's perfectly normal. She's just so used to you protecting her from every splinter and scrape that she ran to you out of habit."

"You dare to criticize me?" The duke half rose from his chair, then thudded back down again when his weak body could not match his ire. "Damn you to hell, Hunt! You don't know what she was like after those bastards finished with her."

"I do," he replied quietly. "She told me."

Belvingham's mouth fell open. "She told you?"

"I know you meant to keep her safe," Rogan continued, "but there comes a time when too much safety becomes dangerous. She had you to protect her. Now you're ill, and she has no more inkling of how to go on in the world than a newborn babe."

"That's why I married her to you."

"And I will watch out for her." Rogan cast another glance out the window. "She's precious, but not helpless. She needs to learn that."

The duke peered closely at his son-in-law.

"Good Lord, Hunt, have you fallen in love with her?"

Rogan gave a jerky shrug. "I don't know. Maybe. I just know I don't intend to let anything happen to her. And that means going after Althorpe."

"He's a snake, and a poisonous one at that!"

"Then the best thing I can do is cut off his head before he bites anybody else."

Belvingham gave a reluctant chuckle. "I admire your confidence, Hunt."

Rogan came around and sat in a chair near the duke's. "Besides discovering Althorpe's secrets, we need to discover how he is poisoning you."

A look of defeat shadowed Belvingham's face. "I've tried. Cook brings my meals directly to me herself, straight from the kitchen. Only Gregson is allowed to fetch my brandy at night. I don't know how the bastard is doing it."

"Well, if he's careful to keep his distance, that means someone near you must know something," Rogan said.

"I trust my staff implicitly," the duke protested.

Rogan's lips curled in a cynical smile. "The facts speak for themselves, Your Grace. Someone in your household had to have helped him. And you and I are going to discover who it is, before it's too late."

Malcolm Gregson sat in the corner table in the common room of the Duck and Crown, his untouched ale before him. Lips pressed in a tight line, he pulled out his pocket watch yet again to check the time.

"Where the devil is he?" he muttered.

He glanced around the tavern. No one paid any attention to him, and that was the way he liked it. He closed the watch with a snap and tucked it away in his waistcoat pocket. Then he reached into his coat pocket and pulled out a tattered length of ribbon, stroking it between his fingers.

What would Edwina think?

His grip tightened around the ribbon, knuckles showing white. His gentle Edwina would hate what he was doing. If she knew the lengths he went to so as to protect their future, she would scold him from here to London, and he would deserve every harsh word.

He was a traitor, albeit a reluctant one.

The door to the tavern swung open to admit several people. A quick glance had Gregson sitting up straight and taking a hasty gulp of his ale. He shoved Edwina's ribbon into his pocket.

He was here.

"Well, young Gregson." Randall Althorpe sat down at Gregson's table, his charming smile at odds with the cold gleam in his eyes. "May I join you?"

Unable to speak, Gregson took another drink of ale.

Althorpe signaled to the barmaid and requested an ale of his own, then looked back at Gregson with an expectant smile.

Gregson wrapped his hands around his tankard,

wishing he were anywhere but here. He could barely look at the duke's heir, so repulsed was he by the man.

"Tell me what brings you here, Gregson." Althorpe nodded his thanks to the barmaid as she set a tankard of ale in front of him. "Have you something more to tell me?"

Gregson nodded.

"Excellent." Randall sipped his ale, never taking his reptilian blue eyes from Gregson. "Tell me then."

Gregson took another bracing swallow of ale. "Our bargain still stands, correct?"

"Of course it does." Althorpe slid a glance around the room. Apparently satisfied they weren't being overheard, he nonetheless lowered his voice. "Just as when you told me of the highwayman's capture, in return for any information you can give me, I promise not to tell dear Uncle that you aren't who you say you are."

"I am Malcolm Gregson," the assistant protested. Then he dropped his eyes to his half-empty tankard. "I just didn't exactly tell the truth about my education and background."

"And your dear Edwina would probably have been beyond your reach," Althorpe sympathized.

Gregson felt his face heat as well as his temper. He controlled both. "Leave my betrothed out of this. Our bargain stands—I provide you with information on the duke's household, and you don't tell His Grace about me."

"And when dear Uncle cocks up his toes, I shall write you a recommendation as the new Duke of Belvingham. Yes, yes, dear sir, that is our agreement. Now what have you heard?"

Gregson stared at Randall Althorpe for a long moment, his stomach clenching in knots. He hated betraying the duke, but what else could he do? He loved Edwina, intended to marry her. If her father discovered that Malcolm Gregson was not the educated man he claimed himself to be— if it came out that he was the son of a fishmonger and that he'd lied to secure a decent position— well then, he knew Edwina would be lost to him forever.

He couldn't let that happen, even if it meant dealing with the devil.

As the minutes passed without Gregson saying anything, Althorpe's expression darkened. "Don't waste my time, Mr. Gregson," he warned softly. "You do not want me as an enemy."

Gregson swallowed hard, then admitted, "I lingered in the hallway and overheard some of the conversation between Mr. Hunt and His Grace. Mr. Hunt intends to question James Black again tomorrow."

"Well, well." Althorpe stroked his thumb along the handle of the tankard. "I shall have to see that does not happen."

"How can you possibly do that?"

Althorpe glared. "I have many connections, Mr. Gregson, some of whom I dare say you would prefer to know nothing about." Gregson paled, and Althorpe raised a brow. "Have you anything else to tell me?"

"I also overheard Lady Caroline and her new husband in the garden." Disgusted with himself, Gregson didn't dare look at Althorpe. "They were discussing their marriage."

Pursing his lips in interest, Randall sat back in his chair, tapping one finger on the table. "And how are the happy newlyweds?"

"Not so happy. They've already quarreled."

Althorpe clicked his tongue in sympathy. "So soon?"

"They were discussing that, and something else." Gregson hesitated, hating to divulge such intimate secrets. "They haven't consummated the marriage."

"Indeed?" Althorpe's brows rose in speculation. "Why not?"

"I believe it has something to do with Lady Caroline." Miserable, he drained the last of his ale.

"Fascinating." His second ale arrived, and Althorpe immediately took a swallow. "So, Hunt hasn't managed to get past those barriers of Caroline's. That might prove useful. Good work, Gregson."

Gregson shrugged off the compliment, lost in his misery.

"If you will excuse me, Gregson, I believe it's best if we not be seen together for very long."

"I have to leave anyway. The duke sent me on an errand at Cathington."

"See that you do a good job there," Althorpe said with a smirk. "That house will be mine shortly." He picked up his tankard and walked away.

Gregson watched him vanish into the crowd, then took Edwina's ribbon from his pocket and slid it through his fingers.

But he found no comfort there.

Rogan arrived home to find Peterson waiting. The irritating fellow paced impatiently outside the door to the stables. Upon seeing Rogan, he stormed straight over.

"A fine thing this is," Peterson ranted as Rogan slid from atop Hephaestus. "Not only do you leave me cooling my heels, but your men will not allow me inside the stables to see to the care of my own mount!"

"She's not yours anymore." Rogan took a moment to check between his horse's front legs to be certain he wasn't overheated. Satisfied, he led the animal into the stables, Peterson trailing behind like an annoying sibling.

"On the contrary, Mr. Hunt, she is mine until funds have changed hands. An event," he pointed out with supercilious sarcasm, "which has not yet occurred."

The man's tone grated. Rogan grabbed a brush and began to brush the grime from the stallion's coat. "You'll get your money."

"So you say! I demand that you write the bank draft now, sir, or I shall take my horse and go."

Rogan spared him a look of disgust. Every time he thought about what Peterson had done to that horse, he wanted to pummel the sneer right off his face. He flexed his fingers, imagining the crunch of bone beneath his fist.

But then he thought of Caroline and pushed the urge away.

"Hunt, did you hear me?"

Rogan didn't even bother to look at him this time. "You'll get your money as soon as I've finished getting Hephaestus settled."

"Don't you have grooms for that sort of thing?"

"I always take care of my own mounts. Watch carefully; you might learn something."

Peterson puffed himself up in indignation. "Mr. Hunt—"

Rogan paused. Fingers clenched tightly around the brush handle, and he pointed the tool at the skinny gamester as if it were a rapier. "Peterson, you take your life in your hands by pushing me."

"I only want what's due me." Peterson cast a disparaging look at the brush and then adjusted the fit of his coat. "It's bad enough that you have caused me to ruin my boots walking across the countryside. Now you expect me to stand and wait in favor of an animal?"

Rogan finished brushing down his mount in silence and gave him a sip of water before he closed the stable door.

"Mr. Hunt, I am speaking to you."

Rogan turned an intolerant glare on Peterson. "You're making noise, but you haven't said anything of interest yet." Before the peacock could puff himself up again, Rogan led the way out of the stables. "Come along then, if you want your money."

"Finally." Peterson sauntered after him. "May I say, Mr. Hunt, that you have a most disagreeable disposition. I don't know how you managed to win a lady as charming as your wife."

"No, you may not say." With a curl to his lip, Rogan led the distasteful wretch into the house to his study. "Have a seat, Peterson. This will only take a moment."

"I should hope so after all the time I've wasted here." Peterson dropped into a chair as Rogan moved behind his desk and pulled out a bank draft. He scribbled out the amount, blew on it to dry the ink, then held out the draft to Peterson, who snatched it eagerly and scanned it. His eyes widened in disbelief. "This is all? That gray is a valuable animal!" Peterson tossed the draft on the desk. "Offer more or I will take the horse and leave."

Rogan flattened his hands on the desk and leaned forward, narrowing his eyes. Anger simmered fit to rend his veins. It was all he could do to not grab the pretentious jackanapes by his neck cloth and eject him from the house. "You will not take the horse, and you will not get another farthing. You damaged that animal, which makes my offer more than generous."

"That horse is poorly trained and needed discipline!"

"It's you who needs discipline, Peterson. Now I suggest you take the money and leave before I give you a taste of what you did to that mare."

Peterson looked as if he would protest more, but a look at Rogan's stone-set face apparently convinced him otherwise. Snatching the bank draft from the desk, he tucked it away in his coat pocket. "I shall not say it was a pleasure doing business with you, Hunt."

"And I shall not wish you to the devil," Rogan shot back. "If you start walking now, you may yet reach Bartholomew's tavern before dark. You can catch the mail coach to London there."

Peterson sneered. "My gratitude knows no bounds."

"My patience does. Good day, Peterson."

The foppish gamester turned away without another word and stormed out of the house. Rogan sat down in his chair with a sigh. As much as he hated paying so generous a price, it had been well worth it to see the back of Peterson. The man was cruel and vicious, and to leave the gray in his care would mean condemning the animal to death.

He took comfort in the fact that Caroline would be pleased that the fellow had left under his own power and not limping and bloody. He hoped she appreciated his restraint, because it had been damned hard to let Peterson walk away without making him pay. Who did the bastard think he was, beating an innocent creature—

His thoughts stumbled, halted, as his gaze fell on a piece of pottery tucked against the hearth.

It was wedged into a corner and easily overlooked by whomever had last cleaned the room, just a small shard of white clay that no one would have considered important. But he knew where it came from, how it came to be there. He remembered the incident last night when he'd brawled with his brother. They'd smashed several figurines and one vase as they attempted to beat each other senseless. The shard he looked at now was no doubt a piece of one of those damaged items.

Who had cleaned the room? Caroline? Tallow or Grafton?

He'd never thought about who cleaned up the messes before. Never even noticed the messes even if he'd been the one to make them. How many servants had picked up after him and his brother and father every time they'd fallen into a fistfight?

He rose from his chair, walked over, and bent down to ease the slice of pottery from where it was wedged. Then he stood, regarding it.

He'd spent the last half hour wishing Peterson to the devil for his abominable treatment of the gray mare.

But was he any better?

* * *

Caroline was ready for bed when the soft knock sounded at the connecting door. Gripping her wrapper closed, she called, "Come in."

Rogan opened the door. He was wearing his dressing gown, and his expression struck her as oddly reticent as he hovered in the doorway. "May I come in?"

"I just said you may," she said with a grin. But when he didn't reply to her jest, her smile slowly slipped away. "Rogan, what's the matter?"

He came over to her and took her hands, searching her face with an intensity that dissolved her levity. "I came for a good-night kiss," he said finally.

Her lips parted in a soft "Oh."

"I want you to know, too, that I will think about what you said today. I want this marriage to work, Caroline."

"So do I," she whispered.

"I want to be the kind of husband you deserve."

Her heart melted. "Oh, Rogan."

"Now kiss me good night, and let us both fall asleep with a sweet memory."

"Yes." She waited, but he didn't take her into his arms. "I thought you wanted to kiss me good night."

"No." His lips quirked with humor. "I want *you* to kiss *me*."

"Oh." Startled, she dropped her gaze to his mouth. "All right."

"Come closer, love. I promise not to move."

She came toward him, longing for the taste of

him with a hunger that surprised her. He guided her hand as she stepped closer to him, placed it on his shoulder. She rested the other on his chest.

"Do you want to kiss me?" he asked softly.

"Yes," she whispered, entranced by his curving lips.

"Go ahead. Kiss your husband good night, love."

She needed no more encouragement, and she stretched up on her toes to press her mouth to his. The kiss was urgent yet sweet, their lips clinging as Caroline swayed on her toes.

They moved apart, and Rogan steadied her with a hand on her arm as she rocked back on her heels. When he slipped his hand around her waist to hold her fast in his embrace, her startled brown eyes met his.

"I don't want you afraid of me, Caroline."

"I'm not," she replied, distracted by the moisture that clung to his lips.

"Good." And with a little smile and a whispered "Good night," he left the room.

Chapter 12

The next day, Rogan left the magistrate's office with a frown on his face.

James Black had been found dead in his prison cell that very morning.

Docket had no explanation for it. No one had come to visit the criminal, so finding him dead in his cell with his throat cut had shocked him.

And it bothered Rogan. Greatly.

He had no doubts at all that Althorpe had something to do with James Black's death.

He was glad now that he had contacted Gabriel Archer. Known as the Avenging Angel, Archer had built his reputation by using his impeccable investigative skills to resolve certain difficulties for members of the nobility, or anyone else wealthy enough to afford him. Ever since he had exposed a traitor to the Crown nine years before, he had been in constant demand for matters that required discretion and excellent performance.

Rogan had no doubt that if anyone could ferret out Althorpe's secrets, it was Gabriel Archer.

He made a mental note to write to Archer and notify him of this latest development as he started for the livery, where he had stabled his horse while he was in the village. He slowed as a glimpse of a familiar carriage caught his eye. The equipage, surrounded by three outriders, stopped in front of the dressmaker's, and his wife descended, her maid at her heels.

Dressed in a becoming yellow dress and a simple straw bonnet, Caroline looked like a ray of sunshine personified. A smile curved his lips as he treasured the opportunity to observe her when she didn't know she was being watched. She looked so petite amid the much taller footmen and outriders. Even her maid topped her by an inch or two.

And when he held her, her head barely reached his chest.

For an instant he imagined enfolding her small frame in his arms, her delicate curves pressed against him. Concerns over Althorpe faded to the back of his mind as an unfamiliar warmth flooded him. He wanted to go to Caroline, to talk to her and watch her smile. Hear her laugh. Before he could move, she went into the dress shop, her maid right behind her.

An ache grew in his chest, and he idly rubbed

the place where his heart beat. Good Lord, he was besotted. When she came into his view, he could think of nothing but her. He could almost smell her perfume, though he stood on the other side of the street. He knew how her lips would curve as she smiled at him, how her soft arms would feel as they embraced him.

Bloody hell. He was *happy*.

Uncertain how he felt about the unfamiliar emotion, he made his way across the street.

"Good afternoon, Lady Caroline." Mrs. Denworthy came forward to greet them with a smile on her face.

Caroline smiled back at the reed-thin woman. "Good afternoon, Mrs. Denworthy. I've come about a new riding habit."

"Worn out another one have you?" the seamstress teased, her deep dimples creasing.

"Yes, I'm afraid so," she replied good-naturedly.

"I have a lovely shade of blue that would look wonderful on you," the dressmaker said. "Let me fetch it."

As Mrs. Denworthy disappeared into the back room, Marie went over to look at the ribbons spilled across a table. Caroline meandered through the familiar shop, touching a muslin here and a radiant satin there. How she loved the different materials and colors! Had she gone on to have a Season in London, she had no doubt she would have gone overboard and ordered a dress in every possible hue and fabric.

A whisper-thin silk in a soft shade of rosy peach caught her eye. She carefully rubbed her fingers across the fabric, captured by its beauty and femininity.

"That shade was meant for you," Rogan said from behind her.

Startled, she whirled to face him and found him even closer than she expected. "Rogan, what are you doing here?"

"Looking for you." Without a care for anyone who might be watching, he dropped a soft kiss on her lips.

"Rogan!" Heat washed through her cheeks, and she glanced around. No one was in the shop but the two of them and Marie, who pretended intense interest in a silver ribbon.

Rogan laughed. "Come now, love. Everyone knows we're married."

"Still, such things aren't done."

He leaned closer, then chuckled as she craned her head out of reach. "I do them. However, if you feel more comfortable pretending we don't like to touch each other, I can play along."

"Rogan, how can you voice such things?" Scandalized, yet excited despite her better judgment, she turned back to the pinky peach silk. "Do you like this color then?"

"As I said, it's perfect for you." He came up beside her and caressed the material mere inches from where her own fingers did the same. "Perhaps a night rail?"

"Out of silk? No, this was meant for a grand evening dress, I'm sure. I'm perfectly content with my regular nightclothes."

He brought his mouth close to her ear. "I'm not."

Heat shot through her. Dear Lord, how could he say such things here? Now? Her pulse skittered madly as she considered what else her bold and passionate husband might do in full view of the public. "Behave," she whispered as Mrs. Denworthy came back with the blue velvet for her habit.

"Good afternoon, Mr. Hunt," the seamstress said. "Have you come to help your wife choose a new riding habit?"

"Yes," Rogan said, approaching the modiste with that charming smile of his. "And a few other things as well."

"Rogan, no," Caroline hissed.

He merely sent her a look that told her he would do what he wanted, no matter what her protests.

"I am pleased to assist you in any way I can," Mrs. Denworthy gushed.

"A ball gown," Rogan said, then pointed to the rosy peach silk. "Made of that material and suitable for a bride."

Mrs. Denworthy sent Caroline a look of feminine approval. "You have exquisite taste, sir."

"There might be a few more dresses I will want made for my wife," Rogan continued. "Perhaps you can show me something . . . ?"

"Of course!" Had her arms not been full of material, Mrs. Denworthy would no doubt have clapped in glee. "Such a generous husband you are, Mr. Hunt."

"Why, thank you."

"We will need to measure, of course. Do let me fetch my assistant." The dressmaker disappeared into the back room again.

"Rogan, what are you doing?" Caroline demanded in a low voice. "I simply came here for a new riding habit."

"You're a beautiful woman," her dangerously handsome husband said, flashing her a charming grin. He lifted her hand and pressed a kiss to the back of it. "You deserve beautiful things."

"I must agree," said a woman in a voice like aged paper. "I have never seen you looking so well, Caroline."

"Lady Jayton." Caroline gave a curtsy to the elderly marchioness, who had just entered the shop with six servants to tend to her needs.

Lady Jayton sent a shrewd glance at Rogan. "I expect you are the cause of the becoming blush on my goddaughter's cheeks, young man."

"I can only hope," Rogan replied, bowing. "I have heard much of you, Lady Jayton."

The marchioness gave a wave of her hand. "Piffle. Pay no mind to gossip, sir, and you will be the better for it." She raised her snowy white brows at Caroline. "And you, child. Have you no kiss for your godmother?"

Obediently Caroline came forward and brushed her lips against the old woman's creased cheek.

"So," Lady Jayton said, "you've married at last, my girl. I regret not being able to attend your wedding, but I have only just returned from the continent." She cast a knowledgeable and appreciative glance over Rogan, taking in every detail from top to toes. "A fine specimen indeed, despite his pedigree."

Rogan scowled but held his tongue.

"We are well suited," Caroline replied demurely.

"And married some days ago. Hmph. That settles it then. A week from Thursday, don't you think?"

"A week from Thursday?" Caroline asked as Mrs. Denworthy came back up front, her assistant trailing behind her.

"Thursday next. A dinner in your honor. Small party, no more than twenty, at Jayton Hall."

"A dinner in our honor?" Panicked, Caroline glanced at Rogan.

He stepped forward. "We're honored, Lady Jayton, but—"

"Excellent. It's done then." The marchioness raised her brows at the dressmaker. "Bring me a chair, Cecelia, and see to my goddaughter's needs. I do believe she will require quite a bit of fashionable new attire. An evening dress, for instance?"

"Quite right, Your Grace," Rogan agreed, abruptly siding with the most powerful peeress in the parish.

"You'll need something new for the dinner party," Lady Jayton said when Caroline opened her mouth to protest yet again. "Humor an old woman, girl."

"And your husband," Rogan chimed in.

Caroline knew when she was defeated. Despite her misgivings about attending any kind of social event, she knew she could never refuse her god-mother. No one swayed Lady Jayton once she had made up her mind.

At least it was only a small dinner party at Lady Jayton's familiar estate.

She turned to the seamstress. "Mrs. Denworthy, it seems I require an evening dress."

"A dinner party." The duke frowned and reached for his ever-present glass of water.

"Papa, you must help me." Caroline paced around the parlor. "I haven't been out in society in years."

"Hmm. Lady Jayton. No one refuses her invitations."

"I know that!" Caroline plopped onto the settee and twisted her fingers together in her lap. "But you remember what happened at my come-out ball."

"I do." The duke sighed. "Do you want me to

talk to her? Perhaps if I explain to her that you do not go out in public—"

"We can't do that." Shaking her head, Caroline rose to pace the room again.

"Why the devil not? I daresay my consequence equals Jayton's, as does my daughter's."

"But not Rogan's."

"Ah." Her father regarded her with a knowing smile. "You don't care what Lady Jayton thinks of you for refusing her invitation, but you don't want your husband to suffer for it."

"Lady Jayton holds a lot of influence in the area," Caroline admitted. "Her cachet would assure that Rogan's business would flourish."

"True. And that's one of the assets you bring to the marriage, Caroline. Your social standing."

She sent him a bland look. "I thought it was a fortune. Or was that a horse?"

The duke cast a warning glance her way. "You both brought things of value to the marriage. Yes, you brought wealth and a horse and your pedigree. And Hunt brings strength with which to protect you when I am gone."

"Oh, Papa." She tried for a teasing smile, but her heart clenched as she looked at his tired, lined face. "I don't need protection."

"Yes, you do," he asserted, his dark eyes fierce. "Hunt will see to it."

Startled by his vehemence, she tried to laugh it off. "I suppose he will. The two of you are so alike."

Her father gave a grunt of disbelief. "You said Lady Jayton's dinner party was a small one."

She nodded. "About twenty people."

He gave a dismissive wave of his hand, but the gesture lacked his usual vitality. "You will attend, of course."

She paced again, tangling her fingers together. "What if the same thing happens? What if I contract a fit of vapors and embarrass my husband?"

"You didn't do that at your wedding," he pointed out.

This brought her agitated pacing to a halt. "You're right."

"I deliberately kept the guest list small," the duke said. "I suspect that part of what bothered you last time was the terrible crush of people. That won't happen at a small dinner party."

"Perhaps." She bit her lower lip in concentration, then cast her father an amused glance. "If it comes to be too much, I can always plead the headache."

He chuckled. "That's my daughter."

With a harsh wheeze, his laughter turned to coughing. His eyes widened, watered. His face reddened as he bent forward in his chair, still coughing.

"Papa!" She flew to his side, kneeling beside his chair. She laid a hand on his back as his body continued to wrack and shake. "Papa, what can I do?"

He waved a hand in the general direction of the

water glass. Caroline snatched it up and handed it to him. He nearly dropped it. She closed her fingers over his and guided the wavering glass to his mouth so he could take a sip, bracing one hand on his back.

He continued to cough, though with less intensity. She sat beside him, calmly guiding the water to his lips while inside her nerves vibrated with fear. Her father was dying, and there was nothing she could do about it.

Slowly the hacking receded, and he drew several shaky breaths. She offered him the glass again, but he shook his head and pushed it aside with a trembling hand. As she replaced it on the table, he fell back in his chair, closing his eyes as he struggled to take breath after breath.

"Papa, is there anything I can do?"

"Fetch Kerns," he rasped, too spent to even open his eyes. "I need to rest."

Knees weak with fear, Caroline scrambled to her feet and raced for the door, flinging it open and sending a nearby footman for the butler. Then she hurried back to her father.

He lay as she left him, his skin unnaturally pale, his lips dry. Fear gripped her by the throat as she tentatively touched her fingers to the side of his neck.

His pulse throbbed, weak but steady, beneath her touch.

She sighed with relief, so overcome she nearly burst into tears. His eyes slowly opened, and he managed a tiny smile.

"I'm not going . . . without a fight," he whispered.

She took his hand in both of hers, unashamed of the tears that lingered, unshed, in her eyes just as Kerns hurried into the room.

"Lady Caroline, is he . . . ?"

"He's weak," she said, gently placing her father's hand on the armrest. "Please take him to his room."

"Very good, Lady Caroline." Kerns signaled, and two footman came forward to assist him with the duke.

Caroline stood back and watched the servants help her father to his feet. One shaking step at a time, he made his way toward the door. As he passed her, he sent her what he no doubt intended to be a reassuring look.

She watched him leave the room, supported by servants. Her father, once so robust and commanding, had become a shadow of his former self. He'd lost a lot of weight, reducing his once-powerful frame to near skeletal. His hands tended to shake, and his dark eyes looked sunken in his face.

But when she looked into those eyes, she saw the spirit of her father there, vital and strong and determined to fight.

She held that image in her mind as the shell of the Duke of Belvingham was all but carried from the room by his loyal retainers. He was slipping away from her little by little. And there was nothing she could do about it.

* * *

Rogan perused the letter that had just arrived via messenger from Gabriel Archer. The missive contained basic facts about Randall Althorpe, though Archer assured him he had barely scratched the surface of the matter. This was just what he had pulled together over the last couple of days—well-known details about Althorpe's life. Now, Archer conveyed, they needed to determine which aspects were truth, and which were fiction.

Rogan shook his head in admiration as he scanned the lines. Althorpe had done a good job of keeping his reputation free of any taint. In fact, if the information Rogan now held was to be believed, Althorpe should be nominated for sainthood.

No man was *that* clear of misadventure.

No, Althorpe's reputation was so clean that Rogan knew a little digging on Archer's part would no doubt produce some juicy tidbit of scandal. A woman, a gambling debt, cheating at cards, bad financial decisions. Something. The duke seemed utterly certain that not only was Althorpe a miscreant, but a murderer as well.

Now they just had to prove it.

Rogan looked up as he heard the front door open. "Caroline?"

"Yes."

She came to the doorway of the parlor without removing her bonnet or gloves. The look in her soulful dark eyes had him setting aside the letter and rising from his chair, all in one smooth movement. "Caroline, what's the matter?"

She sighed and shook her head, stripping off her gloves one at a time. "Papa. He's getting worse."

"I'm sorry." He came to her and rested his hands on her shoulders as she fumbled with the ribbons of her bonnet. "Is there anything I can do?"

"No." She gave him a sad smile that nearly broke his heart, then glanced down at her hat strings, which she had somehow managed to knot. "Oh, botheration!"

"Let me." Gently he pushed aside her hands, then set about the task of unknotting the ribbons. She stood silent as a statue, so quiet that he could almost believe her made of marble.

Finally the knot gave. He glanced up in triumph, the smile on his lips fading as he watched one tear after another trickle silently down her cheeks. "Caroline?"

"He's dying," she whispered as he tugged the bonnet from her head. Her gaze clung to his, her beautiful dark eyes begging him to disagree with her. "He's dying, and I can't stop it."

"I know." He brushed the tears from her cheek with his thumb.

She turned her face into his hand, seeking comfort, then reached for him, gripping his coat blindly as the sobs shook her body. He cradled her to him, pressing her tearstained face into his chest as her grief swept over her.

He should tell her about Althorpe, the duke's wishes be damned. About the poisoning. Perhaps it would make her feel less helpless.

But not now, not while she clung to him and wept with heartache.

There was time for that, he thought, burying his face in her dark hair. He would tell her. Soon.

Chapter 13

L ord Tennsley's horse was a devil.
    While she tied the ribbons of her bonnet,
Caroline watched from her bedroom window as
Rogan worked with the ill-tempered beast. His
great patience with animals struck her as odd
when compared to his strange and inexplicable
furies. It was as if he were two people, one gentle
and the other enraged.

Right now he coaxed Tennsley's skittish gelding to come to him, his posture nonthreatening,
his hands low, palms open. Tallow and Grafton
stayed well out of the way, knowing that only a
master of Rogan's caliber could handle the unpre-
dictable animal. She could almost hear the soothing Gaelic that he sang to the horse. There was
great power in that melodic voice, in the softness
of it, the unspoken offer of safety.

She knew, because he'd used it on her.

Her gaze drifted along her husband's fine form. Dressed in a simple shirt and worn trousers for working with the horses, he presented a handsome picture.

The wind ruffled his ink-black hair and molded his shirt to his brawny chest and arms. She made a sound of pure feminine appreciation, hardly able to believe that such a handsome creature belonged to her. He shifted his weight as he worked with Odysseus, the muscles of his thighs and buttocks clearly defined beneath the form-fitting trousers.

Realizing that she was staring at his rear end, she jerked her gaze away, her face flushed with heat. Her gown suddenly felt too constricting, and she took deep breaths to calm herself. What was she doing, lusting after her husband in the middle of the day? Hadn't he made it clear that she didn't arouse him that way? And even if he did feel attracted to her, she was incapable of going further than a kiss or two.

She turned away and reached for her pelisse. Her fingers shook as she swept the garment around her shoulders, and she forced herself to look down at the fastenings instead of out the window at her husband. Like the gelding, she, too, longed to succumb to the lure of Rogan's call. His presence attracted her more than her fears repelled her. She found herself longing to feel his arms around her, his mouth on hers. She wanted to open her heart and let him lead her to new worlds she had yet to discover.

But always distrust reared its ugly head—a primitive distrust of the male animal, so deeply buried in her memories that she had no control of it. Until she could break down that wall of suspicion, until she could go freely into her husband's arms and offer herself to him, she didn't dare allow herself to get too close.

Besides, he might not want her.

Her fingers stilled. What had happened to that obvious hunger on their wedding night? There had been no repeats of that hot, demanding need in the days they'd been married, just sweet kisses that lingered longer each night before they retired to their separate rooms. Perhaps he had told her the truth, that his arousal had been only a natural occurrence in the morning. Nothing to do with her.

Nothing at all.

And if that were the case, it made it only harder for her to go to him.

Then there was the matter of his temper. It amazed her that a man with such a good heart was capable of such utter rage—and equally incapable of controlling it.

From what he had told her of his family, she suspected that as a child he had simply not been taught to rein in his temper. If anything, it seemed as if his family enjoyed indulging in such dramatics, turning on each other like hungry wolves at the slightest provocation.

When consumed with fury, Rogan seemed to almost enjoy the experience. But afterward he often castigated himself, aware that such behavior was ill-advised, yet incapable of stopping himself.

But *she* could stop him. And perhaps once she had helped him control his rages, and he helped her get past the wall of fear that prevented her from sharing his bed, maybe then they could finally have a real marriage. Maybe.

She shook off the melancholy brought on by such deep thoughts. With her father so ill, she had decided—with Rogan's blessing—to continue her charitable works with Belvingham's tenants. She had decided on a schedule of making her rounds twice a week, much as she had done before her marriage, which still allowed time to manage Rogan's house and keep the accounts. It gave her a sense of normalcy to visit the sick and read to the children at the school. It was as if the clock had wound backward to a time when her father was hale and hearty, and she had nothing to worry about except the weather.

She smoothed her hands down her pale gray skirt and scooped up the books she intended to read to the parish children.

An equine shriek split the air, and she nearly dropped the volumes. Shouting erupted from the yard. She rushed back to the window and looked down to see Grafton leading away an unfamiliar horse, while Tennsley's animal raced around the yard, ears flickering, clearly agitated. The gelding shrieked again, clearly a call of distress.

And grappling around in the dirt outside the fence were two men, one of whom was Rogan.

"Not again," she muttered and hurried downstairs.

By the time Caroline bolted outside, Lord Tennsley's horse was pawing the dirt, snorting like an angry bull. Tallow tried to separate the two men fighting on the ground and got knocked aside for his trouble. Grafton came at a run from the stables.

She wasn't about to get into the middle of two large men trying to pound each other into dust. Disgusted with males in general, she took up her skirts and marched around to the kitchen. When she came back, she lugged along a pail of water, clutching the handle with both hands as she struggled not to spill the sloshing contents.

She put the pail down with a thump and watched for an instant longer as Rogan and Colin (as she could see now despite the dust that covered both men from head to toe) continued to wrestle and—from the looks of it, anyway—twist each other's heads from their necks.

"Stop it!" she shouted. "Both of you, stop right now!"

Neither man paid her any heed. Narrowing her eyes in irritation, she bent down and tried to lift the heavy bucket. Grafton hurried over to her side. With his assistance, she was able to heave the water at the two fighting brothers.

Water splashed over both of them, eliciting howls of surprise. They rolled apart, and both men clambered to their feet as Grafton darted away, clearly unwilling to be associated with the wet, cold call to order.

Rogan—drenched, muddy, and clearly furious—narrowed his eyes at her. "Explain yourself, madame."

She shivered at the warning in his voice. She knew that tone, had heard it the day he bought Peterson's horse. Nonetheless, she faced him. "I had to do something to stop the two of you from brawling like schoolboys."

"Schoolboys, is it?" Rogan's brows lowered, and he planted his hands on his hips as he raked an angry glance over her.

She didn't back away, though part of her screamed to do just that. This was her husband, and they were surrounded by three other people. He wouldn't hurt her.

Not with witnesses anyway.

She swallowed her nervousness and propped her own hands on her hips as she met his glare with one of her own. "What would you call two grown men rolling about in the dirt?"

"Brothers," Colin answered, his amusement plain even through the mud smeared on his face.

"Hush," she snapped, then turned her attention back to Rogan.

Even as she watched, his eyes seemed to lose some of their ferocity. "Did you just tell my brother to hush?"

"I did. And you can do the same."

Colin chuckled and cast a glance at Rogan. "She sounds like Mother."

Annoyed beyond words, Caroline folded her arms and gave Colin a pinch-lipped look of disapproval. "I do believe I asked for silence, sir. You will have your turn to speak."

"You're very brave today." Rogan's low voice whispered along her spine like the cold finger of death.

"And you're very foolish," she snapped back. "Have you even noticed what your altercation has done to Odysseus?"

Rogan whipped around to look at Tennsley's horse, then muttered a curse. Two long strides carried him to the fence, and in one leap he was over it. His pace slowed down as he approached the spooked animal. The soft murmur of Gaelic words drifted to Caroline on the breeze.

"You're a brave woman," Colin said, glancing from Rogan back to Caroline. "Even my father hesitated to take on Rogan in a temper."

"And what of your part?" she demanded. "How did this start? What did you say?"

"I said hello," Colin shot back, clearly offended at the question. "I barely arrived, and Rogan came after me."

She raised her brows. "I find that hard to believe."

His façade of innocence faded under her skepticism. "Well, I did ask him if he'd considered my request. But that was *after* he ordered me off the property."

"More the fool you," she said with exasperation. "Rogan can't be bothered with visitors when he's working with a difficult animal. Frankly, I'm surprised you didn't know that."

"This is important to me! To our family."

Caroline cast a glance at her husband, who once more seemed to be completely focused on the horse. That wouldn't last long, she knew. "I suggest you go inside and clean up and wait for him to finish training Odysseus before you begin pleading your case." She turned to leave.

"Wait, where are you going?"

"Far away from here," she replied with a twitch of her lips. "Grafton, will you please see to Mr. Hunt? And send Marie to me. We're expected in the village."

"Yes, Lady Caroline."

"You're going to leave me alone here?" Colin asked in astonishment. "What if he starts another fight?"

"Just don't break anything in the house." Dismissing her brother-in-law, she headed for the waiting carriage. As she passed the yard, she couldn't stop herself from casting one last glance at Rogan.

And met his eyes—dark, aggravated, and brimming with the promise of retribution.

It had taken a good while to get Odysseus calmed.

Rogan sat in the parlor and sipped his whiskey. That his petite wife had managed to soak him with water and escape unscathed while he was in the middle of one of his rages was a complete miracle. Even now he shuddered to think what he might have done has she not distracted him with Odysseus.

But damn if he didn't admire the chit for standing up to him. Lady Caroline Hunt had spine beneath that delicate exterior, and finally she was beginning to realize it.

"Are you still brooding?" Sitting across from him, Colin enjoyed his own glass of whiskey.

Rogan sent him an annoyed glare. "I could have harmed her. And you, come to think of it."

Colin shrugged off the comment. "Not me. I'm used to your rages."

"Well, I'm not." Rogan rose and put his glass on the table. "I never will be."

"Bloody hell, Rogan, will you get past it already? You have the gift, so you get the temper. It's been that way for generations."

"That's a convenient excuse, nothing more. I never realized that before now. I just need to maintain control before the fury takes hold—or before I start swinging."

"Well, I seem to bring out the worst in you." Smirking, Colin tossed back the dregs of his drink. "I came by to ask you for help, to play on your loyalty to the Hunt name and lend me the money I need to make Hunt Chase a working stable again."

Rogan arched a brow at his brother. "Lend?"

"All right then. Give."

"You and Father should have considered that before you sold off everything."

"By the devil, Rogan, do you intend to hold that foolishness over my head forever? Father was the one who sold everything. Yes, I helped, but I want to restore Hunt Chase to what it once was. Doesn't that mean anything to you?"

"Maybe it will. Eventually."

"Oh, for pity's sake. Why do I think I can reason with you?"

"There's the door." Rogan gestured with his glass before moving to refill it.

"I'm not leaving." Colin thumped his glass down on the table. "You care about Hunt Chase, too, Rogan. I know you do. What Father and I did was wrong, but I'm trying to make it right. Help me. Give me the money to make our legacy great again."

Rogan didn't answer. With a frustrated growl, Colin got to his feet and stalked toward the door.

He intended to let his brother leave. Intended for him to go back to his empty house and impoverished existence and reap what he'd sown. But then he thought about it, imagined what it would be like to have Hunt Chase restored to its former glory, a sister operation to his own breeding stables.

In his heart of hearts, he knew it was what he really wanted.

"Wait." He turned to face his brother as Colin paused, one hand on the door latch. "I have a proposition for you."

Colin raised his brows in a skeptical expression Rogan knew had frequently been seen on his own face. "Will I have to pummel you again once I hear this?"

Rogan bared his teeth in a challenging smile. "I believe *I* pummeled *you*, dear brother. But it does not signify. I will give you the funds to set Hunt Chase to rights, but in exchange, you will work here for two months."

"Work? Me? Curse you, brother, but I am no groom to be employed at your whim!"

Rogan arched a brow. "Aren't you? The money is yours, Colin, for two months of your time."

Colin opened his mouth to protest again, then slowly closed it. Finally he said, "Done."

"I'll expect you here by week's end. That should give you enough time to set affairs in order at Hunt Chase."

Caroline crept into the house with all the care of a drunken spouse unwilling to wake a scolding wife. As silently as she was able, she removed her bonnet and gloves. She'd stayed in the village as long as she could, but she knew she had to return home, to face Rogan.

Enough hours had passed that his anger should have cooled, but at the same time, she knew that there was bound to be a confrontation. No doubt he would lecture her, paint himself the devil incarnate, and warn her to stay clear of him when his temper flared.

She tiptoed past the parlor, but just as she reached the staircase, she heard the door open behind her.

"Caroline."

She winced. Rogan's voice, stern and uncomfortably patient. As if he were her parent or her priest. Well, he wasn't. Enough of that. A woman had to take a stand if she didn't want to be treated as a helpless twit for the rest of her life.

She turned to face him, unnerved despite her resolve by his austere visage. Nonetheless, she managed a look of polite inquiry. "Yes, Rogan?"

He swept an arm toward the parlor. "A word, if you please."

Her stomach knotted at that quiet, controlled tone. She'd rather he raged; at least then she knew what he was truly thinking. Feeling much like a chastised schoolgirl, she slipped past him into the parlor.

He closed the door behind them, and the quiet *snick* of the latch echoed like the clang of a cell door.

"Sit down." He indicated the settee, and she sat, folding her hands in her lap out of sheer habit.

Rogan sat down in the chair across from her. He looked at her for a moment with a troubled frown on his face. Then he loosely linked his fingers together and said, "What the devil did you think you were doing this morning?"

The words, though soft, struck with the force of multiple pistol shots.

"I was breaking up your fight with your brother," she answered calmly. "And you will note that my method was quite successful."

His lips thinned. "This is no laughing matter, Caroline. When I am . . . like that, you need to stay away from me."

"I'm not laughing, husband." His patronizing tone grated. She stiffened her spine, preparing for battle. "I do not take violence on the part of males lightly, as you will recall. And I will not let you ruin your business when you are not in your right mind."

"That's not your responsibility," he said. "I'm supposed to protect you, not the other way around."

"Well that's just nonsense!" Her own temper flared. "I'm sick to death of the men around me treating me like I'm a brainless ninny who has no sense of self-preservation! Do I need to remind you of what I've survived?"

"I know what you've been through." He leaned closer, his eyes narrowing. "Do I have to remind you what that did to you?"

She sucked in a sharp breath. "I'm aware of my problems, Rogan. But hiding from them isn't going to help me solve them."

"This isn't a negotiation," Rogan said, frustration showing for the first time on his handsome face. "When you see me lose control, you get away. No discussion."

"There *will* be discussion!" She got to her feet and propped her hands on her hips. "You talk about yourself like you're some kind of wild animal who will devour me if I get too close. And that's just ridiculous, Rogan. You're my husband, not some lunatic."

"Damn it, Caroline, you must listen to me!" He jerked to his feet and took her by the shoulders. "When I'm like that, I have no control. I fear I will inadvertently hurt you. Please, do this for me."

She raised a hand to his cheek. "You will never hurt me, Rogan."

As if in pain, he closed his eyes and turned away from her touch. "Please, Caroline. Promise me."

"What demons haunt you?" she whispered. He opened his eyes, and she saw a familiar torment in that gray gaze. A torment she had seen too many times in her own mirror. "Tell me, Rogan. Let me help."

"This is madness." He pushed away from her and strode to the other side of the room to lean an elbow on the mantel, his face hidden from her. "Your father and his machinations be damned, I should never have married you."

Her stomach seemed to drop to her knees. Her mouth went dry. "What . . . what did you say?"

"I said I shouldn't have married you, blast it!" He spun to face her, his handsome visage twisted with suffering. "I am a penniless second son prone to uncontrollable raving, and you are an heiress haunted by the ghosts of your ravagers.

We should have known this wouldn't work. I'm no good for you."

She took a deep, calming breath. "I think you have been very good for me."

He gave a harsh laugh. "You're in danger every time I lose my temper. And you won't heed me when I tell you to run and hide. Dear God, Caroline," he whispered hoarsely. "I live every day in fear that I will harm you."

"What makes you think that?" Slowly she began to inch toward him.

He closed his eyes. "I've done it before."

She stopped. "Done what?"

"Isabel. I killed her." He clenched the hand resting on the mantel into a fist, pounded it against the marble. "I was furious at her for betraying me. And I killed her."

"Rogan." She waited until he met her gaze. "Who was Isabel?"

"A woman I knew during the war. I thought I loved her."

"What happened?"

"She was using me, pretending to love me to get information for the enemy. When I found out, I confronted her. She laughed," he added softly.

"Then what happened?"

"We argued." Anguish roughened his voice. "I lost all control. I couldn't see clearly, couldn't think clearly. There was yelling, and she shoved me. I pushed her back. She tripped and hit her head on the hearth and died."

"Oh, Rogan." She came over and rested her

hand on his arm. "It was an accident. You mustn't blame yourself."

He shrugged her off. "Don't you see? No one is safe from me, not even the people I love." His hard expression wavered as tenderness touched his gaze. "I couldn't bear it if I hurt you."

"I trust you," she whispered.

He stroked his knuckles down her cheek. "You shouldn't."

"Rogan, has it ever occurred to you that we can help each other? That maybe two damaged people like us might actually belong together?"

"Damaged." He nodded. "That's how I feel. Defective. Wrong somehow."

"No more than I do." She took a step toward him, and this time he didn't pull away. She laid her hand on his chest. "Before I met you, I would never have had the courage to do this small thing. You're helping me, Rogan, even if you don't realize it."

"Caroline." He closed his hand over hers, holding it fast over his pounding heart. "You astonish me."

She colored. "Nonsense." She dropped her hand, her own heart skipping around in her chest. Standing so close together, she could smell the citrusy scent of his body, practically feel the warmth coming off him. To her shock, she could barely resist turning back and smoothing both hands along that broad chest with wanton abandon.

"You have such faith."

"It's all I have." She raised her eyes to his. "Without it, I would be lost."

"I was lost before you."

The gentleness in his voice melted her insides like butter in a skillet. She could only stare at him mutely, undone by the growing desire in his eyes. He was so handsome, and he was *hers*, and she could barely stand the fact that terrors within her kept her from being a true wife to him. And she wanted to. All she had to do was reach out and touch him . . .

He seemed to sense her response to him. His mouth curled in a lopsided grin that made her knees weak. "What are you thinking, love?"

Unable to answer in simple English, she stepped forward, stood on tiptoe, and kissed him, wrapping her arms around his neck.

For an instant he didn't move, and her heart sank. Then his arms clamped around her, and he crushed her to his body, taking over the kiss with an ardor even she couldn't deny.

Hot desire flooded her in a rush. Every detail swamped her senses: his scent, the heat of his body pressed chest-to-thigh with hers, the obvious hunger of his mouth. She waited for the fear, expected it even. But it didn't come.

All she felt was glorious need as it crashed inside her like an ocean wave.

"Caroline." He whispered her name between kisses, dipping his head to nibble at her neck. "Caroline, are you sure?"

"Yes." She tangled her fingers in his hair as he brushed his lips over a sensitive spot beneath her ear.

He swept his hands down to her hips and held them as he once more captured her mouth with his. His tongue touched hers, and she opened gladly, eagerly kissing him the way he'd taught her.

Long moments later, he broke the kiss. "I was supposed to be chastising my wife," he murmured with amusement.

"I admire your methods." She studied his face, his mouth glistening from their kisses, his hair in disarray from her hands. His gray eyes looked almost black and glittered with pure male hunger. A twinge of alarm rose in her mind, but she squelched it. Rogan was her husband. He wouldn't hurt her. "Kiss me again, Rogan."

He complied most readily, scooping her into his arms even as his mouth descended. Her mind blurred and her heart raced as she let herself be swept away by his embrace.

His strong arms made her feel protected, not trapped.

"You are so beautiful," he murmured, nuzzling her hair. He pressed a kiss to her temple, to her cheek, then settled on her mouth again. She returned the long, slow kiss, her body aching for something she couldn't name. She stood on tiptoe and curled her arms around his neck. He pulled her tightly against his body.

The warning bell rang again, and once more she pushed it aside. She wanted to be in Rogan's arms, wanted to feel like a woman. *His* woman.

He clamped one arm around her waist and cupped the other hand around the back of her head, holding her still while he plundered her mouth. His breath came in harsh pants as he came up for air, then descended right back into passion.

He stumbled forward, and her back hit the wall near the mantel. She gave a squeak of alarm and clamped her fingers in his shirt as he settled heavily against her. Cupping her bottom in both hands, he tilted her hips into his, pressing his hard erection into the softness of her belly.

She was trapped. Pinned to the wall.

He rubbed against her slowly. His hardness fit snugly into the vee of her thighs, rigid and insistent. Her heart skipped in her chest. Alarm shot through her like an icy sword. He was too close. It was too much. Always before she'd been able to escape his embrace. Had the room to step away if need be. But this time . . .

She was trapped. Helpless. Crushed against the wall. No! *No!*

"No!" she rasped, ripping her mouth from his. "No, please, no!" Her caressing hands turned to claws as she raked at his shoulders.

"Caroline!" She struggled in his arms, terror seizing her in its relentless grip. He tried to pull her closer, but she shoved at him, desperate to be free.

"Let me go!" she cried. "Please let me go!"

He set her down and took a step backward, keeping his hands lightly on her shoulders. "Caroline, you're free. It's all right. You're free."

She sagged back against the wall, folding her arms around her middle and curling into a defensive posture. Her sobs shook her entire body.

She would never be free.

Chapter 14

Rogan stood by helplessly, uncertain what to do. The panic had come on her so suddenly. He wanted to comfort her, but he didn't want to make the situation worse.

"Caroline," he said quietly, "it's Rogan. You're at home, Caroline. Do you hear me?"

She sniffled and took a deep, shuddering breath that tore him up inside.

"It's me, Caroline." He gently cupped her cheek. She tried to turn away. "No, look at me. Look at me, love."

She opened her eyes and looked at him, her big dark eyes rife with torment. Tears clung to her spiky lashes as she continued to hug herself.

She nearly broke his heart.

"That's it." Gently he stroked her hair. "It's

Rogan, love. You're not in that terrible place any-more. It's just me, just your husband."

Awareness slowly brought the sanity back into her eyes. "Oh, God," she choked. "Will I never be free of this?"

"Shhh. Calm yourself." He continued to stroke her hair, kept his touch gentle. "It's all right, love. I went too fast."

"No." She sniffled and slowly straightened from where she huddled against the wall. "It was . . . I couldn't escape . . . I was pinned to the wall. Always before I could escape." A strangled sob escaped her throat, and her knees buckled. She staggered backward.

Rogan swept forward and gathered her into his arms, pulling her clear of the wall.

"No," she whispered, weakly shoving at his shoulders. "No more."

"I'm just holding you, love, so you don't fall down." Rogan kept his touch light, one arm around her waist to support her. He caressed her face with gentle fingers. "Come back to me now, Caroline. Leave those monsters behind."

"I thought I had." Misery made her lips tremble as she looked up at him. "I thought I could. I'm sorry, Rogan."

"None of that." He tried to smile. "What's important is that you're safe. You need to under-stand that. Believe it."

She swiped at her teary eyes with the back of her hand. "I haven't felt safe in years."

"You're safe with me. I won't let anything happen to you."

"I want to believe that." She closed her eyes, rested her forehead against his chest. "I liked kissing you," she whispered into his shirt. "It felt nice. And then . . . monsters."

"No monsters here. Just me." He cradled her against him, dropping a kiss on top of her head.

"They're always waiting for me," she sighed.

"We'll beat them. Look at us. I'm holding you, and you're all right."

"Mmm." She cuddled closer to him. "You're right. Just don't hold me too tightly. And no more walls."

"I won't. We'll stay just like this." He kept his embrace loose, and she stayed in his arms. "I like to hold you, love."

"I like it, too." She nuzzled her nose into his chest, then glanced up at him. "It's fading away."

"Good." He smoothed his hands up and down her back, his hands trembling with the effort to keep his touch nonthreatening. He pressed another butterfly-soft kiss to her temple. "We'll take all the time you need."

"I hate this." She laid her cheek against his chest. "I wanted to be a wife to you, Rogan. It felt normal to kiss you, to want to touch you. I didn't expect this to happen."

"Thought you were cured, hmm?"

She sighed. "Yes. And look at what happened."

"Yes, look at what happened. You kissed me—

most passionately, I might I add. I held you, and you weren't frightened."

"No, I wasn't," she realized, her voice full of wonder.

"A few weeks ago just one kiss would have had you fleeing in terror," he pointed out. "Look how far you've come already."

"You're right." She pulled back so she could look into his face. "I can kiss you, and it doesn't bring back the bad memories."

"Progress. You also let me hold you, and there was no panic."

"True."

"So when did the fear take over?"

"When you—" She halted, her face flushing red. "When you pinned me against the wall."

"Then I'll take care not to do that again."

She shrugged with impatience. "That part doesn't concern me as much. It's . . . well . . ." Her voice trailed off, and she glanced away, cheeks bright red.

"You have to tell me, Caroline. Else how will I ever be able to prevent it from happening?"

She closed her eyes and gestured toward his groin. "When that gets . . . um . . . hard. That frightens me."

"I see." He gave a sigh and cuddled her a little closer. "I'm not certain what to do about that, love. I get excited whenever you're around, and that's the result."

"What?" Her eyes popped open. "You told me

that's a natural state for a man. That it had nothing to do with me."

"And so it is. But alone in a room with you, and you kissing me—" He lowered his voice. "That had everything to do with you."

"Good heavens!" She pulled out of his embrace.

He coaxed her back with an arm around her waist and cupped her chin in his hand. "I want you, Caroline, make no mistake. But I'm no blackguard to be forcing you. We'll do this in your time."

Her lips curved, and she touched a finger to his chin. "Your Irish accent is showing, husband."

"It happens when I'm emotional."

"I take it you're emotional now."

"Of course I am." He took her fingers from his face and brushed a kiss across them. "I've a beautiful woman in my arms."

"A damaged woman." She sighed, resting her cheek against his chest. "I so wanted to be a true wife, Rogan. But I'm afraid. And I hate being afraid."

"You're not afraid now."

"As long as we stay like this." She stroked her palm down his chest, paused over his thundering heart.

"We can stay like this as long as you want. You can be the leader."

"I can?" She glanced up at him, clearly intrigued by the idea.

He smiled down at her. "I'll stay still, and I'll

keep my hands here." He rested his hands on her hips.

She pursed her lips and considered him. "You won't move?"

"Not a muscle."

"You'll let me do anything I want?"

One side of his mouth curved in a rakish grin. "Absolutely."

"I can touch you . . ." She stroked her hand down his chest again, watching him from beneath her lashes, "and you will stay where you are?"

"Yes." The end of the word came out in a hiss as she smoothed a hand along his waist.

She had the ability to arouse him. The notion fascinated her. Intrigued her.

Curious, she again trailed her fingers along his side, following the waistband of his trousers. He stiffened, but his hands remained safely on her hips. She slanted a look at him. "Do you like this?"

"Very much." His gray eyes glittered with male hunger, but he kept to his word and didn't move.

"What about this?" She took a step closer to him, leaning her body lightly against his.

He swallowed hard. "Yes."

Dizzy from her ability to affect him, she trailed a finger along his lower lip and down his chin. His hands clenched, then relaxed again. She pressed a soft kiss on his lips, her questing hands continuing to explore his torso. "You are a very handsome man, Rogan. I find myself thinking very unladylike thoughts when I see you."

"Indeed?" His eyes slid closed as she nipped at his throat.

"Indeed." She experimentally closed her teeth on his shoulder. "See?"

"Very unladylike," he agreed with a low growl.

Her hands hovered near his flat stomach. "I want to be with you, Rogan. I want you to teach me what loving is all about. Not what I learned from . . . them."

"Dear God, Caroline," Rogan groaned, burying his face in her neck. "You'll drive me mad, to be sure."

To her surprise, this brought a smug little smile to her lips. "Good."

He raised his head and caught a glimpse of her face. Then he chuckled. "Discovering your power, are you?"

"Apparently." She tilted her head back to look at him, and he took the opportunity to nibble her neck. She gave a husky little laugh and let her head fall back farther to give him better access. "I thought you were supposed to stay still."

"I did. My hands are still on your hips."

"But your mouth—" She gasped as his teeth raked along her throat. "You're not playing by the rules."

"I'm making new ones."

Caroline laughed for the first time in a long while and let her husband kiss her.

Rogan walked up the stairs, leading Caroline by the hand. He glanced back at her, and she smiled at him, her lips swollen from his kisses, her dark eyes alight with discovery. His fingers tightened around hers, and she squeezed his back.

They wandered down the hall, fingers entwined, Caroline leaning into him slightly. He stopped outside her bedroom door.

She sighed and turned her face into his shoulder. "Home at last."

"In a sense." He tilted her face up with a gentle finger beneath her chin and searched her eyes. He saw no panic there, no fear. Just contentment and affection. "I think it's time for the next step."

Wariness darted across her face for an instant. "What's the next step?"

"I think you should let me hold you tonight."

She shifted, putting a few more inches between them. "It might be better if you tell me exactly what you mean by that."

"I mean that you should get ready for bed. Put on your night rail, brush your hair. Then come to my room and let me hold you while you sleep."

"That's all?"

He chuckled at her skeptical tone and traced a finger along the slope of her cheek. "That's all. I've come to the conclusion that the best way to deal with your fears is for us to become used to each other."

"Perhaps you're right." Her gaze met his, her eyes dark with worry. "I'd like to sleep in your arms tonight. But are you certain you can . . . um . . . refrain?"

"I'm a grown man, not some stripling wet

behind the ears." He gathered her closer, dropped a kiss on her temple. "Holding you in my arms tonight would give me great pleasure, love."

She relaxed against him. "All right."

He stroked a hand down her hair. "Go on, then. Marie is no doubt waiting for you."

"No doubt." She slowly pulled out of his embrace, her expression apprehensive but resolved. "I'll get ready for bed."

"And then you'll come to me." It wasn't a question.

She nodded, her lips curving. "Then I'll come to you."

Hope lightened Caroline's heart as she went about her duties the next day.

She had passed the night in blissful slumber, curled up against the warmth of her husband throughout the night. She hadn't realized a man's body gave off so much heat, and she'd awakened toasty and comfortable with Rogan's arm slung across her waist.

He looked so young while he slept, she thought now with a smile at the memory. Perhaps it was because those fierce eyes were closed. But the important thing was that she had spent the whole night with him wrapped around her, and she'd slept as peacefully as a babe.

And she would do so again tonight.

Humming softly, she had decided to attack the pile of correspondence congratulating them on their nuptials, which waited to be addressed.

With Rogan gone to the village to see his solicitor, she had applied herself to the task on this dreary, rainy day. The project had taken hours, as Caroline often found herself staring into space and reliving some sweet memory from the night before.

Once she finally managed to plow through the pile of letters, cards, and invitations, she discovered herself to be out of sealing wax and went down to Rogan's study to obtain some. As she pushed open the door to the masculine sanctum, the heavy wood furniture and bold colors seemed to discourage the presence of a female. She hurried to Rogan's desk, feeling for all the world like a thief.

She found the wax immediately, but even as she clutched it in her hand, she found herself standing still, absorbing the familiar, citrusy scent of her husband that lingered in the room. Heat swept through her as surely as if he had touched her, and with an amused little smile, she sat down in his great leather chair and let herself absorb the vestiges of her husband that infused the room.

Besotted, that's what she was. As surely as any schoolgirl.

She giggled, a sound that had not passed her lips in more years than she could count, and then spotted the day's post piled on the desk. She pulled the stack toward her and flipped through it, setting aside those social letters and invitations to which it was a wife's duty to respond. She set the rest back where they had been, and as she pulled her hand back, she knocked a book off the desk.

The volume landed on its edge, and the pages exploded open, expelling several folded pieces of paper that she assumed Rogan used to mark his place. Sliding from the chair, she crouched down on the floor and began to gather up the papers.

A name on a partially open paper caught her attention: Randall Althorpe. Puzzled, she unfolded the letter the rest of the way and scanned it, but the contents only bewildered her further.

Why would Rogan have hired an investigator to look into cousin Randall's background?

The question continued to plague her, long after she had set things back to rights and left the room.

Something was afoot, she determined as she dripped wax on her letters to seal them. And given Rogan's tendency to protect her, she doubted he would tell her about it. It was time to stop being afraid, to look around her and see what was truly there. To make her own discoveries and decisions.

The best way to gain information, she knew, was through the social whirl. And what better place to start than Lady Jayton's upcoming dinner party?

Jayton Hall glittered with lights and swelled with music. Caroline clung to Rogan as they approached the dance floor, trying not to think about the dozens of people who jammed the ballroom.

"This is no intimate dinner party," she whispered to him.

"Apparently not." He smiled down at her. "You're doing very well, love."

"Well, I haven't fainted yet," she said with a wry grin.

"I'll catch you if you do," he promised as they took their places on the dance floor. He rested his hand at her waist and took her other hand in his, his gray eyes gleaming with humor and affection. "Don't step on my toes now."

Her laughter trilled behind them as the orchestra struck up a waltz, and Rogan swept her off into a whirling, twirling adventure.

He was an excellent dancer, and she had already gotten so used to his touch that she was able to completely relax in his arms as he led her in graceful twirls around the room. His warm hand clasped hers with an intimacy she hadn't expected, the hand at her waist a firm guide. His legs brushed against the skirt of her new peach silk dress, and she found herself wishing he could come closer still. The warmth of his body, his familiar scent, his engaging grin—all of it tempted her to surrender to him.

Surrender completely and totally, and learn what it was to be a woman.

"You look quite fetching, love," he said, his eyes

gleaming with male appreciation. "I knew that color would suit you."

"And you look quite handsome." She sent him a flirtatious glance. "I hope I won't have to engage in unladylike behavior should one of the other ladies in attendance attempt to catch your eye."

"I see no one but you." He pulled her a tad closer, holding her gaze as the heat built between them.

Ensnared by the passion that had flared up without warning, Caroline was too breathless to reply. The music seemed to fade away. All she saw was Rogan's eyes; all she felt was his strong hands guiding her, his warm body straining toward hers. Desire bubbled up from deep in her belly.

And there was no fear.

His fingers squeezed her waist. She leaned into him on the turn, her breast brushing his arm. Tingles swept through her at the fleeting contact. One side of his mouth quirked in a knowing smile, and on the next turn he swept his hand from her waist to her hip and back again.

She glanced up at him. The same heat that rushed through her veins was reflected in his eyes.

She slid her hand along his shoulder in a deliberate caress. He responded by pulling her close against him for an instant as they twirled. Her leg brushed his. His fingertips teased the upper swell of her bottom. She caressed his hand with her thumb.

Her body hummed with arousal by the time the song ended. When the music stopped, she and Rogan stood frozen for an instant, both of them flushed, both of them breathing a little too hard. It could be said that the exertion of the dance had produced these reactions.

They knew better.

When the orchestra swung into a country dance, Caroline jerked as if awakened from a sound sleep. She met Rogan's heated gaze for an instant, then blushed and stepped out of his arms. "If you'll excuse me, I must refresh myself," she whispered.

"I'll procure you a glass of punch." His low voice wrapped around her like an embrace.

She nodded, her mouth dry, her limbs quaking from sheer desire. Unable to speak another word, she went to seek out the ladies' retiring room.

Dancing with Caroline had proven more stimulating than he'd expected. Before acquiring Caroline's promised glass of punch, Rogan took a moment to step outside into the cool night breeze.

He needed cooling.

He walked out into the garden, sucking in a deep lungful of the brisk evening air, waiting for his hungry body to settle down. The seductive movements of the waltz had more than aroused him. Had they not been dancing in public, he would have been tempted to drag his wife off to the nearest bed.

Caroline was a pretty armful, that was certain. It was all he could do to remain patient and wait for the day when he could make her his. Some times were more difficult than others, but all he had to do was remember the sheer terror on her face when she spoke of her kidnapping, and his ardor faded as if he'd been soaked with ice water.

While Caroline appeared to be progressing with her intimacy dilemma, Rogan wasn't getting very far with his other responsibility—Randall Althorpe.

How could a man so obviously deceptive, a man who had murdered at least one person to their knowledge, manage to evade the authorities for so long? Even Gabriel Archer's initial investigation had uncovered nothing but an immaculate history, fictitious though it was. Archer had assured Rogan he was working to uncover the truth about Althorpe, but Rogan feared it might be too late. The duke was worsening, and unless they could discover how to prove Althorpe was involved, they had no chance of saving his life.

And Althorpe—the villain of the piece—would become the ninth Duke of Belvingham.

At least Caroline was safe from him now. As long as she was married to Rogan, there was nothing anyone could do to harm her.

Caroline stood frozen on the terrace. Though she had not succumbed to panic or the vapors, her nerves were still strung to the breaking point from both the close confines of the crowd and the aching desire that had left her shaken. The cool spring night had beckoned to her, a welcome respite from the stuffy ballroom. Once she had stepped outside, the pressure lifted from her mind, and she could once more think clearly.

At least until Mirabella Aston and Felicity Winters had entered the room.

"I can hardly believe Lady Jayton opened up the ballroom after so many years," Felicity said, her high-pitched voice distinctive even from Caroline's place on the terrace.

"Yet she did it for Belvingham's daughter," Mirabella replied. "Astonishing that the lady would even continue to acknowledge Caroline, much less throw a ball for her."

"Lady Jayton is Lady Caroline's godmother," Felicity replied. "No doubt it was the family connection."

"Either that or she was simply thrilled that her goddaughter had finally landed a husband." Mirabella gave a nasty little laugh. "I thought for certain that girl would be a spinster forever."

"One would think it would be easy for a duke's daughter to find a suitable husband," Felicity said. "Especially an heiress."

"But not a *ruined* heiress."

Felicity gasped. "Mirabella, you know what the duke said."

Caroline moved closer to the doorway and peered into the room. Felicity and Mirabella were gathered around a mirror, artfully refreshing their appearance.

At Felicity's comment, Mirabella's pretty face twisted into a sneer. "The duke would say anything to restore his daughter's reputation. But everyone knows she was held captive by those men for days. That they did things to her."

"No!" Felicity's blue eyes widened in horror. "I had just heard that she was mad. Collapsed at her own debut ball, you know."

"It's both," Mirabella declared. "She's been locked away at Belvingham for years now. No doubt His Grace despaired to ever find a man to wed her." She lowered her voice. "I heard not even the fortune hunters wanted anything to do with her!"

"Now you're jesting!"

"I'm not."

"Rogan Hunt must have been desperate for her fortune then," Felicity said. "Though his own reputation is somewhat questionable."

"The Hunts are perfectly respectable, if somewhat reckless and foolish," Mirabella replied, her voice arch with authority. "But Mr. Hunt himself does have a tendency to cause scandal."

"He's all but caused one by marrying her," Felicity said, clearly thrilled to be in possession of news that Mirabella had not yet heard. "My brother says that he married her for a horse!"

"A horse!" Mirabella's mouth dropped open. "You're jesting with me."

"It's true." Felicity tucked a springy curl back

into place. "Mr. Hunt is trying to recreate the Hunt stables. Apparently the horse was Hunt bred."

"How lowering," Mirabella mused. "'Tis not bad enough to be considered soiled goods, but to have a man marry you for a *horse* is the worst sort of debasement."

"And he elevated himself in the process," Felicity said. "Now that he's related to the Duke of Belvingham, he has become quite popular with the local gentlemen. They all want Mr. Hunt to train their horses."

"I heard Mr. Hadley is furious!" Mirabella gave a little snicker. "Did you hear about his fight with Mr. Hunt?"

"What fight? When? Was there actual fisticuffs?"

"The most common sort of brawl," Mirabella confirmed. "It was at the Hound and Horn. Apparently Mr. Hadley made comments insulting Lady Caroline's honor—"

"What did he say?" Felicity squealed.

"Just the truth, that she was ruined beyond all repair. If her father had not been a duke, I daresay Lady Caroline would have had to find other means of surviving."

"Mirabella!" Shock and excitement warred in Felicity's voice. "How can you even imply such a thing?"

"I overheard my mother saying so to Lady Lorrington and Mrs. Stanhope. So it must be true."

"Imagine, she might have had to make her living as an actress or something worse. How fortunate that Mr. Hunt came along when he did."

"How fortunate that she has a father who can buy her a husband," Mirabella corrected. "Come, we must get back to the ballroom. I am certain Sir Peter Warren intends to ask me to dance tonight."

The two girls bustled out of the room, but Caroline did not go back inside. She leaned against the cool stone of the house, her cheeks hot with mortification. Was this what people said about her? Was this what they truly thought of her?

How could she not have known?

Ruined. That's what they said. Her stomach clenched with nausea. How they must have laughed at her.

Her father had sheltered her from all the talk, had wrapped her in the silken cocoon of Belvingham Manor and protected her from the truth.

People thought her mad. Ruined so badly that not even the most desperate of fortune hunters would wed her. And they had said such things to Rogan's face.

A choking sob escaped her throat. Dear God, Rogan. What did they say about him for marrying her? Fortune hunter at best. Madman at worst.

Yet he had defended her.

A tear trickled down her cheek, and she swiped it away with an impatient hand. If the two giggling misses had heard the rumors, then it stood to reason that everyone down in the ballroom had also heard the gossip. How many of them believed it? How many of them smiled to her face and then talked behind her back?

She really hadn't missed society that much after all.

She closed her eyes against the welling moisture behind her lids and took deep breaths to regain control. She couldn't go back downstairs like this—it would only confirm the rumors and give the gossips more to chew on.

She wanted Rogan, wanted his arms around her and his strength to lean on. They would leave the ball with their heads held high.

Determined, she pushed away from the wall and reentered the retiring room. She took a moment to check her reflection, but except for the paleness of her cheeks and the slight redness of her eyes, she looked positively normal.

Not at all like someone whose world had just tilted.

She pinched her cheeks in an futile effort to bring color back to them, then turned away from the mirror. She needed to return to the ballroom, find Rogan, and leave Jayton Hall as soon as possible.

She only hoped she didn't encounter Mirabella or Felicity on the way. The notion of pulling both women's hair out by the roots tempted her, and she had no desire to add to her reputation as a madwoman.

Chapter 15

Caroline was unusually quiet on the ride home.

"Are you well, love? I thought the headache was just a ruse."

"It was." Caroline gave him a wan smile that told him for certain that something was wrong.

Frowning, Rogan took her hand in his. "Did someone insult you?"

"Whatever gave you that idea, husband?" For an instant she held his gaze, her big, dark eyes unfathomable.

"Logic." He caressed her hand with his thumb. "Was it the crowd?"

"Yes." She glanced away from him. "It was the crowd."

It sounded believable, but Rogan knew she was lying.

They rode the rest of the way in silence. When they reached the house, Rogan helped Caroline out of the coach. She wouldn't meet his eyes and slipped away from him to walk to the door. But despite her leisurely pace, he wasn't fooled.

Something was bothering her.

He followed her into the house. "Caroline."

She stopped just before the stairs. "Yes?"

"You're not telling me something."

"*I'm* not telling you something?" She whirled on him. "I believe it is *you*, husband, who is keeping secrets!"

His blood chilled. "What do you mean?"

"Why didn't you ever tell me what people say about me?"

Her soft voice—so like that of a lost little girl—slipped past his hardened defenses. He stiffened. "Did someone say something to upset you at Lady Jayton's?"

Caroline sighed and stripped off her gloves one at a time, placing them on a nearby table. "Rogan, stop answering my questions with more questions. I thought you of all people would tell me the truth."

The weariness of her tone only deepened his feeling of guilt. "Your father and I thought you were better off not knowing."

"My father? I should have known." She dropped her wrap on the table with her gloves. "You didn't think I might want to know what people really think of me before socializing with them? That they think I'm soiled goods? That my husband married me for the price of a horse?"

Rogan narrowed his eyes. "Who said that?"

"Does it matter? The stories—true or not—are out there circulating among my neighbors. I wonder how many of them are having a good laugh at the heiress that the fortune hunters wouldn't even pursue?"

"Caroline—" He reached out to her, but she didn't take his hand. He dropped it, unsure what to say to her; he just wanted to make the sting go away. "You know as well as I do that facts get distorted once they become gossip. You shouldn't give a thought to any of it."

"Don't patronize me," she warned in a low voice. She looked at him, her eyes fierce. "My father has locked me away in his castle for the past five years. I allowed him to do it, to protect me from the real world. But not anymore. I'm all grown up now, Rogan, and I won't faint at the first ugly rumor that concerns me."

"I've always known you were stronger than your father allowed," he said. "I wanted to tell you, but I didn't know how. Some of those rumors . . ." He clenched his jaw and stopped himself before profanity slipped past his lips. "There was no need for you to hear some of that."

"There is every need!" she shot back. "How can I defend myself if I don't know what's going on? How can I hold my head up knowing that people are laughing at me behind their hands?"

"You're right."

His acknowledgment seemed to take some of the wind out of her sails. "I need to hear all of it, and you're going to tell me." She folded her arms across her chest. "So, did you really engage in a tavern brawl when Mr. Hadley insulted my honor?"

"Bloody hell," he muttered.

Caroline merely raised her brows at him.

"All right, yes, I did. Hadley insulted you, and I couldn't let that lie."

"That was the day I picked you up in my carriage, wasn't it?" She shook her head. "Rogan, you could have told me right then what had happened. Do you think me so soft-witted that I wouldn't have understood?"

"I didn't know." Rogan swept a hand through his hair, exasperation biting at him. "You seemed so fragile. I didn't want to unnerve you."

Her lips thinned. "I'm growing very tired of everyone telling me how fragile I am."

"I did what I thought was right."

"You were wrong." She began to tick off on her fingers. "Let me see . . . there was the rumor that you married me for a horse, which we know is true."

"Blast it, Caroline, you know there's more to it than that."

"And people are saying that even the fortune hunters didn't want me, but you got your horse and a better social standing by sacrificing your bachelorhood."

Her sarcastic tone stung. "Now wait a minute—"

"They speculate that my kidnappers ruined me, that no decent man would want me, even with my fortune."

"That's bloody well not true," he burst out. "You're a beautiful woman with a good heart. Any man would want you."

"And do you?" Her lips curved in a blatantly seductive smile. "I'm a bride who has yet to be bedded, husband. What do you suppose people would say to that?"

The sexy lilt in her voice and that slow, warm glance set his blood humming. That peach silk evening dress looked about as substantial as tissue paper, and he struggled with the urge to peel it from her body. "Are you asking me to bed you, wife?"

"Maybe you should." She lifted her chin, though her fingers twisted amid her skirts. "At least then I would feel as if I were a proper wife."

"I would be more than happy to accommodate you," Rogan said, trailing a finger along her bared shoulder. "But you know there are reasons why we have not yet consummated this marriage."

"I know." She took in a shaky breath and glanced down at his finger where it traced patterns on her skin. "Your patience is truly magnificent."

"I'm not nearly as patient as you think I am." He crowded her back against the table, then nipped at her neck. "I want you more than I want to breathe," he rasped, lost in the taste of her.

"Don't squash me against the table," she gasped, pushing at his hips even as she leaned her head to the side so he could continue to nuzzle her neck.

"I won't." Before she could blink, he lifted her and seated her on top of the table, putting them practically nose-to-nose. He grinned at her. "Better?"

"Interesting."

He chuckled. "It's about to become even more so." Dipping his head, he placed a kiss between her breasts bared by the low neckline of the gown.

She made a squeak of surprise and gripped his arms. "Rogan!"

"Patience, love." He laughed again and nuzzled his nose against her breast. She jerked backward with surprise, jostling his head, but he knew he had affected her, had felt the hard little nipple poking his cheek.

"What are you doing?" she panted. "We're supposed to be having a quarrel."

"We're done quarreling." He cupped her breast through the dress and regarded her with searching eyes.

"Good heavens, what are you doing?"

"Making love to my wife." He tugged on the neckline of the dress until one small, creamy breast popped out. She went to cover herself, but he grasped both her hands in his and held them fast to the table. Then he ducked down and teased her hard little nipple with just his lips.

"Dear Lord." Her head fell back, and she unintentionally arched into his mouth. He licked the pink, pebble-hard nub, then began to suckle.

"*Rogan!*" Breathing hard now, she half-heartedly tried to pull her hands from his. "We must stop. What if someone comes?"

"Who? Grafton and Tallow are abed, and your maid awaits upstairs." He grinned up at her like a pirate, and she could feel her resolve melting. "You wanted to be treated like a woman, didn't you?"

"You're a devil," she muttered. "A wicked, wicked devil."

"Just a man." He traced a string of kisses up to her throat. "A man who very much wants to take his wife to bed."

"I don't know—"

"Let's find out," he interrupted, desire roughening his voice. "What say you, Caroline? Are you ready to be a wife?"

"Are you going to lie to me anymore?"

He chuckled against her skin. "You are a very single-minded woman. No, I won't hide things from you anymore."

"Then I'd like to try." She pulled her hands free and cupped his face, looking into his eyes. "I want this, Rogan. I just don't know if I can—"

"Shhh. Don't fret about it. We'll do what we can and work with the rest."

"But I don't think I can—"

He placed a finger over her lips to silence her. "Hush, love. Relax and let me teach you. I promise we'll stop whenever you say."

She hesitated only for a moment, then nodded.

With a low growl of triumph, Rogan scooped her into his arms and mounted the staircase.

Caroline clung to him, misgivings fluttering like butterflies in her stomach. What if she wasn't ready? What if she grew distraught? Perhaps teasing Rogan into bedding her had not been the wisest course of action. She wasn't even sure why she'd done it. The words had just spilled from her mouth.

He carried her up the stairs as if she weighed nothing, kissing and caressing her all the way. She clung to his neck, her fingers twisting tightly together. She was both nervous and hungry for him, excited to be treated as a proper wife rather than an invalid. She wanted to be able to give something to Rogan, something only she could give.

He stopped outside his bedroom door, then bent and kissed her until her head spun. By the time he managed to push open the door, desire had flushed most of her doubts from her mind.

He laid her on the bed, stroking his hand down her throat and chest, coming to rest on her belly. She could only watch him and try to remember to breathe, while delicious feelings swamped all thoughts and reason from her mind.

"I want to undress you, love," he murmured. "I want to see all that lovely fair skin of yours."

Heat flooded her cheeks. The look in his eyes, the tone of his voice. He wanted her, and the knowledge sent a thrill shooting between her legs. Her body erupted to life, and she reached up her arms to him.

He knelt one knee on the bed, his gray eyes so dark with need that they looked black. He coaxed her to sit up, bringing her closer for his kisses as he worked the fastenings of her dress. The peach silk gaped away, and he tugged at the low neckline until both her breasts and her shoulders were bared to his gaze. He stroked one soft mound and then the other, kneading gently with his fingers while he made her dizzy with kisses.

By the time he peeled the gown off her arms, she was too hot and hungry to protest. All she wanted was for him to touch her—anywhere, everywhere. His slow, tender caresses didn't trigger any of her horrible memories and instead eased her into the strange new world of desire with barely a murmur of protest.

"Beautiful," he whispered.

She felt beautiful. He tugged the dress down and off, leaving her clad in just her thin shift. The straps of the nearly transparent garment dangled down her arms, and her breasts lifted softly above the rest of it where it bunched around her middle. He stroked his fingers down the slope of one pale mound, the brush of his fingers against her bare skin making her more and more aware of her body. Her limbs felt strangely heavy, and time seemed to slow. Her blood ran like fire through her veins, despite the steady, almost leisurely beat of her heart.

He took one of the pins from her hair. She helped him, pulling free the pins and ribbons until her hair fell in tangled curls around her shoulders. He made a low sound of approval and buried his face in the dark mass.

She stretched her arms up, feeling alive and female and gloriously powerful, then lay back on the bed. Her lips curved in a feline smile as he stood there looking at her, desire plain on his face. "Do you intend to undress, husband?"

His eyes narrowed at her seductive purr, and he began to strip off his coat. "Absolutely."

The power of Woman rushed through her as she noticed his hands were shaking. How odd that such a small female could shake the control of such a strong man. But she could see it in his trembling fingers and fierce expression, hear it in his harsh breathing.

Testing her wiles, she shook out her hair and leaned up on her elbows. His eyes immediately drifted to her naked breasts, and he fumbled with the buttons of his waistcoat. Thrilled with the results of her little experiment, she caught his eye and slowly licked her lips.

He stopped undressing, arrested by the movement. "Caroline, what are you doing?" he asked hoarsely.

"Waiting." She let her head fall back, her hair brushing her shoulders. Then she settled back into her former position and gave him the tiniest smile. "I've been waiting for you for a long time."

He yanked at the waistcoat, buttons flying everywhere. She laughed, a throaty, seductive sound even she didn't recognize. He tossed what was left of the garment to the floor and jerked at the knot of his neck cloth.

"Shall I help you?" She climbed to her knees on the bed and reached for the cravat. Her shift slipped down a little more and caught at the curve of her hips.

He placed his hands on her waist, bare flesh to bare flesh, and tilted his head back a little. "Be my guest."

The unfamiliar feeling of strong hands around her middle sent another jolt of excitement shuddering through her. Biting her lower lip, she struggled with the knot of his neck cloth. His fingers flexed around her waist—once, twice. She finally jerked the cloth free and dropped it to the floor.

"Caroline." He swooped down and claimed her mouth in a hot kiss that made her brain shut down completely. All she could do was cling to his shirt and fly with him.

As if she had turned a key, his passion erupted. His hands swept over her body as his mouth engaged hers in a lusty tangle of lips and tongues. He tugged at the shift, shoving it up around her hips and leaving her lower body exposed.

"Rogan—" His kiss stopped her words, and her thoughts spun away. He eased her down onto her back, still kissing her, one hand stroking over her from neck to knees. He lingered at her belly, leaving his large, warm hand there for long moments.

She arched her hips, following her instincts, her eager moans captured by his mouth. His hand coaxed her thighs apart, slipped between them.

The first inkling of alarm cut through her passion-clouded mind. She grabbed his wrist and pulled, tearing her mouth from his. "Rogan, stop."

He froze, meeting her gaze. "Are you all right?"

"It was starting."

"Why?"

"Where your hand was." She knew she was blushing but didn't care. "It makes me nervous."

"All right." He moved his hand to her thigh. "Is this better?"

"I think so." She reached up and curled her hand around his neck. "Kiss me again. Chase away the ghosts."

He bent down and kissed her tenderly, their lips clinging as he pulled back. "Better?"

"Yes." She took a deep breath, shocked to discover the fear had faded.

"I want to show you what loving can be like," he said. "But I can't do that if I can't touch you."

"You are touching me."

He gave her a very adult smile. "Not the way I want to."

Heat flooded her face. "But if you do that, and you're on top of me . . . it won't work, Rogan."

"Then let's try something else." He got off the

bed and considered her for a long moment. "Do you trust me not to hurt you?"

"I know you don't *intend* to hurt me." She shrugged, uncomfortable. "But part of me doesn't believe that about any man."

"I need you to trust me. I promise to stop if you want me to." He grasped her by the hips and slid her until her legs dangled off the bed.

"What are you going to do?" Trying to ignore the twinge of panic, she propped herself on her elbows again and frowned as he knelt down beside the bed. "What—"

He parted her knees, lightly stroked the insides of her thighs.

"Rogan . . ." Her muscles tightened.

"Hush. It's all right." He placed a butterfly kiss on her knee, on her inner thigh.

"You're not going to . . . dear Lord, I can't even say it." She crossed an arm over her eyes as he slowly kissed his way along her leg. Her heartbeat sped up, but she kept reminding herself that this was Rogan, that he wouldn't do anything she didn't want him to do.

Then she felt the questing touch between her legs, and she gasped at the fleeting sensation. He came back again, another tentative caress. A keening sound escaped her throat, and she straightened her arms at her sides, fingers digging in and gripping the coverlet.

"Let me show you," he murmured. "This is what it should be like."

She wanted to know the truth so badly. She relaxed her thigh muscles, but her fingers gripped the blankets even more tightly. This was nothing like she'd experienced before, at the hands of the kidnappers. That had been rough and humiliating and disgusting. But this—the feather-light brush of his lips, the tender tracing of his fingers along her inner thigh—this didn't make her cry or sick to her stomach. Once more he touched between her legs, and this time she didn't panic.

She wanted to know.

Drawing a deep breath, she relaxed, her knees parting a bit more. Rogan smiled down at her, his hand still teasing between her legs, inspiring all kinds of unfamiliar hungers. Then he touched one specific place, a place where all the blood seemed to center, and she moaned aloud at the jolt of desire that rippled through her. One jolt fed another jolt, and her mind soon grew foggy with increasing sensation.

"That's it, love." He leaned closer, a satisfied smile on his face as he watched her expression. "Hold fast now." Bending down, he pressed a kiss right between her legs.

She gave a squeal of surprise and tried to sit up. He gently urged her back again with a hand on her chest, then began to lick the most sensitive part of her body.

"Dear sweet Lord." Caroline closed her eyes as wild sensation rolled through her in waves. His soft hair brushed the insides of her thighs as he skillfully teased her with his mouth. She had never in her life imagined that people did such things to each other. It was so wicked. So indecent.

So incredibly delicious.

He hooked her knees over his shoulders and continued to pleasure her with tongue, lips, teeth. All the while his hands roved her body, stroking her legs, holding her hips still for his ministrations.

Pressure built. She found herself arching her hips, trying to get closer. He scooped his hands beneath her bottom and lifted her to his mouth, finding the hard little bud hidden in her female folds and rubbing his tongue against it. The wonderful friction nearly pulled her out of herself, jerking her from growing pleasure to pure, demanding lust in seconds. She gave a startled cry, lost in the delightful torment, dying to reach a place she couldn't describe. She needed something . . . something . . .

The pressure changed, his tongue curled, and her body exploded, sending her hurtling into sweet oblivion with his name on her lips.

Caroline returned to herself slowly.

Rogan lay beside her on the bed, head propped on one hand while the other hand rested on her thigh. He was smiling. "Are you back, love?"

"Good heavens." She blinked at him, trying to bring him into focus. "Is that what all the fuss is about?"

He chuckled. "Quite."

"Oh." She frowned at him. "You're still dressed."

"I know." His mouth curved in a lopsided grin. "I thought it was safer, so I wouldn't get carried away."

"Carried . . . ? *Oh*." She flicked a glance toward his lower body. "Are you . . . well, all right?"

"Are you?"

"I am . . . I don't know what I am. Barely coherent, that's for certain." She rolled onto her side to face him, casting him a speculative look. "I meant, did you—" She made a sound of exasperation. "I don't think you felt what I did."

"Not quite." He traced a finger along her nose. "I very much enjoyed watching you, though."

"That doesn't seem fair. Don't you want to . . . um . . . finish things?"

He stilled. "Do you?"

She opened her mouth to say yes, then hesitated. "I don't know. I thought I was ready."

"We can try." He reached for the fastening of his pants.

Caroline grabbed his hand. "No. No, I don't think it would work." She blew out a long, shuddering breath. "Panic again. Apparently I'm all right as long as you remain properly dressed."

"Well that certainly throws my plans out of kilter." He smiled as he said it, but Caroline didn't smile back.

"I want to share your bed, Rogan. I truly do. But this reaction of mine—I'm afraid I may never get past it."

"You will." He pressed a kiss to her forehead. "Don't worry about me, love. This isn't the first time I've been frustrated, and I doubt it will be the last."

"But I don't want you to be frustrated." Gathering her courage, she stroked her palm down his chest. "I want you to feel the way I did. Men do feel that way, don't they?"

"They do." He put his hand over hers, held it fast over his heart. "One step at a time, love. Perhaps you should think about going to bed."

"I should, but I don't want to." She curled her fingers against his chest. "I want to sleep in your arms again."

He gave a rough laugh and sat up on the bed. "That would be dangerous, sweet wife. Best you retire to your own bed, before I forget my good intentions and ravish you now."

She started to laugh, then saw the gleam in his eye and realized he was only half jesting. She jerked into a sitting position, then flushed as her shift sagged around her waist. She tugged at it, trying to cover her breasts.

"Let me help." He assisted her with turning the garment around—it was on backward, having shifted from rigors of their embrace—and she managed to get a strap pulled up over one arm. Before Rogan tugged the other into place, he leaned forward and took her exposed nipple in his mouth, suckling just long enough to make her insides melt again, before releasing her and slipping the strap up her arm.

"Rogan." Her body hummed, and she gave him a look that begged for more and promised retribution all at once.

He just grinned at her, the rogue, and helped her get her dress back on. Once she was fully buttoned and hooked, he handed the hairpins to her. "I'm not much of a lady's maid," he said with a grin.

She closed her fingers around the pins, studying his face for some sign of torment or frustration. "Are you certain you don't want me to stay tonight? I enjoy sleeping in your arms."

"Caroline." He stroked his fingers along her arm. "If you stay I will have you naked and under me before you can say no." He looked directly into her eyes, letting her see the hot lust that simmered in his. "I want nothing more than to be inside you, love. And until you want that as much as I do, until you crave it more than food, more than air—until you want it so much that none of your fears can possibly stop the inevitable—that's when it will happen. I don't want you frightened of me."

"I'm not frightened of you." She leaned in and kissed his lips, then smiled. "I'm frightened of me. Good night, Rogan."

"Good night, love," he replied, wondering as he watched her leave the room how much cold water might be found in the kitchen at this late hour.

Chapter 16

Caroline clicked her tongue at Melody and urged her to a trot with a tug of the lead rope. The gray picked up her pace, trotting smoothly in a circle around the paddock.

Dressed in her oldest riding habit, Caroline surveyed the mare's progress with satisfaction. She had worked with Melody each day, gaining the horse's trust after her abuse. Taking Rogan's advice, she had retrained her from the beginning, going back to rudimentary exercises. The horse had quickly progressed, and Caroline had had a chance to evaluate how well trained the animal was. She was a fine mare who had fallen victim to abusive owners. She doubted Peterson had been the first.

As with Caroline, the physical wounds had healed, but the emotional ones still festered.

But she appeared to be making progress on the emotional front. She clicked her tongue again, sending Melody into a swift canter. Her encounter with Rogan last night had been a revelation. The terror that had once gripped her seemed a mere shadow, easily pushed aside. Rogan had shown her that sharing their bodies could be beautiful and moving, not necessarily scary and humiliating. Her father was right: she had thought she knew what sex was all about, but it turned out she didn't know anything at all.

She was rather glad Rogan had gone to attend to some business today; looking into his eyes after what they'd done together gave her a tendency to blush. Yet at the same time, she felt beautiful and female and found herself daydreaming at odd moments about the kisses they'd shared.

Footsteps crunched on the dirt surrounding the paddock. With a sigh of annoyance, Caroline turned, saying, "You gentlemen know not to approach me when I'm working with Melody."

But it wasn't Grafton or Tallow standing outside the fence.

"Randall, what are you doing here?" She called out a command to halt Melody's canter and reeled in both horse and rope as she hurried to the fence. She searched Randall's expression for any hint of dire news. "Heavens, is it Papa?"

"Dear girl." Randall cast a disbelieving eye over her shabby attire. "Can your husband not spare a bit of coin to dress his wife properly?"

She pulled up short. "Bother my wardrobe! Is Papa all right?"

Randall's brows came together. "I assume so. I haven't seen him today."

"So he's all right then." She let out the breath she'd been holding. "When I saw you here, I thought—"

"Oh, dear girl!" Randall shook his head and gave her a pitying smile. "You thought I had come with bad tidings."

"I did." She managed an answering smile. "I'm glad I am mistaken."

"Still, this isn't exactly a social call. I haven't come to talk about your father, Caroline. I've come to talk about your husband. About your marriage." He gave her a sad, solemn look. "And the news may yet be dire indeed."

"What are you talking about?"

"Perhaps we should go inside." Althorpe glanced from Caroline to the gray and back. "And I would recommend tea at such a time."

"I'll see to it. Just let me put up Melody." She called softly to the horse, soothed her nervousness with caresses. "Randall, Melody is afraid of men, so please back away from the gate."

With raised eyebrows, Randall did as she asked. She led Melody into the stables and tended to her most basic needs, then hurried back outside. Randall waited where she'd left him, his arms crossed, his expression impatient.

"Come inside," she said. "I'll ready the tea tray."

She settled Randall in the parlor, then went into the kitchen to prepare a pot of tea. Mrs. Cox, the cook who came three days a week, had made a batch of lemon biscuits, and she took some of those as well when she brought the tray back to the parlor.

"Ah, biscuits," Althorpe said, helping himself to two and setting them aside. "Shall I pour?"

"If you would," she replied, afraid her trembling hands would cause her to drop the pot.

Her cousin poured tea the way he did everything else: with a refined elegance that gave him a bit of a haughty air. She had never really felt comfortable around Randall, and sitting alone with him in the parlor, waiting for him to impart what might be bad news, was not helping matters.

Finally they each had a cup of tea and some biscuits.

"Caroline," Randall said. "I hope you will take what I am about to say in the best possible context, as one concerned relative to another."

"Good heavens, Randall, what's wrong?" Caroline set down her teacup with a little clink, unable to keep up even the pretense of drinking.

"I hope you won't consider me too presumptuous, but I've come upon some information about your husband's history of which you may be unaware."

A chill ran through her as suspicion reared its head. Why would Cousin Randall, who for most of her life had considered her either an inferior female or a veritable lunatic, suddenly develop such concern for her welfare?

And now that she thought about it, why would Rogan feel the need to engage an investigator to look into Randall's past? Something was going on between the two men, and in typical overprotective fashion, Rogan had told her nothing about it.

Her growing anger with her overbearing husband steadied her nerves. Randall was here now, his face the picture of gentlemanly concern. Now was her chance to learn what Rogan was hiding from her.

"I've shocked you, haven't I?" Randall said, apparently attributing her silence to feminine sensibilities.

Caroline gave him a reassuring smile. "I'm afraid you did startle me. I cannot fathom what 'history' you refer to, cousin."

"I was afraid you might not know." Randall sighed and gave her a sympathetic look that she found hard to believe. "Your husband's volatile temper is well known all through the area, Lady Caroline."

She dropped her gaze to her teacup in mock modesty, masking her sudden interest in his words. "I'm certain you don't heed the loose tongues of gossips, Randall."

"Normally no." He leaned forward in his chair, the picture of earnest concern. "But my own sources have confirmed the rumors. Caroline, I'm afraid for you."

She gave a little laugh, all the while noting his every flicker of expression. "Rogan has treated me very well, cousin. You worry for naught."

"I'm afraid I must disagree. Are you aware that while your husband was at war on the Continent, he killed a woman?"

Having heard the story from Rogan's own lips, she was unsurprised at this revelation, but she gasped anyway. "How can you say such a thing to a new bride, sir?"

"I do hate to be the bearer of ill tidings, cousin, but I fear for you. My contacts tell me that Hunt supposedly loved this woman, yet he killed her during one of his rages. I can't help but fear what he would do to his gentle wife."

"Thank you for your concern, Randall, but there is no reason to fear for me."

Randall looked down at his hands. "There is more, but if you do not believe me about this, how will you believe the even more incredible tale I wish to relay?"

"I don't disbelieve you," she said. "I just don't think I am in any danger."

Randall raised his brows. "Forgive me for dis-agreeing, cousin, but I believe you should be on your guard." He paused, his expression reflecting some sort of inner struggle. "Caroline, may I be honest with you?"

"Of course, Randall. I prefer honesty."

"It's no secret that Hunt married you because you are an heiress."

"I suppose that had something to do with it."

She gave him a gentle smile. "It's done all the time, you know. A destitute man marrying an heiress is hardly illegal."

"No, it isn't." Randall suddenly jerked to his feet and began to walk about the room, his hands behind his back. "This next piece of news is so disturbing that I hesitate to relay it."

"Honesty," she reminded him.

"Very well." He stopped pacing and faced her, his expression grim. "Caroline, I fear Rogan has poisoned your father."

"What!" She set down her cup and saucer with a clatter and rose to her feet. "What nonsense is this?"

"It's not nonsense. Your father is dying, Caroline. He was a vigorous, healthy man before this mysterious illness laid him low in a matter of weeks. Rogan is a known killer, and I believe he is hastening your father's death in hopes of increasing your portion of the Belvingham fortune."

"You're mad. Rogan would never hurt my father."

Randall stepped closer to her, locking her gaze with his. "Men would do many desperate things for money, my dear innocent cousin," he whispered.

A tremor rippled through her. There was something in Randall's voice, in his eyes, that drew all her defenses into play. "But poison, Randall?" Her voice broke, and she turned away from him.

Dear God, could it be? It would explain the suddenness of Papa's illness, the confusion of the physicians, the rapid decline of Papa's strength. But Rogan?

"No," she whispered. "No, it can't be."

Randall came up behind her and laid a hand on her shoulder. "Dear cousin, I know this is a shock to you."

"Yes," she choked out. Tears welled in her eyes despite her will to stop them. Someone was deliberately trying to kill her father. Murder him.

But it wasn't Rogan.

She turned back to Randall, not even bothering to hide her distress. "I'd like to be alone now, if you don't mind. I'm sure you understand."

"Are you certain?" He peered into her face, his eyes watchful and concerned. "Shall I call someone for you? Your maid perhaps?"

"No, thank you. I'll just go up to my room. Please forgive me."

He waved a dismissive hand. "Don't be foolish; you've had a shock. I'm only sorry my news has brought you to this end."

"It's not your fault, Randall. You were only doing what you felt was best."

"But if there's anything I can do—"

Someone cleared a throat. "Am I interrupting something?"

Caroline turned to see Colin standing in the doorway of the parlor. She swiped the tears from her cheeks. "Hello, Colin. I didn't realize you were coming to visit today."

"I'm not visiting, I'm staying for a while." He sent a hard look at Althorpe. "And who's this?"

"This is my cousin, Randall Althorpe. Randall, this is Colin Hunt, Rogan's brother."

"Ah. The master of Hunt Chase, I take it?"

"As a matter of fact." Colin came into the room, his canny dark eyes on Caroline's face. "Is something the matter?"

"It's nothing." Caroline tried to smile at him. "I didn't know you were coming, so I'll need to have the maid air out the other bedroom—"

"It can't be nothing," Colin said, cutting her off. "You're crying." He cast a narrow-eyed glance at Randall, looking very much like Rogan in the process. "Has this fellow upset you?"

Althorpe stiffened. "I brought news of her father. Family business," he added meaningfully.

"I'm family now." Colin caught Caroline's gaze. "Bad news, I take it?"

She nodded, words jamming in her throat.

"The duke isn't doing well," Randall said. "We fear he will not be long for this world."

"I was just going upstairs," Caroline whispered.

"You do that," Colin said, his voice gentle. But the look he sent Althorpe was not. "I'll see your cousin out."

"Thank you," Caroline whispered.

She fled the room before the tears came in force, leaving the two men glaring at each other.

It was nearly dusk before Rogan arrived home.

His meeting with Lord Traversleigh had proven most successful. His Lordship would be delivering two horses in the next couple of days for training, and more than that, he seemed interested in purchasing the first foal when Rogan began breeding Destiny with Hephaestus.

Between the money from Caroline's dowry and what Lord Traversleigh planned to pay him, he could begin to purchase stock for his new breeding line. Everything was falling into place.

He walked Hephaestus into the stables. Grafton and Tallow had no doubt gone to have their dinner, and Rogan enjoyed the simple pleasure of removing his horse's tack himself. As he brushed down the stallion, he heard the sound of footsteps behind him.

"Your wife had company while you were gone," Colin said.

Rogan stopped and glanced at his brother, who leaned in the doorway of the stall. "If you were talking about anyone but Caroline, that remark would lead me to some interesting conclusions."

"Her cousin Althorpe, was here."

"Althorpe?" Rogan set down the brush and turned his complete attention to his brother. "What happened? What did he do to her?"

"Just brought her some bad news about her father." Colin frowned as Rogan swiftly locked the stall and pushed past him to head for the house. He hurried after him. "What's the matter?"

"What did he say?" Rogan didn't slow his pace. "What did he say *exactly*?"

"He said he brought bad news about her father."

"The duke is dead?"

"No, I don't think so. Otherwise I doubt she would have been up in her room all this time." Colin caught up with Rogan and kept pace with him as he headed for the front door.

"No, she would have gone with haste to Belvingham." Rogan went into the house and glanced into the parlor. She wasn't there.

"She went upstairs, Rogan, and I don't think she ever came down again."

Rogan paused at the bottom of the stairs and looked up. "Thank you, Colin," he said without turning. "I think it's better if I do the rest alone."

"I understand." Colin glanced up as well. "I didn't like the look in Althorpe's eyes, brother."

"What look?"

"Let's just say I've seen friendlier eyes on a snake. Call me if you need me."

"Thanks." As Colin left the house, Rogan began to climb the stairs.

The quiet knock at her door startled Caroline.

"Caroline?" Rogan said. "May I come in?"

She rose slowly from her seat near the window and went to the door. When she opened it, Rogan was standing there, concern etched on his handsome face. She stared at him for a long moment, then turned away, leaving the door open.

He followed her into the room. "Caroline?"

She turned back to face him, folding her arms across her chest. "Rogan. How was your meeting with Lord Traversleigh?"

"Forget Traversleigh. Colin told me that Althorpe was here today. What did he say?"

"He had a lot of things to say. Now I want to hear what you have to say."

Her directness brought a frown to his face. "You sound angry with me."

"I don't know how I feel right now." She met his gaze squarely. "You've been keeping things from me, Rogan."

"What did Althorpe say?"

"What did Mr. Archer have to say?"

She could see she'd startled him. He narrowed his eyes. "How did you find out about him?"

"Why didn't you tell me about him?" she shot back.

"Answer the question."

"You answer mine."

They stared at each other for a long moment.

"What did Althorpe say to upset you?" he asked again, softly.

She had difficulty holding on to her outrage when he spoke to her so gently. "Lies," she replied. "He told me lies. Just like you did."

"I've never lied to you, Caroline."

"Lies of omission are still lies. Why didn't you tell me you were investigating Randall? And don't you dare say it was to protect me!"

He lifted a brow. "It was."

"Dear God, not again!" She spun away, rage bubbling up, rage that had been simmering inside her for years. "I'm not a child, Rogan."

"I know you're not a child."

"Yet you keep things from me as if I am. Randall tells me my father is being poisoned. Is that true?"

"He told you that?"

"It's true, isn't it? And you've known all along. In fact, Randall says you are the one doing the poisoning."

He stilled, and his eyes grew watchful. "And what do you think?"

She rolled her eyes. "I'm not an idiot, Rogan. You've hired one of the best investigators in London to look into Randall's affairs, and then Randall himself comes to visit and tries to convince me that my husband is a murderer." She gave a humorless little laugh. "He even brought up . . . what was her name? Isabel."

He stiffened. "I told you what happened with Isabel."

"Yes, it was an accident. But my father's illness is deliberate."

"I'm not trying to kill your father, Caroline."

"I know that." She sent him a chiding look. "It's Randall, isn't it? He's hurting Papa."

"That's what we believe."

"We?" She glanced back at him, puzzled. Then realization swept over her. "Papa knows."

"Yes."

She let out a long sigh. "I can't believe he didn't tell me. Then again, of course I can. He was trying to *protect* me."

"He loves you. Of course he was trying to protect you."

"And what of today?" She stalked over to him, thrust her face as near his as her lesser height would allow. "I was alone in a room with my enemy, and I didn't even know."

He cupped her cheek. "I would never let him hurt you."

"But you weren't here." She backed away from him, and his hand fell to his side. "If Randall can so easily poison a powerful man like my father, what's to stop him from harming me?"

"He has no reason to harm you."

"And where is this poison coming from? Why hasn't Randall been taken into custody?" She clenched her fists at her sides. "Make him tell you how to cure my father."

"We haven't been able to prove anything." Rogan dropped his chin, weariness weighing on him. "Archer is the best, and if there is any under-handed business to be found about Althorpe, he will find it. In the meantime there is nothing we can do until we have some sort of proof."

"I can't just sit here and watch him *die*!" Tears stung her eyes; grief welled up to choke her. "It was bad enough when we merely thought him ill. To know that someone did this to him is unbear-able." She came to him, clenched her hands on the lapels of his coat. "Please help him, Rogan. I can't lose him."

"I know, love." Tenderly, Rogan pulled her into his embrace, cradling her as if she were precious. His gentleness struck at the raw anguish deep inside her, and it spilled out in a torrent—anguished, bitter sobs that soaked the fabric of his coat in moments. She clung to him, barely able to stand on her own, and he held her, rocked her, until the storm wore itself out and she sagged in his arms, spent.

Chapter 17

The nightmare started as a pleasant dream.

She rode Destiny, laughing as the mare charged like lightning across the green fields of Belvingham. But suddenly the white clouds darkened to gray, filling the sky until not a hint of blue could be seen. Caroline pulled up on Destiny, alarmed.

Suddenly they were everywhere—laughing, leering men who clawed at her riding habit and tried to rip her from the saddle. She cried out, kicked and fought and bit in a desperate effort to escape.

They laughed at her.

Up on the hill, she saw her father sitting in his favorite chair. Randall appeared and offered him an apple. He took it and smiled, and as he went to bite into it, a snake came out of Randall's coat pocket and began to slither toward her father.

"Papa!" she screamed, but then the men surrounding her dragged her from her mount and shoved her to the ground, their greedy hands making free with her body. "Papa!" she screamed again, straining to see past the bodies of her abusers.

"Where's your papa now?" one of them sneered. He pointed, and she saw that her father was gone, and Randall now sat in her father's chair.

"Caroline!" Rogan's voice seemed to come from far away.

"Papa," she whispered. "Don't go."

"Caroline, wake up."

She couldn't take her eyes from her father's chair, from her father's murderer. Even when the dark men tore at her clothes, she couldn't look away.

"Save him, Rogan," she wept. "Save him." And then she awoke to find her husband sitting on her bed in his dressing gown. She blinked away the tears that had welled even in sleep. "Rogan?" she croaked, her throat raw.

"Wake up, love. You're safe." He stroked a hand over her cheek, tucked a stray strand of hair behind her ear. Though he smiled, his eyes were shadowed with concern.

"It was a dream." She closed her eyes in relief, but then she remembered and opened them again, anguish flooding her. "No, it wasn't. Randall is trying to kill Papa."

"We're doing everything we can." He scooped her unresisting into his lap and cuddled her close.

Gratefully, she burrowed her face into his strong chest. "I don't know what would have happened to me if you weren't here to hold me," she whispered. "Without Papa, I am alone."

"No, you're not." He stroked a hand over her tattered braid. "You have me. You even have Colin, though he's a troublesome piece of work to be sure."

Her lips curved in a weak smile. "Your Irish is showing, husband."

"That doesn't surprise me a bit."

She turned her head to look up into his face. Those soulful eyes of his held so many emotions, it was hard to sort one from the other. His mouth formed a grim, unsmiling line, but when she reached up to touch his lips with her fingertip, some of the bleakness left his expression.

"What are you about?" he murmured as she slowly traced his lower lip.

"My father wanted you to marry me so you could protect me," she mused in a soft voice, "didn't he?"

He swallowed when she trailed her finger along his chin and down his throat in a slow, lazy pattern that left a trail of tingling sensation in its wake. "That was one of the reasons," he managed to say.

"What else?" She leaned up, pressed her lips against the pulse pounding at the base of his throat. "Besides Destiny and my dowry."

"I wanted to." His hands slid down, closed around her waist. "Caroline—"

"You wanted to marry me?" She shifted in his lap, noted the gradual hardening beneath her. And wasn't afraid.

"Yes, I wanted to marry you." He leaned down and touched his forehead to hers. "Now sit still before I forget I'm supposed to be comforting you."

"Do you think I'm pretty?" She shifted ever so slightly in his lap, watching with satisfaction the hunger that flickered in his eyes.

"I think you're beautiful." He pressed a chaste kiss to her forehead. "You'd best go back to sleep now."

She gave a long-suffering sigh. "Rogan, you're treating me like a child again."

"Believe me, I'm well aware that you're no child."

"I'm not a simpleton, either." She cupped one hand along his cheek. "You want me, Rogan."

"That's no secret." His voice roughened, and he cleared his throat. "Enough playing. Back to bed with you."

"Good God!" she snapped. "You're still talking to me like I'm some schoolroom miss!" She struggled out of his lap and got to her feet, whirling to face him. "Look at me, Rogan." She smoothed her hands down over her body, her thin night rail clinging to every feminine curve. "This is the body of a woman, not a little girl. And this woman wants you."

"You're overwrought," he protested, yet his eyes followed every movement of her hands.

"Of course I'm overwrought! My father is dying, murdered by my cousin." Caroline came closer, cupped his face in her hands. "And if it weren't for you, I'd be all alone in this, vulnerable to Randall's whims. You saved me."

"I don't want your gratitude." He took her wrists and pushed her hands away. "This isn't a game of 'even the score,' Caroline. You don't need to offer yourself to me to reward me for protecting you."

"Reward you?" Furious now, she planted her hands on her hips. "Let me explain something to you, Rogan Hunt. I want you. I. Want. You."

He got to his feet, towering over her with a grim expression on his face. "You learned some disturbing news today, Caroline. This is not a good idea."

"What will it take to convince you?" She slid her hand down his chest and toyed with the knotted sash of his robe. "We're married, Rogan. Don't you think we should act like it?"

His hand covered hers, stilling her fluttering fingers. She met his gaze, not hiding anything, hoping he could read the honest desire in her eyes. Silence stretched on, one heartbeat at a time, until finally he guided her hand to the end of the sash. She tugged. His dressing gown fell open.

Caroline felt only the tiniest tremor of anxiety as she looked at Rogan's bared flesh. He was a beautiful man, his powerfully built chest covered

with a sprinkling of dark hair that arrowed down-
ward along his flat abdomen. She followed that
trail with her eyes, not even hesitating as it led her
to the source of her fear.

He had the muscled thighs of a horseman, she
noted absently as she studied his lower body. But
it was his sex that fascinated her, thrusting boldly
from the nest of dark hair. Even as she watched, it
moved, growing stiffer.

"A man can't hide his desire," she mused. "I
imagine that can be inconvenient sometimes."

"Caroline," Rogan said in a strangled voice.
"That's a hell of a thing to say."

She glanced up at him and flashed him a nervous little smile. "Please hold still, Rogan. I'm
exorcising my ghosts."

She reached out and touched him.

He hissed in a breath, and she snatched back
her hand. "Are you all right?" she asked.

"Yes." His jaw clenched, he nonetheless
attempted a smile. "It feels good, that's all."

"It does?" She gave him a speculative look. "As
good as you made me feel?"

"Almost."

"I see." She reached out again but hesitated a
few inches from her target. "Don't move," she
reminded him.

He met her gaze, need glittering in his eyes. "I
wouldn't move an inch, even if Prinny himself
ordered me to."

She closed her fingers around him. His erection
was hot in her hand, the skin smooth as velvet,

which surprised her. She glanced up at his face.
He was looking down, watching her hand. She
trailed her fingers along the length of him and
was satisfied to see the flare of pleasure that
swept across his features.

The knowledge flooded her senses, embracing
the feminine cravings she had long suppressed.
She stepped closer to him, still stroking him with
her fingers, and laid a hand on his bare chest.

"I want you, Rogan. Not out of gratitude. Not to
win your protection. I want you because I trust
you. You're the only man I have ever wanted to
give myself to willingly."

"Caroline," he choked, stroking a hand over
her hair. "I don't deserve you."

"Ah, but you're saddled with me for life." She
leaned up on her tiptoes and stopped with her
mouth barely touching his. "Shall we not make
the best of it?"

"You will stop me." He cupped a hand around
the back of her head, his gaze deadly serious. "If I
do a single thing that makes you uncomfortable,
you tell me immediately."

"You'll be the first to know," she murmured
with a smile, then closed the distance between
them.

The first kiss started as a slow exploration, as if
they were lovers touching for the first time. But
after only a few moments the heat took over. He
pulled her close with one arm around her waist
and the other still cupping her head. His kiss was

long and deep and terrifyingly intimate, but she opened up to him, gave him what he asked for, closed her eyes and blindly put her trust in him.

Long-suppressed desire raised its head and howled. Passion exploded, flooding both of them with hot demands. Caroline clung to Rogan as her emotions swept her away to a world of hungry mouths and heated touches. His body fascinated her, and she explored it first with her hands, then with her mouth.

The first touch of her lips on his chest made him groan, her shy uncertainty devastating him with its innocence even as it inflamed his need for her. Curious as a kitten, she licked here, touched there, rubbed her nose in his chest hair. His hands clenched around her waist, heart pounding as he let her explore to her heart's content. The slow, leisurely pace drove him mad, his body clamoring for more, for her.

He tangled her long hair in his hands. She slid a glance at him, her dark eyes alight with feminine mysteries, and he tugged her face back to his, kissing her hard as he swept her against him. Her body warmed his, the slide of her nightdress an erotic caress against his naked skin.

He cupped one small breast in his hand, teased the nipple to hardness with his thumb. A quiet mewl escaped her lips. He moved his hand away, thinking she was afraid, but she arched her back, pressing the soft mound into his palm again. He groaned and dipped his head to nip at her neck.

"Make me your wife, Rogan," she panted, trembling with the force of her emotions.

His wife. He wanted nothing more than to bury himself in her welcoming body, to claim her as his. But she was a virgin and had more reason than most to fear what was to come. He needed to be gentle, to ease her into womanhood.

But her small hands sweeping over his body clouded his mind with desire, and her questing fingers over his erection made his eyes practically roll back in his head with pleasure.

"We have to slow down," he mumbled, gliding his mouth down her throat to her shoulder. "I need to be careful."

"No." When he pushed the strap of her night rail down her arm, she helped him by slipping free of the other one. The night dress pooled around her feet, and she stood naked before her husband. "I want to feel everything."

"Caroline," he breathed. Almost reverently, he reached out to touch his fingertip to her burgeoning nipple, then gently pinched it, watching how she gasped, how her eyes slid half closed. He bent forward. "Caroline," he said again, against her flesh, then took the pale pink bud in his mouth.

"Good God, Rogan." Heat flared between her legs, and passion clouded her brain. She clung to him as he suckled first one breast, then the other. By the time he lifted his head, both of them were breathing hard, barely coherent.

He kissed her, hard and fast, silently demanding her complete surrender. She gave it willingly, arching into him as his hand slid along her spine, down the curve of her hip. Then his fingers slid between her legs, parted the moist folds waiting for him. Her knees nearly buckled as he caressed the tiny knot that seemed to be the center of all her pleasurable feelings.

She parted her thighs wider, clung to him. He laid her down on the bed.

She was ready for him. Her musky scent tickled his senses, clung to his fingers. Impatiently he shrugged off the dressing gown. Naked, he knelt on the bed.

As he started to cover her, she slapped both hands against his chest, stopping him. Her eyes held a flicker of fear. "Rogan . . ." she whispered, her cheeks growing the faintest shade of pink. "Please, not like this."

He shifted his weight to the side and stretched out beside her. "Have you changed your mind?" He dropped a kiss at the corner of her mouth, managing to keep his voice steady though his body raged to take her. Here. Now.

"No, I haven't changed my mind, but you can't . . . if you lie there, on top of me—" She stumbled to a halt, too mortified to continue.

"That's all right. There are other ways."

"Are there?" she asked hopefully.

"Certainly." He rolled onto his back, dragging her with him until she sat up, straddling him. "Do you like this better?"

"Hmm." She appeared to ponder the matter, even as she dragged both hands through his chest hair. "Like riding a horse."

"Almost." He slid his hands up her supple thighs to firmly grip her hips. "Now ride *me*, wife."

Color swept her cheeks, but her beautiful doe eyes sparkled with fascination at the idea. She lifted up and balanced with her hands on his stomach, but couldn't quite get the deed done. "Help me, Rogan," she whispered.

Half mad with wanting her, he slipped his hand between her thighs. She was damp, and as he stroked open the petals of feminine flesh, his head spun with the delicious scent of aroused female. Her head fell back as he caressed her, her long hair tickling his thighs. Her eyes slid closed, lips parting on a soundless sigh of pleasure as he pressed his sex to that open heat. It was all he could do not to slide inside, hard and deep.

It was her first time, he reminded himself, trying to ignore the instincts that screamed at him to thrust home. Sweat misted his forehead and his muscles trembled with the effort to hold back. "You do it, love," he rasped. "Take as much time as you need."

Her eyes opened, dark pools of heated desire. He couldn't take his eyes from her face as she began to lower herself onto him, an inch at a time.

She bit her lower lip in concentration, and for some reason the sight of those small white teeth aroused him beyond reason. He shuddered as her body yielded to him, as he slipped deeper and deeper inside that welcoming heat.

When she felt the pressure that signaled the proof of her innocence, she paused, fingers curling into his chest. "Help me," she breathed.

Barely capable of coherent thought, he gripped her hips and with one powerful thrust, tore through that virgin membrane. She gave a cry of alarm, eyes moistening with tears of pain. He froze, buried deep within her quivering body. "That's the worst of it," he murmured, reaching up to swipe a lone tear from her cheek.

She took in a deep, measured breath. The seconds ticked by with agonizing slowness. She shifted slightly, her inner muscles flexing around him. He gave a hiss of pleasure, and she stopped, watching him with unconcealed curiosity. Then she did it again.

"Dear God, Caroline," he choked.

Feminine awareness crept into her eyes. Her lips curved in a tiny smile, and she began to ride him with an unhurried pace that made all coherent thought flee his mind. He clenched his teeth, unable to take his eyes from her as she drove him mad with her sinuous movements. But soon she, too, got caught up in it. Her teasing smile faded, and her dark eyes widened as the delicious torment built. He felt the beginning ripples of her climax around him, and he helped her along with a stroke of his thumb between her thighs. She gave a high, keening cry, stunned pleasure stamped on her face as she went over the edge.

He was right behind her. One stroke, two. He couldn't get deep enough, close enough. Then it ripped through him, and with a hoarse shout, he emptied himself inside her.

She slumped forward, melting over him like molten wax and burying her face in his throat. He raised a trembling hand to stroke her hair as the pleasure continued to wash over them in ever-slowing ripples.

Utterly content, they slipped into sleep.

Banging on the bedroom door woke them hours later.

"Bloody hell," Rogan muttered, shoving aside the covers. He scooped his dressing gown from the floor and thrust his arms into it.

In the bed, Caroline, snuggled deeper into the pillows, her eyes only half open. "What is it?" she asked sleepily.

"It had better be death or fire," Rogan snapped. "Or one of the horses." He jerked open the door. Tallow stood there, his face grave.

It was death.

Chapter 18

Belvingham already felt like a tomb.

Rogan stood near the doorway of the duke's bedroom as Caroline rushed to her father's bedside. Dr. Raines stepped away from the bed as Caroline crouched beside it, taking her father's hand in both of hers. Rogan met the doctor's gaze, and the physician sadly shook his head in answer to the unasked question.

The duke was going to die.

Rogan let out a harsh breath. The duke was a manipulative busybody, but his motives had always been pure. Everything Belvingham had done, he had done to protect Caroline. He would miss the old man, interference notwithstanding.

He looked back at the bed, at his wife staring stricken at her father's pale face, and knew he had to be there for Caroline when the end came.

"He's as comfortable as I can make him," Raines murmured, joining Rogan near the doorway. "I've dosed him with laudanum so at least he won't be in pain."

"Do you have any idea what's killing him?" Rogan asked quietly, not taking his eyes from Caroline.

Raines gave a sigh. "None. His heart isn't good, but that could be the result of whatever illness he's contracted. I wish I could tell you more, but I've never seen the like."

"Poison," Rogan replied softly.

"What . . . are you certain?" the physician whispered back, stunned.

"That's what the duke thought." He looked at the doctor, knowing his own cold fury must clearly show on his face. "Can you find out?"

"I . . . If I am allowed to examine the body, then yes, probably."

"Good." Rogan glanced back at the heartbreaking tableau at the bed.

"Don't you think you should ask me, Hunt?" a voice murmured from behind him. "After all, I will be the authority here should dear Uncle pass on to his reward."

Rogan jerked around to find Althorpe in the doorway. The smaller man's blue eyes glittered with malevolent victory for an instant before he turned a sorrowful gaze on Dr. Raines.

"You must be the physician," he said with the perfect combination of grief and courtesy. "I'm

Randall Althorpe, the duke's cousin. I take it he is not doing well."

Raines shook his head, and Rogan wondered how he would react if he knew he spoke to the duke's killer. "I'm sorry, Mr. Althorpe, but I don't expect him to last the night."

"How terrible," Althorpe murmured. "I'm so glad I happened to be in the area when I heard the news. I might have missed my chance to say good-bye."

"That's right, I believe you paid a call on my wife yesterday," Rogan said, keeping his tone as polite and disinterested as he could manage.

"I did," Althorpe said with the barest of smiles. "My dear cousin seems quite happy in her marriage."

"Quite," Rogan agreed, then turned his attention back to Caroline before he gave in to the temptation to plant the bastard a facer.

"If you'll excuse me, I should like to speak a private word with the duke." With a polite smile, Althorpe pushed past the two men and made his way to Belvingham's bedside.

Caroline looked up as Althorpe approached. For one instant, it was all she could do not to leap to her feet and claw his eyes out for what he had done to her father. She glanced at Rogan, and he gave her an imperceptible shake of his head. No, this was not the time and place to confront her father's killer.

But the right time would come, and Randall would pay.

"Caroline." Althorpe cast a sympathetic glance at the duke. "How is your father?"

"Dying." Even the most basic civility was beyond her now. She clasped her father's hand and turned away from his killer.

"I share in your grief," he murmured.

Liar! She nearly shouted the word, but instead she pressed her trembling lips against her father's hand. That Randall could commit so heinous a crime and then spew polite insincerities nearly made her sick to her stomach.

The duke's eyelids fluttered, then opened slightly. His dark eyes glittered with emotion as he saw Caroline at his bedside. "Daughter," he whispered.

"I'm here, Papa." She bent closer, brushed a kiss to his pale cheek. "Try not to talk."

"Must." His fingers tightened in hers for just an instant.

"I am here, too, Your Grace." Althorpe took a step closer.

Outrage flared in the duke's face. "You . . . no."

"It's all right, Papa," Caroline said, sweeping a soothing hand across his forehead. "Rogan is here."

His eyes flicked to her face. "Rogan?"

"Rogan," Caroline called. "Papa wishes to see you."

Rogan came over to the bedside, jostling Althorpe out of the way. "Pardon me, Althorpe."

Randall's eyes narrowed to slits, but Caroline ignored him. She reached up with her free hand to take Rogan's. Their fingers entwined, and her nerves steadied.

The duke stared up into Rogan's face. "Protect . . . her."

"With my life," Rogan vowed.

The duke looked over at Caroline. His lips parted as if to speak. Then he sucked in a startled breath, eyes widening. And was still.

"Papa?" Even as his fingers fell slack in hers, she refused to believe. She leaned closer, hysteria mounting to choke her. "Papa?"

"He's gone, love." Rogan crouched beside her and turned her face to his. "He's gone."

"No." Tears streamed down her face. She glanced over at her father's pale, still form. "His eyes are open. He's looking at me."

"Allow me." Althorpe stepped closer, reaching for the duke.

Caroline surged to her feet and slapped his hand away. "Don't you touch him," she snarled.

Althorpe's hand clenched, and his expression hardened, then cleared. "You are distraught, cousin."

"She is," Rogan agreed, standing. "Perhaps we should all leave the room and let Dr. Raines care for His Grace now."

The physician came forward. "Lady Caroline, will you allow me to tend to your father?"

Beyond rational speech, she could only nod. Rogan gathered her close and escorted her to the door as the doctor went to the duke's bedside and gently closed his eyes. Althorpe lingered.

"Your Grace," Dr. Raines said, startling every-one in the room. Caroline and Rogan froze in the doorway. They looked back at the doctor; he was looking at Althorpe. "Would you be so kind as to step outside so that I might tend to things here?"

Even Randall looked taken aback by his new title. Then a small smile curved his lips. "Of course, Doctor."

Caroline began to sob in earnest, undone by this final proof that her father really was dead.

Caroline passed the next few days in a fog. At night she lay in Rogan's arms, sometimes taking comfort from his mere presence, and other times she turned to him in the night, searching for the hot passion that would make the pain fade away for a little while.

Her father's funeral took place on a damp, cloudy day. The gray sky and moist chill in the air suited her mood as she watched her father's coffin interred in the family plot. Rogan held her hand, the warmth of his flesh her only connection to the world around her.

Althorpe, now the new Duke of Belvingham, was of course present at all the functions attached to her father's death. His sober face fooled the local gentry who came to pay their respects, but it didn't fool Caroline. She knew what he was, what he had done. And deep inside her, couched in grief, anger burned. And a hunger for vengeance.

The will was to be read at Belvingham by Mr. Tenloft, the duke's man of affairs these past twenty years. The slim, balding man expressed his sincere sympathies as Rogan assisted Caroline into a chair. On the other side of the room, Althorpe lounged, his watchful blue eyes missing nothing. Her father's secretary, Gregson, was also present. Apparently the new duke had elected to keep the services of the eager young man. The housekeeper, cook, and butler all stood at the back of the room.

Mr. Tenloft sat behind the duke's desk and donned his spectacles to read the will. It began with the usual monetary gifts to the servants and charities. Cook began to sob into her apron when it was revealed that the old duke had left her enough money that she could retire if she wanted.

"To my secretary, Malcolm Gregson," Mr. Tenloft continued, "I leave the sum of five thousand pounds, that he might marry his lady and provide for her in the event the next duke chooses not to retain his services."

Gregson's mouth fell open in shock. "But . . . that's a fortune!"

Althorpe glanced at him. "A welcome windfall, though I have already decided to retain Mr. Gregson as my secretary."

"To my daughter, Lady Caroline Hunt, I leave the rest of my personal wealth, totaling approximately three hundred and twenty-five thousand pounds—"

"What!" Althorpe leaped to his feet. "What nonsense is this, Mr. Tenloft?"

The solicitor peered over his glasses at Althorpe. "It is no nonsense, Your Grace."

"But three hundred and twenty-five thousand pounds? That's practically the entire financial value of the estate!"

"Indeed." Tenloft's mouth tightened, and he looked at Caroline. "Lady Caroline, while your father's titles and estates pass to your cousin with the entailment, you should know that the duke's personal wealth was not part of that entailment." He turned back to Althorpe, who had opened his mouth to speak. "This three hundred and twenty-five thousand pounds is the personal wealth of the former Duke of Belvingham, and as such it can be distributed to his discretion. In this case, he chose to leave it to his only surviving child. Or, rather, her husband, as the law dictates that he will have control of the funds."

"Impossible!" Althorpe glared at Rogan. "How am I to run these estates without adequate finances?"

"The lands draw a modest income that will serve to provide for their care and maintenance," Tenloft said. "If you are frugal, that is."

"Frugal!"

The solicitor straightened the papers before him. "This concludes the reading of the will."

"It concludes nothing!" Althorpe glared at Caroline and Rogan. "This matter is not finished."

"It is," Tenloft said, meeting Althorpe's gaze without flinching. "This will is completely legal and has been witnessed and filed in the appropriate manner. You will not be able to overturn it, Your Grace."

"We'll see about that." With a sneer, Althorpe stormed from the room.

"Did you know about this?" Caroline glanced at Rogan in her mirror as she sat at her vanity table, brushing her hair.

Clad in his dressing gown, Rogan closed the connecting door behind him. "Yes, your father told me."

"So my inheritance was yet another reason to wed me."

"No. I originally refused his offer."

"Indeed?" She set her brush down, her gaze never leaving his reflection. "Then how is it I am your wife?"

"Do you really want to talk about this now?"

"Actually, I do." She turned in her chair and regarded him. "Why did you marry me, Rogan? I know it was my father's doing, but you don't strike me as a man who is easily intimidated."

"I had no intention of marrying anyone. I didn't want to let anyone that close to me. You know why."

"Isabel," she mused. "And your rages."

He took a step closer to her. "I wanted you the minute I first met you. But you had been so hurt already, and I didn't want to put you in danger. Besides, how could a second son ever hope to win the daughter of a powerful duke?"

"So you didn't marry me for a horse. You married me for three hundred and twenty-five thousand pounds."

"I married you because I wanted you."

She rolled her eyes, cynicism drowning out the constant throb of grief. "Rogan, please. We've always been truthful with one another."

"I'm being truthful." He took her by the shoulders, yanked her out of the chair. "Caroline, I've always wanted you. Damn it, woman, I fell in love with you."

"What?" She goggled at him, so stunned by his confession that she nearly forgot to breathe.

"I love you," he repeated, stroking a hand through her hair. "I didn't want to, fought it even. But it happened anyway. I can no more stop loving you than I can stop breathing."

"Heavens," she whispered. Her heart warmed and expanded, practically bursting from her chest. She couldn't stop staring at him. "You love me."

"I will protect you," he vowed. "From villains, from Althorpe, even from myself."

"I don't need protecting from you," she said, her insides melting like hot butter. "But my cousin . . ." Anger and grief twisted her features, hitched her breath. "We cannot let him get away with this."

"I know." Rogan cupped her face and kissed her. "But there's more about your cousin that you do not know."

"What?" She pulled back from him, searched his face. "I thought we no longer kept secrets from each other."

"Come sit down." He tugged her toward the bed, but she dug in her heels.

"No, you sit down if you need to, Rogan. I want to hear what you have to say." She folded her arms. "I keep telling you I'm not some meek little miss."

"No, but you're not as brave as you think you are, either."

"Just tell me what you know. I'm tired of secrets."

Rogan sighed, and she watched the indecision play over his face. Finally he said, "Your father believed that Althorpe was responsible for the death of your brother. And for your kidnapping."

"What?" Though she had expected bad news, his revelations still shocked her. "Randall killed my brother? And he . . . Good Lord." She lifted a trembling hand to her mouth. "Good Lord, he did that to me. Hired those men. Monster," she choked out.

"I suspect he's been trying to clear his way to the title and the Belvingham wealth for some time now. Killing your brother so he could become the heir, kidnapping you for money. Your father found out about it."

"So he killed Papa."

"Yes, he did." Rogan gathered her close as her eyes grew damp with tears. "But your father saw to it that he didn't get what he wanted. He didn't get the money, and he didn't get you."

"But he's the duke now." She clenched her hands in Rogan's robe. "I want him to pay for what he's done, Rogan. I know you've been working on it."

"I hired Gabriel Archer to assist me. If there's

anything shady about Althorpe, Archer will uncover it."

"Let me help." She looked up into his face, her big dark eyes pleading. "We can trap him, Rogan."

He scowled. "Absolutely not. I won't have you in danger."

"I can't just sit here and do nothing! According to you, Randall killed my father and brother *and* put me through the most hellish experience of my life. I need to help see him brought to justice."

"I can't risk you."

"You'll be there to protect me, but I must help."

"No." He pressed a soft kiss to her lips, his eyes deadly serious. "I love you, Caroline. Don't ask that of me."

"I love you, too." She nearly laughed out loud at the surprised pleasure that washed over his face. "Silly man. Did you think I could trust someone as much as I trust you, give myself the way I gave myself to you, and not love you? You saved me from a life of fear, Rogan."

"You saved me from a life of loneliness."

"You've given me hope." With a tremulous smile, she traced a finger down the front of his robe, tenderness welling up in her despite the bitterness of the truths that had been spoken tonight. "We have each other, Rogan. No one can take that from us."

He caught his breath as her fingers dipped inside his robe. "No one," he agreed, and led her to bed.

Chapter 19

Caroline was going through the account ledgers when Malcolm Gregson came to call. She smiled with genuine welcome when she found him at the front door. "Mr. Gregson, good afternoon."

"Lady Caroline." He lingered in the doorway, his hat in his hands. "Pray forgive me for intruding on your grief. I only intend to stay a minute. His Grace has sent me on an errand."

Caroline winced at hearing the title, knowing it was no longer her father's. "That's quite all right, Gregson. Do come in."

The secretary glanced around. "Your husband is not at home?"

"He's outside in the stables." She stepped aside so that he might enter, then closed the door. "Did you have business with him?"

"Not exactly. My business is really with you."

"Come into the parlor, and we can discuss it."

"No," Gregson said, stopping her in her tracks. "I really do only have a moment. Please allow me to address this matter here and now."

When a long moment passed and the young man said nothing, Caroline prompted, "What is it, Mr. Gregson?"

The skinny secretary pulled a length of ribbon out of his pocket, and stared at it for several seconds. Then he shoved it back into his coat, stiffened his spine, and met her gaze. "Lady Caroline, I wish to return the five thousand pounds your father left me."

"What? Gregson, don't be silly."

"I don't deserve the duke's generosity. Not after I betrayed his daughter." His jaw worked with emotion. "I told Mr. Althorpe—I mean, His Grace—that your marriage was not yet . . . er . . . legal."

"I beg your pardon?"

Gregson flinched at her icy tone. "I overheard your conversation with your husband in the garden that day. That you and he hadn't . . ."

Caroline's face heated. "Sir, that is a private matter!"

"I know. But Mr. Althorpe—I mean His Grace—he found out something about me I didn't want your father to know. And he threatened to tell him if I didn't do what he said."

Caroline's blood froze in her veins. "What exactly did my cousin ask you to do, Mr. Gregson?"

"Just to tell him things, pass him secrets." He looked down at his shoes. "I lied to your father about my background, Lady Caroline. He thought I was from a fine family with a good education. But my father was a fisherman, and I learned everything I know on my own, from books."

Caroline's lips thinned. "My father would not have cared about such trivialities."

Gregson's eyes widened in earnest. "But he would have cared that I had lied to him. And then he would have dismissed me, and I would not be able to marry my dear Edwina." He took the ribbon from his pocket and looked down at it. "But neither could I marry Edwina with funds that I did not earn."

His true remorse touched her. "Gregson, did my cousin ask you to do anything else, give you anything for my father?"

He frowned in puzzlement. "No, nothing. Just asked me to pass on information."

"And did you tell him anything else?"

Gregson shrugged. "Sometimes he asked questions about the workings of the house. Sometimes about the family. But now that the will's been read, His Grace is flying into the boughs about how he was cheated of his rightful inheritance, raging about how he's going to get it back. I don't think he's right, of course, but as his secretary I must do his bidding." He pulled an envelope from inside his coat. "I am to deliver this to Mr. Tenloft. It is a letter claiming His Grace—your father—was not in his right mind when he wed you to Mr. Hunt. And since the marriage hasn't been . . . well, completed, so to speak, he plans to annul your marriage and take control of your fortune."

"Then he is doomed to failure," Rogan said from the doorway. He strolled into the house and bent to kiss Caroline on the lips. "My wife and I are quite legally married."

She smiled up into his eyes. "Quite."

Gregson's shoulders sagged. "I'm glad to hear it. I didn't want to cause trouble."

"You were afraid," Caroline said. Rogan's expression darkened, and he opened his mouth to say something, but she laid her hand on his arm, silencing him. "Please do keep the funds, Mr. Gregson. Despite what you did, you were a loyal employee to my father for several years, and I do believe he would want you to have it."

"Thank you, Lady Caroline." Gregson bowed, his face the picture of relief. "I'm glad my foolishness will have no dire consequences. And I would like you to know that I intend to resign my post immediately."

"Gregson, no!"

"I must, Lady Caroline. I cannot remain after the way I betrayed your father."

"Oh, Gregson," she whispered sadly.

"Before you speak to the duke," Rogan suggested, "might I suggest you deliver your letter first? This way Althorpe will find out through legal means that our marriage cannot be annulled, and you will not be implicated for coming to us with the truth."

"An excellent suggestion. I will do that, Mr. Hunt." Gregson bowed to Caroline. "Lady Caroline, it has been an honor to serve your family. I will miss you." He nodded at Rogan. "Mr. Hunt."

"Gregson." Rogan nodded right back. "Good luck."

"Thank you. Good day." Gregson donned his hat and then slipped at the front door.

Caroline glanced at her husband. "That was well done of you, husband. I thought you would have torn the lad to bits."

Rogan shrugged. "I've been practicing self-control. Besides, it will be more fun to watch Althorpe squirm when he realizes this tactic will not work."

"You are truly a clever man."

Days later, Randall Althorpe, Duke of Belvingham, crumpled up the letter from the solicitor and threw it into the fire. Then he grabbed a small figurine from his desk and threw it in as well. It smashed in the hearth, sending sparks flying.

"Damn it," he muttered.

There was only one thing to do now. In order to regain what was rightfully his, he had to get rid of Rogan Hunt.

And any other loose ends that might bring about his downfall.

* * *

Rogan was unfastening his trousers when his wife burst into his bedchamber.

"Rogan, I found it!" She clutched one of the account books to her chest, her eyes wide with excitement.

Rogan raised a brow and glanced down at his half-fastened trousers. "I didn't realize it was lost."

She jerked to a halt, wisps of hair clinging to her flushed cheeks. Her mouth fell open. "You . . . I . . . That's not what I meant, you wicked man!"

He burst out laughing, something he hadn't done in a long time. "The look on your face was priceless!"

A blush burned her cheeks. "You're a devil, Rogan Hunt."

"I'm sorry, love." He came to her and pressed a kiss to her forehead. "What did you want to show me?"

Her piqued expression cleared, and her face once more grew animated. "When we first went over the accounts, you told me that you had lost some funds. Well, I found them."

"What? Where?"

"It was a mathematical mistake. See? That number for the purchase of the feed is not an eight but a three. You thought that money lost, but it's right here." Eagerly she flipped the pages of the book, showing him this column of numbers and that one, chattering an explanation all the while.

Watching her, Rogan felt his heart tighten in his chest. She looked so excited, so thrilled to be able to help him. He loved her more than he ever thought possible, and he had never expected to feel this way again.

She glanced up and caught him staring. "What's the matter?"

"You are my heart," he said simply and touched her cheek.

Her face softened. "And you're mine."

He slid his hand behind her neck and pulled her into his kiss, tenderness all but choking him. She leaned into his body, and the book fell to the floor with a thud as she wrapped her arms around his waist. He lifted his mouth from hers. "You dropped your book."

"So I did," she murmured, not taking her eyes from his face.

He rested his forehead against hers, closed his eyes, and took a deep breath. Her scent enveloped him and made his heart lighter. "Thank you for fixing that for me. My accounts are in much better shape since you took over the ledgers."

Caroline beamed up at him. "I'm happy to help."

"Are you?" He kicked the book aside.

"Rogan! That book is the key to your business, you know."

"Never mind that." With a wicked gleam in his eye, Rogan pulled her into his arms. "Has it escaped your attention, wife, that I was in the middle of undressing when you burst into my chamber?"

She cast her glance over him. "My goodness, indeed it has." She tugged on the tail of the untucked shirt, her fingers inches away from where his trousers were unfastened.

"That was quite rude of you." He watched her face, fascinated by the flickers of curiosity and hunger in her expression. "I believe you owe me an apology."

She slid him a seductive glance. "I'm sorry, Rogan."

"Not good enough." He shook his head in mock disappointment. "I must demand restitution."

"Tell me what I can do," she breathed and stroked whisper-light fingers along his waist.

He arched a brow at her even as his body responded enthusiastically to her touch. "You're a forward chit, Madam Wife."

"You've made one of me."

"And a good thing." He curved his hand around her neck. "Kiss me, minx."

She stood on her toes to reach his mouth, pressing her small, feminine body against his. He dragged her closer with a hand on her bottom, the kiss leaping from playfulness to hot desire in the space of a second. She moaned in the back of her throat, meeting him mouth to mouth, tongue to tongue.

Passion flared, and she gave herself into his hands.

His fingers plucked at the fastenings of her dress as she shoved greedy hands up under his shirt and stroked his back. He buried his face in her throat, nipping and sucking on the tender flesh as she clung to him, knees weak. He stripped the dress down her arms, trailing his mouth down over the smooth slopes of her breasts above her chemise. The dress fell forgotten to the floor.

Caroline's eyes slid closed, and she clung to him, trying to stay upright. How was it he could so easily melt away her every defense? He took one step backward, then another, edging her toward the bed. She went willingly, unafraid.

Rogan had given her this, freedom from the fear. He'd taught her to be a woman, to trust him. To love him.

He pushed the straps to her chemise down her arms, and she helped him strip the fragile garment from her body. His eyes darkened as he gazed at her.

She reached out and tugged at the shirt. He helped her strip it off him, and she eagerly tangled her fingers in the hair on his chest as he took her mouth in a hard kiss.

He tipped her back onto the bed, parting her thighs to cup her moist heat. She shuddered and reached for him, running her hands along his muscular arms as his fingers stroked her to readiness.

Then her hands fell limply to her sides as her head spun and she surrendered to the demanding desire that swept through her. He bent forward to take her nipple in his mouth, sucking strongly as his fingers continued to torment her. She gripped the coverlet with white-knuckled hands, lifting her hips into his touch.

"Please," she whispered, clinging to the only English word that still made sense to her.

"Please what, love?" he murmured against her flesh.

With a soft cry of need, she arched her hips even more as his thumb found a particularly sensitive spot. "Please."

"What do you want?" He pulled back to watch her face as she began to writhe. "Tell me."

"You," she managed, grabbing his trouser leg. "Just you."

He left her to strip off his trousers, and she gave a whimper of protest. But then he was back, edging the blunt head of his erection against her aching flesh. "I'm here, love."

He scooped her knees over his elbows and leaned on the bed, opening her and pushing inside in the same smooth movement. She moaned as he filled her, deeper than ever before.

"That's right, love," he whispered, closing his eyes as her feminine flesh embraced him in welcome. He began to move, slowly at first, her legs still hooked over his elbows.

"Rogan," she moaned, tilting back her head as arousal swept through her. "Please, please, please—"

"I've got you," he murmured, losing himself in the delicious heat of her. "Come with me."

"Yes-s-s-s," she whispered, giving herself up to the pleasure of having him inside her.

Words faded. Hands clung, and lips moved in silent supplication as the need grew hotter and hungrier by the second. She thought she would die if he didn't go deeper, harder, faster. Then he did. Somehow he did. The spark grew, burst into an inferno. She tightened her inner muscles around him, keening her pleasure with abandon.

As she melted around him in climax, he slowed and bent to kiss her lips. "I love you," he murmured.

She nodded, beyond speaking, her body still vibrating with the power of their coupling.

"Hold on to me," he murmured, then suddenly thrust in earnest, wildly, eyes shut tightly and face taut with hunger.

She gasped, clung to his arms as he worked toward his pleasure. Then he groaned, expression twisted as if in pain as the peak of his release tore through him.

He remained poised there, muscles straining. Then he slumped over her, sweaty and sated. She ran her hands over his damp back and smiled, feeling every inch a woman. Then suddenly it struck her.

"Rogan!" She nudged his shoulder. "Do you realize I'm lying here beneath you, and there's no sign of panic?"

He muttered a sound of assent.

She poked him harder. "Rogan!"

"No more ghosts," he murmured sleepily.

"Yes," she whispered with wonder. "No more ghosts."

Much later they moved beneath the covers of his bed and fell into deep, satisfied slumber.

Shouting woke them from a sound sleep. Befuddled from sleep, Caroline struggled to make sense of the sudden chaos even as Rogan jumped from the bed and grabbed his trousers.

Then the jumbled shouting from outside sharpened into one, coherent word. "Fire!"

The screams of panicked horses split the night amid the cacophony of urgent human voices. Rogan grabbed his shirt and thrust his arms into it, his face grim, then shoved his feet into the nearest pair of boots. "The stable's on fire."

"Dear God!" Caroline thrust aside the blankets.

"Stay here," Rogan commanded, heading for the door.

"But—"

"I don't want you hurt." With a last look of warning, he slammed out of the room.

Caroline stared at the closed door. "I don't want you hurt, either," she murmured. Then she went to her room to dress.

Rogan raced for the stables. Fire blazed, lighting up the night, and smoke curled into the sky. A shadow followed by a horse ran out of the burning building. Grafton.

"How many left?" Rogan shouted.

"Five!" Grafton called back, racing away from the blaze with the spooked animal.

Rogan charged into the burning building, bracing his arm over his mouth to keep from inhaling the smoke. He saw Destiny, her ears rolling back and forth as she pranced in panic. He pushed toward her stall.

His foot hit something; he stumbled. He looked down and saw Colin crumpled on the floor.

"Hell of a night to get drunk," he muttered, bending over his brother. "Colin, get up, you lazy sot."

His brother didn't answer, didn't move. He clapped a hand on Colin's shoulder and shook. His brother's head lolled, and it was then he noticed the lump near his temple.

Someone had coshed him over the head and left him to burn in the stables. The fire had been set deliberately, Rogan had no doubt about it.

A simple stable fire had turned into attempted murder.

"Colin!" He grabbed Colin's limp arm, dragged it around his shoulders. "Colin, can you hear me?"

Nothing.

Cursing beneath his breath, he got to his feet and started dragging his unconscious brother toward the door, the screams of the trapped horses stabbing him like a thousand swords.

Tallow appeared in the doorway, raced for a nearby stall to release the animal locked in it. Rogan left him to it, dragging his brother out into the cool night air.

"Rogan, what happened?" Caroline came running up, her hair tumbling loose around her shoulders.

"I told you to stay inside," he growled. "But since you're here, see to Colin while I get the horses."

Caroline fell to her knees beside her brother-in-law while Rogan raced back into the stables.

Hours later Rogan stood looking at the charred ruins of what had once been very fine stables. They had managed to get all the horses out unscathed, but the buildings were a loss. Only the simple miracle that Grafton had been coming back from a late night at the tavern and sounded the alarm had prevented him from losing everything; the horses alone were worth a fortune.

Not to mention his brother's life.

Caroline came up beside him and laid a hand on his arm, silent as she looked at the smoldering ruins of his dreams.

"How's Colin?" he asked quietly.

"Dr. Raines says he'll be fine as long as he stays in bed for a couple of days." She buried her face in his arm. "Had he been trapped in there, he would have died."

He slipped an arm around her shoulders. "I know."

She turned distressed eyes to his. "He regained consciousness for a few moments and insisted on talking. He said that whoever hit him called him by *your* name."

Rogan's jaw clenched. "The bastard."

Caroline jerked back in surprise. "Colin?"

"No. Your cousin."

She opened her mouth as if to protest his conclusion, then slowly closed it. "Of course," she
said. "If something happens to you, he can get to
me."

"And your fortune." He squeezed her to him in
a one-armed hug. "That's all he's ever wanted,
Caroline, was money."

"The things he has done to get it are uncon-
scionable." She gazed out over the destruction.
"He must be stopped, Rogan."

"Don't worry." He dropped a kiss at her temple
and stared out into the smoking night. "He will
be."

Chapter 20

Malcolm Gregson gathered his courage around him. The knowledge he possessed sickened him, as did his part in recent events. Reaching into his pocket, he clenched his fingers around the tiny vial, then dropped it, appalled at his own thoughts.

How could he contemplate such an action? But contemplate it he had, enough that he had purchased the instrument of his potential damnation. Did he now have the courage to use it and right the wrong he had helped to perpetrate?

Perhaps.

But not today. Cursing his own cowardice, he knocked briskly on the door to the duke's study and entered when bid.

The new Duke of Belvingham sat behind his

desk, papers strewn before him. He glanced up. "What is it, Gregson?"

Gregson resisted the urge to reach again for the vial in his pocket. "Good morning, Your Grace."

"Get to the point." Althorpe held up a paper and squinted at it.

"I am giving my notice, Your Grace."

Althorpe looked up with a start, then slowly lowered the paper he had been reading. "I don't believe I heard you aright."

Gregson winced at the menace underlying the lazy tone. He glanced at the cup of coffee at the duke's elbow, then jerked his gaze back to his face. "I am giving my notice."

Althorpe leaned forward. "And why would you contemplate such a thing?"

"I—I—" Gregson swallowed hard.

"You heard what Hunt said to the good doctor," Althorpe finished with a penetrating stare. "Didn't you? Come, admit it. I saw you standing outside the room."

Malcolm contemplated lying, then opted for truth. "Yes."

"And do you suspect I am the guilty party?"

"I choose not to take sides."

"Yet you tender your resignation."

Gregson shifted nervously. "I thought it best."

Althorpe stood. "Have a care, Mr. Gregson. You yourself played a part in this."

Gregson's face flushed. "To my everlasting shame."

Althorpe laughed. "Little did you know. Come,

Mr. Gregson. Did you not bring Uncle his pipe in the evenings?"

"Of course I did."

"Then 'twas you who administered the herb that made dear Uncle so ill." Althorpe laid a hand over his heart, his face a mockery of grief. "Every time dear Uncle smoked that pipe, he took a step closer to St. Peter."

Gregson gaped. "I've never heard of such a thing!"

" 'Tis a rare Chinese herb that is deadly when smoked." Althorpe chuckled. "Have no fear, Mr. Gregson. I've burned the rest of the tainted tobacco. No one will ever know."

"*I* will know!"

"But *you* brought him the pipe every night." Amusement plain on his face, Althorpe reached for one of the discarded papers. "Accept it, Mr. Gregson. You killed the Duke of Belvingham."

"No," Gregson whispered, horrified.

"And that is what I shall say—grief-stricken, of course—should you attempt to tell anyone the truth. And who will they believe, a mere secretary who lied about his background? Or the Duke of Belvingham?"

His heart sank as he realized he was trapped. Once more he thought about that vial in his pocket. Once more he resisted the temptation.

"No more talk of giving notice," Althorpe said. "Even if you did somehow escape England, my informants will track you down. Now be a good fellow and fetch me more coffee, will you?"

And as Gregson turned to obey, he thought longingly of justice.

Caroline sat in the study with the accounts spread across the desk. Carefully she tallied up a long column of numbers, then sighed at the total. The fire had done tremendous damage, and would cost a pretty penny to fix.

Thank God for her inheritance.

She looked up as Rogan entered the room, his expression sober, his every step weary. "Were you able to salvage anything?"

"We got most of the saddles, some of the tack." He sank into a chair, fatigue slowing his movements. "We're going to have to replace everything else, right down to the last lead rope. Damn it!" He pounded a fist on the arm of the chair.

She rose and came to him, laying a hand on his shoulder. "At least we have my inheritance."

"Our one stroke of luck." He reached up and covered her hand with his. "I'm sorry. I didn't mean that the way it sounded. Like it was lucky that your father died."

"I know what you meant." With her free hand, she toyed with the ends of his hair.

"How's Colin?" he asked.

"Dr. Raines has confined him to bed with a concussion. I checked on him about a half hour ago, and he was sound asleep."

"Good." He leaned his head back into her touch, closed his eyes. "I was afraid he might be seriously injured."

"He'll be fine. But what about you? Have you eaten? The sun's gone down, and I don't recall seeing you come in for luncheon."

"I didn't. There was too much work." He tugged her hand from his shoulder to his lips. "And now that you've reminded me, my stomach is about to revolt."

"Mrs. Cox left a cold platter for you."

"Anything sounds good right now."

"Then let me go, and I'll fetch it."

His lips quirked. "I don't want to. I rather like you here with me." He pressed another kiss to her palm.

"You have to eat, Rogan."

"Are you mothering me, love?" He grinned up at her, a spark of mischief lighting his otherwise dispirited eyes.

"I'm just taking care of you. Isn't that what a wife is supposed to do?"

"It is," he agreed, then startled her by tugging on her arm so she tumbled into his lap. He chuckled at her squeal of surprise. "Perhaps you can take care of me from there."

"You're a madman," she declared, laughing, and tried to rise.

"No, you don't." He pulled her back into his arms. "Why don't you sit here and tell me how your day went."

She gave him an arch look. "I helped Mrs. Cox plan the week's menus, cleaned out the spare bedroom, and went through your correspondence. I also worked on the accounts for a while."

"Quite a busy day. Perhaps we both need to relax."

"I need to fetch your dinner." She squirmed in his lap, trying to wiggle free.

A new spark entered his eyes, one she recognized well. "Or perhaps we need to play."

"Rogan, you must be starving!"

"I am," he said with a leer and buried his face in her neck.

She giggled. "You know I'm ticklish there!"

His muffled "I know" was all she got in the way of response. Then he started kissing beneath her ear, and the air left her lungs in a rush. "Rogan," she breathed, her eyes sliding closed with pleasure.

"Yes, love," he murmured and drew her into a sweet, searching kiss.

She forgot about the fire, forgot about the account books, forgot about Rogan's dinner. Her hands slid around his neck as if drawn there, and she clung to him, drowning in the delight of his hands and mouth.

He murmured soft compliments in her ear as his hands swept over her body, lingering on her curves, teasing the sensitive spots he had come to know so well.

She arched into his touch, and when he slid a hand up her leg, under her skirt, she moaned.

With a wicked smile, he pulled the pins from her hair, letting the beautiful dark mass tumble around her shoulders. He gazed into her eyes, and his grin slowly faded to be replaced by a more serious expression. Tenderly he swept a stray curl behind her ear. "Caroline, I could lose everything I have tomorrow, as long as I still have you."

"Oh, Rogan." This time *she* kissed *him*, so overcome with emotion that she didn't have the words to express it.

He clasped her to him and eased them down onto the floor. Caroline found herself on top of him as he leaned against the base of the chair, his hair mussed from her passionate fingers, his hollow-eyed face lit by a bright, loving smile. He pulled her to him, kissed her again with her hair falling down around them in a silken curtain.

He plucked at the fastenings of her dress. She gasped when she realized his intention and pulled back, uncertain. "Rogan, we're in the study!"

"No one's here. Grafton and Tallow have turned in for the night, my pesky brother is confined to bed, and Mrs. Cox has gone home." He buried his face in the hollow of her throat, sending a quiver of delight through her body. "We're all alone."

"But—"

"I need you, love." He pulled back so she could see his face. Hunger and melancholy warred in his beautiful gray eyes. "I *need* you."

She cupped his face. "Oh, Rogan."

"Don't deny me, love."

"No." She shook her head, kissed his lips. "Oh, no."

He took over the kiss, deepening it. Caroline gave herself over to his hands, tugging at his clothing even as he pushed hers aside. He took her nipple in his mouth, and she tangled her fingers in the hair on his chest. Urgency swept through her, built as passion coursed through her veins. His hands and mouth were everywhere, driving her higher. When he slipped his fingers inside her, she dug her nails into his shoulders and threw her head back with a deep, throaty moan.

That sound seemed to snap his patience. He jerked open his trousers, positioned her over him, and pulled her down, sinking into her warm, willing flesh.

She quivered with pleasure, finding the rhythm with the encouragement of his hands on her hips. He grew more demanding, and she rode hell-for-leather, matching his deep thrusts with her own movements. He slipped his hand between them, stroked her most sensitive spot, and in moments she was clenching around him with a loud moan, her body shuddering as the climax ripped through her.

"Yes, yes, yes," he groaned, then buried his face in her shoulder and thrust hard and fast, his own hoarse cry echoing hers as he found his own release.

She slumped across him, and they sat there for long moments, hearts pounding in tandem, his shaking hands stroking her perspiring back.

Then his stomach growled, loud and long.

Caroline giggled, and he joined her, his laughter muffled against her throat. "I think I'm still hungry," he said.

"I can't see how that could possibly be," she purred, which set them both chuckling again.

"I need to eat," he said finally, raising his head. His eyes looked clear and bright, the shadows from before completely banished. "And afterward, I want you to take a ride with me."

She glanced at the night-darkened window. "At this hour?"

"I enjoy riding at night." He playfully patted her bottom. "And so do you, apparently."

She blushed beet-red, her mouth opening and closing but no words escaping. Finally she swatted his shoulder. "Wicked man!"

"I am," he admitted. "But I still want to ride with you in the moonlight, love." He swept her back in a lazy caress. "Please."

She couldn't refuse him anything when he looked at her like that. "All right," she agreed, and leaned forward to kiss him.

They galloped over the moonlit fields like a couple of children on holiday. Caroline rode Destiny, the only other horse who could possibly keep up with Hephaestus. She and Rogan alternately raced each other and galloped in tandem, both of them laughing and throwing teasing taunts back and forth.

They were just heading back to their home

when a shot rang out through the night, followed by a woman's scream.

Rogan glanced at Caroline, clearly concerned, but then more shouting ensued, and with a look of grim determination, he turned his horse in the direction of the fracas. Caroline pounded right behind him.

They discovered the source of the ruckus very close to their own home. A coach was stopped in the middle of the moonlit road, where two ruffians had apparently stopped it. One was unfastening the horses, and the other held a pistol pointed at a man and a woman. As they drew closer, Caroline recognized the man as Malcolm Gregson.

Rogan thundered down on the man with the pistol. The fellow looked up at the sound, but before he could aim the weapon at this new threat, Rogan kicked it out of his hand and sent it skidding beneath the coach. Gregson dived after it, as did the other villain.

Rogan pulled up on Hephaestus and dismounted. He grabbed the second brigand, who had scrambled beneath the coach, by the back of his coat and flung him aside, allowing Malcolm to grab the pistol.

Some yards away, Caroline sat frozen in fear, the tableau before her reminding her too forcibly of her own recent attempted kidnapping. Now, as then, Rogan engaged one highwayman in a fist-fight, punches flying and bones crunching. The other miscreant made his way toward the petite blond woman who stood petrified near the coach.

"Stay away from her!" Gregson cried, pointing the pistol at him.

The villain lunged, grabbing the girl. She cried out as he swung her in front of him as a shield. "Go ahead and shoot," the brigand taunted.

Gregson didn't waver, but his young face revealed his indecision.

It was the despairing whimper of the girl that galvanized Caroline. She kicked Destiny into a gallop and charged the fellow holding the girl.

She had only a moment to enjoy the highwayman's look of astonishment before she raised her riding crop and brought it down on his face with all her strength.

The fellow howled and released the girl, who darted behind Gregson. The young man curved one protective arm behind him as if to shelter her, the other hand holding the pistol steady on the cursing, injured villain.

Caroline pulled up on Destiny and surveyed the scene. Rogan had subdued the other highwayman and even now dragged him over to stand with his bleeding cohort. He took the pistol from Gregson, pointing it at the two criminals. Dismounting, Caroline hurried over to her husband.

He glared at her as she came to his side. "What the bloody hell did you think you were doing?"

She jutted her chin at him. "Helping."

"You could have been killed."

"So could you."

"I want you safe."

"I want you safe, too."

"Damn it to hell, woman!" Rogan raked his hand through his hair, bleeding knuckles and all, yet kept the pistol aimed steadily at the highwaymen.

"Stop cursing, Rogan. There's a lady present," Caroline said mildly, then walked over to Gregson. "Is everyone all right?"

Gregson nodded. "Thank you—both of you—for saving us."

"What happened?" Caroline asked.

"This is my fiancée, Miss Edwina Price," Gregson said, tugging the pretty blond girl forward. "I've resigned my position with His Grace and told Edwina the truth." He smiled down at her. "She's agreed to come with me to America and be my wife."

"How lovely. It's nice to meet you, Miss Price."

"This is Lady Caroline, Edwina. And that is Mr. Rogan Hunt."

"Oh! We were coming to see you," Edwina said.

"To say good-bye," Malcolm added. "Then this happened." His young face hardened. "I have my suspicions as to what this is all about. I can't help but notice that the coachman ran off at the first sign of trouble."

"Quite the coincidence," Rogan said. "Let's get these two to the magistrate, and we'll go back to our home and discuss the matter."

"Miss Price could no doubt use a cup of tea," Caroline said with a smile.

The girl nodded. "Oh, yes. And may I say, Lady Caroline, that you were incredibly brave just now, the way you attacked that highwayman. I wish I were as courageous as you are."

"Thank you," Caroline murmured, stunned at the unexpected compliment. She glanced at Rogan, who gave her a proud grin.

"Foolish," he said, "but courageous. Well done, love."

By the time the magistrate had been summoned to collect the two highwaymen, it was well past midnight. Mr. Docket took the two men into custody, though both insisted they had been hired by a man they couldn't identify, whose name they didn't know.

Caroline came down the stairs from readying the guest room as Rogan closed the door behind the magistrate and his prisoners.

"Althorpe," Rogan said, coming to meet her at the bottom. "I'd stake my life on it, yet as usual, there are no clues left to follow."

"He's clever," Caroline agreed, walking down the last few steps. "Blast him."

Rogan chuckled and slipped an arm around her shoulders, walking her back toward the parlor. "Now, love, is that any way to talk in front of our guests? You'll shock Miss Price."

"They couldn't hear me out here anyway."

They entered the parlor, where Gregson and his

fiancée sat sipping tea and recovering from their ordeal. Gregson got to his feet when Caroline entered the room. Miss Price hovered over her tea, clearly rattled.

"I've made up the guest room for Miss Price," Caroline said. "Unfortunately, Mr. Gregson, you will have to make do with the butler's pantry. My brother-in-law is injured and is taking up our last spare room."

"Luckily," Rogan interjected, "we have no butler."

"We're grateful for any assistance you can provide," Gregson said. "I cannot thank you enough for your assistance."

"Given the circumstances," Rogan said, "I believe your idea of starting anew in America is a good one. You should be safe there."

"And in America, a man is judged for his abilities and not his pedigree," Miss Price added. "My Malcolm will do well there."

"Edwina's father wasn't happy when he learned the truth about me," Malcolm said. "He wanted Edwina to break the engagement. But she loves me."

"I refused," Miss Price said with a vehement nod of her head. "I love Malcolm, and that's that."

"She gave up everything for me." Malcolm cast his fiancée a look of pure adoration. "So we're headed to Scotland first, to get married. Then on to America."

"I wish you both much happiness," Caroline said.

"Thank you," Gregson replied. He turned his attention to Rogan. "Mr. Hunt, I could not help but notice that our hired driver abandoned his hack at the exact moment the brigands arrived. I suspect this was a carefully planned robbery, no doubt designed to result in our deaths."

"I suspect you are correct, Gregson."

"And I believe His Grace is behind it." Malcolm looked at Caroline. "He recently told me how he poisoned your father, Lady Caroline, and I am disgusted at my part in his plan. I hope that some-day you can forgive me."

"Althorpe admitted that he poisoned the duke?" Rogan asked. "That doesn't seem like him."

"But we can't prove it," Caroline whispered, grief grabbing her unexpectedly.

"He's a horrible man," Edwina said. "And now he's tried to hurt my Malcolm."

Gregson laid a hand on her shoulder. "And you, pet. He's tried to hurt you, and for that I will never forgive him."

"It's late," Caroline said, clearing her throat of the sorrow that choked her. "Let's all retire and think on this some more tomorrow."

"You can take our coach to Scotland in the morning," Rogan said. "And I promise you, our driver will not abandon you."

"Thank you," Malcolm said, gratitude heavy in his voice.

"Rogan will show you to your room, Mr. Gregson," Caroline said. "Come with me, Miss Price, and I will get you settled."

As Miss Price said a fervent good night to her fiancé, Rogan touched Caroline's hand. "Are you all right?" he murmured.

She nodded, the grief slowly receding. "I'll be fine."

"I'll help you."

She smiled up at him, moved by the concern in his eyes. "I know."

Chapter 21

Rogan woke slowly to sunlight in his eyes and a persistent thumping. After a moment of confusion, he realized someone was knocking on the door.

"Come," he called, sitting up in bed. He ran his hands over his face as Grafton stuck his head into the room.

"Visitor for you," he said. "Fellow by the name of Archer."

"Archer? What's he doing here?" He raked his fingers through his hair. "Put him in my study. I'll be right down."

Grafton nodded and disappeared.

Rogan cast a glance to the other side of the bed where Caroline still slumbered. His lips curved, and he couldn't resist brushing a kiss on her cheek.

"Mmmmm." She shifted, turned toward him. Her eyes drifted open. "Good morning."

"Good morning, love."

"Is it morning?"

"It is, but you don't have to get up. Go back to sleep." He threw back the covers and sat up.

"Don't go," she mumbled and laid a hand on his bare back.

He smiled down at her, wanting nothing more than to climb between the covers again. "I must go, love. Mr. Archer awaits downstairs."

"Archer?" She stretched lazily, and then her eyes popped wide open as his words apparently sank in. "Gabriel Archer the investigator?"

"The same." Rogan stood and walked to the basin atop his bureau. He poured water from the pitcher and splashed some on his face.

"Do you think he discovered something about Randall?" Caroline sat up, clutching the sheet around her. "Do you think we can actually have him arrested for Papa's murder?"

Rogan wiped his damp face with a towel. "I don't know if that will ever happen, love. We have no proof of that."

"But we *know* he did it." She scrambled to her knees, her eyes fierce.

"What we know and what we can prove are two different things." He came to her and cupped her face in both hands. "We may never be able to prove he killed your father, Caroline, but Archer must have found something, else he wouldn't be here. Chances are we can have Althorpe arrested for some other crime he has committed, perhaps even for some other murder."

"I hate that." She rubbed her cheek against his palm. "I want him to pay for what he did to Papa."

"I do, too. But we have to be realistic."

"Very well," she said with a sigh. "As long as he is imprisoned for *something*. Let's go see what Mr. Archer has to say." She scooted to get off the bed.

"You don't have to come," Rogan said as she got to her feet. "What he has to say might be disturbing."

"I want to come. I owe it to Papa to see this man brought to justice." Dragging the sheet behind her, she headed for her own room to dress.

Gabriel Archer looked more like a devil than an investigator. Known as the Avenging Angel, he was tall and lean with a long-boned face. Dark eyes glittered with shrewd intelligence over sharp cheekbones, and his wide mouth seemed more inclined to sneer than smile. He dressed in an elegant, subtle, and tasteful style, his clothing clearly the work of London's most talented and expensive tailors. As Rogan and Caroline entered the room, Archer turned his gaze away from the portrait of a Hunt ancestor that hung above the mantel.

"Good morning, Lady Caroline," he said, sketching an elegant bow.

"Mr. Archer," she said with a nod.

Archer held out a hand to Rogan. "And to you, Mr. Hunt. I'm Gabriel Archer."

"Archer," Rogan acknowledged with a brief shake of the hand. "What brings you here?"

"His Grace, the Duke of Belvingham." Archer produced some papers from inside his coat. "I've found the proof you need to send him to the gallows."

Caroline hurried to peer over Rogan's shoulder as he unfolded the papers.

"I can hardly credit it," Rogan said, scanning the documents. "A witness to Stephen Ware's murder?"

"My goodness," Caroline whispered. Her stomach knotted, and she turned away to seek a chair. "He really did kill Stephen, then."

"I'm afraid so," Archer replied, his voice compassionate. "I'm sorry you had to find out about it like this."

Rogan swiftly knelt beside her chair and placed a hand over the one she pressed to her queasy stomach. "Are you all right, Caroline? Can you listen to the rest?"

She squeezed his hand and nodded, afraid to speak lest she embarrass herself.

"All right." He stood and faced Archer. "If there is a witness, where has this fellow been hiding?"

"The 'fellow' is the daughter of Lord Brackenridge, now Lady Krenton. She was something of a bluestocking and had taken to hiding in trees to read her books. She was up in the branches when Althorpe killed young Stephen."

"Why didn't she say anything?"

"She was afraid of scandal. Althorpe didn't know about her, and she liked it that way. But now that she's married to old Krenton, she's decided to clear her conscience."

"How fortuitous." Rogan raised his brows at Archer. "I don't suppose anyone persuaded her to do such a thing."

A small, knowing smile touched Archer's lips. "Perhaps."

"I know Lady Krenton," Caroline said quietly. "She grew up in this parish. She's an honest woman."

"This is enough to start an inquiry," Rogan mused. "Certainly enough to bring to the magistrate."

Archer's face grew serious. "Keep in mind that the new duke is not only a killer but a powerful man. He may well have the magistrate under his control."

"Then we'll find another. We have the bastard," Rogan said with a vengeful grin. "He may never pay for murdering Belvingham, but he can certainly be brought to justice for doing away with Belvingham's heir." He turned to Caroline. "Will that do, love? Is it enough to see him brought to justice for Stephen's death?"

"It will have to be enough," she replied. She closed her eyes as grief welled up. For Papa. For Stephen.

"I will see to it those papers get into the right hands," Archer said, reaching for them.

"I'd like to go with you," Rogan said. "I want to be there when they arrest the bastard."

"I want to go, too," Caroline said, standing.

"No, love." Rogan came to her and smoothed his hands down her arms. "I don't want you any-where near Althorpe."

"I want to see him pay for what he's done," she insisted, her voice breaking with anguish. Tears welled, and she swiped them away. "Please let me come."

"Look at you, love." Rogan pulled her into his embrace while Archer pretended sudden interest in the paintings. "You're still distraught over your father's death, and who could blame you? You need to stay here and see to our guests. Let me handle this."

"I would like to come." All three of them glanced at the door where Malcolm stood. "If His Grace is about to have justice served to him, I would like to be there to see it."

"What about Scotland?" Rogan asked.

"My fiancée will understand. Maybe I can help. I can certainly tell the magistrate what I know."

Archer stepped forward. "What do you know?"

"Nothing incriminating, unfortunately," Rogan said. "I'm sorry, Gregson, but spying on the duke's household is hardly a crime that will put Althorpe in prison."

"But this is." Archer held up the papers.

"Yes," Rogan agreed. "Come along if you want, Gregson. Caroline is going to stay here and watch over Miss Price, right, love?"

Reluctantly she nodded. "Just promise me we can attend his trial," she said, her voice raspy from unshed tears. "No matter where it is or when. Promise me."

"I promise." He kissed her forehead, then looked into her eyes. "You will stay here and be safe, agreed?"

She nodded. "Agreed."

"Very well. Let's go, gentlemen."

Archer tucked the papers away. "We'll stop for the magistrate on the way."

The men had been gone for an hour when the messenger arrived.

A lad of fourteen or so stood panting at the door, his horse lathered and exhausted nearby. "I'm looking for Mr. Archer," he told Caroline when she opened the door.

"He's not here right now."

"I've got an urgent . . . message for him." The boy sucked in a breath, his face red from hours of hard riding.

"I know where to find him."

"Where is he?" The young man sagged against the doorjamb, pulled a folded, sealed paper from his pocket. "I need to . . . get this . . . to him. Urgent."

"You look too exhausted to ride anywhere else, young man. Why don't you take a few minutes and have some lemonade before you go after Mr. Archer?"

"Can't. Have to . . ." The boy's eyes rolled backward in his head, and he collapsed in a heap on the doorstep.

"Young man, are you all right?" Caroline bent down and shook the boy, but he was out cold. A breeze blew the letter from his lax fingers, and she snatched it before it could get swept away.

An urgent message for Gabriel Archer, a messenger unconscious at her feet, and a horse so exhausted it could barely stand. None of this boded well.

"Grafton!" she shouted, racing toward the ruins of the stables. "I need your help!"

The haughty butler, Kerns, opened the door upon their knock. "Good afternoon, gentlemen." His gaze fell on Malcolm. "I am instructed not to allow you in the house, Mr. Gregson."

Docket stepped forward. "You had best let him in, because he's with me, and I need to have a few words with His Grace."

"I see." Kerns didn't betray his feelings by so much as the flicker of an eyelash, but he did step backward and open the door wide. "Do come in."

Kerns left them cooling their heels in a drawing room while he went in search of his employer.

"Remember," Docket said. "No accusations. If we make one mistake here, it could ruin everything."

"I agree," said Archer. "Let Mr. Docket do the talking."

The butler returned. "His Grace is taking breakfast on the terrace. Please follow me."

The new Duke of Belvingham lounged on the terrace, eating a splendid morning repast. Upon seeing his visitors, he smiled. "Good morning, gentlemen. To what do I owe the pleasure?" Then his gaze fell on Gregson. "What the devil are you doing here, you traitor?"

Gregson stiffened but said nothing.

"I would like to have a word with you, Your Grace," Docket said. "And Mr. Gregson is here at my invitation."

"Is that so?"

"Your Grace, I would like to question you about certain matters that occurred some years ago in which you may have had some involvement."

"Well, that's specific enough." Althorpe grinned.

"You won't be laughing for long," Rogan said.

Randall clasped a hand over his heart in mock fear. "Dear me. What's the matter, Hunt, trouble on your little farm?"

Rogan narrowed his eyes. "Would you like to say anything about that?" He clenched his fists at his sides, so tempted to simply pummel the truth from the murdering weasel. But unchecked rage would get him nowhere, and they needed to make certain they had Randall cold. He was too adept at slipping out of the noose.

"I would simply like to express my sincere condolences on the loss of your stables," Althorpe said. "Such a setback for a fledgling business like yours."

"Yes." He bared his teeth in a smile. "Good thing I married an heiress."

Althorpe's face hardened.

"Your Grace," Docket said. "If I might direct your attention to my inquiry."

"And which inquiry would this be?" Althorpe lifted his coffee cup and sipped at the steaming black liquid.

"The inquiry into the death of Stephen Ware."

"Death?" Althorpe set his cup down with a clink. "Am I to understand that you suspect me of having something to do with my young cousin's death?"

"It's merely an inquiry brought about by some new evidence."

"What new evidence?"

"A witness," Rogan said.

"Indeed?" Althorpe smiled, and dread knotted in the pit of Rogan's stomach.

"Lady Caroline Hunt," Kerns announced.

The men were all clearly taken aback as Caroline came out onto the terrace. Only Althorpe seemed unsurprised to see her, though he stood out of courtesy.

Rogan came over and took his wife's arm. "What are you doing here?" he muttered.

"A messenger brought this urgent letter for Mr. Archer," she said, producing the missive. "The poor boy collapsed in trying to deliver it, so I thought I should bring it right over."

"It didn't occur to you to send Grafton or Tallow?"

"Actually, no." She turned away from her husband's scowl and presented the letter to Gabriel. "Here you are, Mr. Archer."

"You just wanted to see what was going on," Rogan murmured.

She flashed him a quelling look and watched Archer open the letter.

"While Mr. Archer opens his post, might we continue with the inquiry?" Docket said.

"Yes, let's." Althorpe folded his arms and regarded them with a smug smile.

A sudden crash diverted everyone's attention. Gregson looked back at them with reddened cheeks, Althorpe's coffee cup shattered on the stone floor of the terrace. "Forgive me, Your Grace," he begged.

"You dolt! I'm glad you resigned. Saves me the trouble of sacking you."

"Apologies, Your Grace. Allow me to fetch you another cup of coffee."

"Fine." Althorpe waved a dismissive hand at his former employee and turned back to Docket, supercilious smile in place. "You were saying, Mr. Docket?"

"I was saying that I would like to proceed with the investigation. Now—"

"There will be no investigation," Archer said softly.

"What?" Docket spun to face the investigator. "Mr. Archer, you assured me—"

"There will be no investigation." Archer held Althorpe's gaze. "Lady Krenton is dead. A hunting accident."

"Dead!" Rogan glared at Althorpe, who placidly took the cup of coffee from Gregson. "Rather convenient."

"Such distressing news," Althorpe said with a smirk, then sipped his coffee.

Docket cleared his throat and straightened his jacket. "Well, then. Sorry to have bothered you, Your Grace."

Althorpe nodded his head graciously. "Misunderstandings occur."

"This is more than a misunderstanding," Caroline exclaimed. She met Althorpe's smug gaze as he continued to sip his coffee. "Do you really think you can get away with something like this?"

"Get away with what?" Althorpe's expression was pure innocence.

"What you did to my father and brother. What you did to me."

"Dear girl." Althorpe cast a meaningful glance at the others before draining his coffee cup. "Clearly your ordeal has left your mind addled. If she were my wife, Hunt, I would see her safely ensconced in an institution so she doesn't hurt herself or others."

"Luckily she's not your wife," Rogan growled. Rage simmered through him, but not the uncontrollable, killing rage he had so long feared. This was clean, and it was cold. But he knew if he got his hands on Althorpe, he would kill the bastard.

Caroline marched over to her cousin and glared at him. Then she slapped him across the face.

"Someday your sins will catch up with you, Randall."

Randall's eyes narrowed. "Be very careful, my girl."

Rogan stepped forward. "Don't even think about threatening my wife, Althorpe."

"Threatening her? She just struck me!" He turned to Docket. "Did you not see that, Mr. Docket?"

"Lady Caroline is clearly overwrought," the magistrate replied.

"Oh. I see how the wind blows." Althorpe blinked in confusion, swayed. His coffee cup crashed to the ground. "This is a conspiracy."

"Hardly," Docket spluttered.

"What have you done to me?" Althorpe grabbed Caroline by the arms, shook her. "What have you done to me?"

"Release my wife, Althorpe!" Rogan started forward, but Randall swung Caroline in front of him with an arm around her throat. Rogan froze.

"Try and rescue her, Hunt. I'll snap her neck like a twig."

"Your Grace, what are you doing?" Docket asked, trying to placate a man who was clearly becoming unhinged. "Are you well?"

"They've done something to me," Althorpe hissed. "They're conspiring against me! Arrest them!"

"I can't arrest them, Your Grace."

Rogan clenched his hands, wishing he could wrap his hands around Randall's throat and

choke the life from him. "If you hurt her, I'll kill
you, Althorpe."

"That's Lord Belvingham to you, Hunt." Randall took another step backward, hauling Caroline with him. "And any move you make against
me will result in your wife's untimely death."

"Don't try anything stupid," Archer warned.

"Your Grace, if you would simply release Lady
Caroline—" Docket began.

"And then what would happen? No, I think the
lady will come with me. She's the best chance I
have of actually escaping your devious plan." He
took another step backward.

Rogan stepped forward. "Stay where you are."

Archer inched along the wall, trying to get
around to Randall's left. Randall spotted him and
jerked Caroline back another step, toward the
railing. "I don't think you want to do that, Mr.
Archer."

Archer froze. Rogan seized the moment to step
forward as Docket slipped around to Randall's
right.

Randall glanced from one man to the other.
"Keep moving, gentlemen, and Lady Caroline
dies."

The three men stopped.

"You can't escape," Docket said again.

"I am the Duke of Belvingham. I can do anything I want." Randall grinned at them, and the
gleam of insanity in his eyes made the blood chill
in Rogan's veins. He backed up against the railing of the terrace, then sat Caroline on the edge of

the balustrade. His arm around her waist was all that kept her from falling.

"Stop!" Rogan barked, flinging out an arm to hold back Archer. He gazed at his wife, at the fear in her eyes. "Don't move, any of you."

"Do you have a man in the garden?" Randall taunted Docket. "Are your men even now prowling through the hedge maze down below? Somehow I don't think so." He hauled Caroline closer, glanced over the edge of the railing. "I believe I can manage to land safely on those hedges there. Of course if I don't, Lady Caroline will break my fall."

Rogan stepped forward. "Randall, don't."

Randall's eyes narrowed. "I believe the proper form of address is 'Your Grace,' Hunt. Have you no respect for your betters?"

Rogan pushed back the rage that urged him to leap forward. "Your Grace," he choked out, realizing finally that Randall was not quite sane. "Please don't harm my wife."

"How the mighty have fallen," Randall chuckled. "Now I suggest you and Mr. Docket and Mr. Archer step back. We wouldn't want me to accidentally let Lady Caroline fall."

Rogan glanced at the other two men and waved them back. Docket fell back obediently, but Archer held his gaze for a long moment before following suit. Rogan looked back at Randall. "There. Now release my wife."

"I don't know," Randall mused with a taunting grin. "I—" He gasped suddenly, his eyes bugging.

He glanced at Caroline, then at the men around him. His face grew very, very red. His entire body began to shake.

Rogan surged forward, but not in time.

And he watched in horror as Randall's eyes rolled back in his head, and both he and Caroline tipped over the edge of the railing, her scream of terror ripping through his heart as she vanished from sight.

Chapter 22

Rogan paced outside Caroline's bedroom, glancing up every few moments in hopes that the door would open. But it remained firmly closed. Gregson leaned against the wall nearby, quiet and subdued.

"Still no word?" Colin came down the hall, concern etched on his face.

"No." Rogan cast yet another frustrated glance at the door. "What could be taking so long?"

"Easy, brother." Colin squeezed Rogan's shoulder in a surprising gesture of solidarity. "She's alive, that's what matters."

"Which is more than I can say for Althorpe." Rogan turned away from the firmly closed door, images of that morning's horror still fresh in his brain. "I nearly died myself when Caroline went over that railing."

"It was horrible," Gregson whispered.

Colin glanced at the secretary. "What's with him?"

"I don't know. He's been like that since it happened." With barely a glance at the young man, Rogan began his pacing again.

Colin leaned against the wall and folded his arms. "It's a good thing she landed in that hedge."

"It broke the fall," Rogan agreed, "but she's still unconscious."

"Have some faith," Colin said. "If she had fallen a few inches to the left, she would have landed on the stone path like Althorpe. Is it true he went completely mad?"

"I don't know what happened," Rogan said. "He started spewing nonsense like a bedlamite, then collapsed as if he'd contracted apoplexy."

"Maybe it was something he ate," Gregson said.

Rogan and Colin both looked at the pale young man. "What are you talking about?" Rogan asked.

"Maybe His Grace ate something that didn't agree with him." The young man shrugged. "Or drank something."

The implication hit Rogan like a blow to the chest. "You put something in his coffee."

"He deserved it," Gregson whispered. "After what he did to His Grace."

Rogan narrowed his eyes at Malcolm. "You poisoned him, and now my wife might die."

"I didn't mean for that to happen," the young man explained, anguish in his eyes. "I used something that would affect him quickly, but I had intended for it to happen after we left."

Rogan clenched his fists, the urge to *hit* something almost more than he could bear.

"He was trying to right a wrong," Colin said softly. "He made the wrong choice, but his heart was in the right place."

"I'm sorry," Gregson said, his voice hoarse. "I'll never forgive myself if something happens to Lady Caroline."

"If something does happen to her," Rogan said tightly, "you had best run farther than America."

He closed his eyes and turned away from the guilt-ridden young man, the events of the morning replaying themselves in his head. When he and Archer and Docket had come upon Althorpe's broken body, Randall's skull crushed like ripe fruit, his heart had very nearly failed him. He'd caught sight of Caroline's skirt in the hedge nearby, and he'd all but torn the shrubbery to bits to get to her.

She'd lain so still, looked so pale. He'd been certain she was dead.

It was Docket who'd pulled him away when he would have crushed her in his arms. It was Archer who'd checked for her pulse and said the words that brought Rogan's world back into alignment with a snap. "She's alive."

Relief had flooded him, stealing the strength from his limbs. He'd sat on the ground, cradling his wife in loving arms while Docket summoned some servants and set about cleaning up the mess that had once been Randall Althorpe. Through it all Gregson had watched, white-faced, clearly frozen with shock. Archer had sent for the Belvingham carriage and had also dispatched an urgent messenger to Dr. Raines when Rogan insisted on taking her home to her own bed. Dr. Raines had arrived with all haste and banned everyone from the room while he examined Caroline.

And Rogan slowly went mad while he waited to hear if she would live or die.

He looked at his brother, taking comfort in the connection of family. "If anything happens to her . . ." He couldn't finish, the words clogging his throat.

"Don't borrow trouble," Colin advised, just as the door opened.

Dr. Raines smiled at Rogan. "She's awake and asking for you."

Suddenly he could breathe again. In the corner, Gregson made gave a weak moan of relief. "Is she all right?"

"She's bruised, and she's broken her wrist. She also took a nasty blow to the head on the way down, so I'd like her to stay in bed for a day or two. But all in all, she'll be right as rain."

"Thank God." Rogan closed his suddenly stinging eyes. "Can I see her?"

"I just said you could." The doctor moved aside as Rogan charged into the bedroom.

Caroline lay propped up against the pillows in her night rail. She was still pale, and her right wrist was bandaged. But she managed a weak smile when she saw him, and her dark eyes were full of love.

He dropped to his knees beside the bed, clasped her uninjured hand between both of his. "Dear God, Caroline," he rasped and buried his face against their clasped hands.

"Rogan," she whispered, her heart nearly breaking with love as she felt the tear that trickled over their joined hands. "It's all right. I'm all right."

"I nearly lost you."

"You'll never lose me. I love you."

He looked up at her, and the sight of this strong, powerful man with moisture clinging to his eyelashes squeezed her heart. "I love you, Caroline. You've changed my life, made me unafraid to feel again."

"You brought me back to life," she replied. "You taught me to trust and to love and so many other things. I was alone in darkness before you came into my life."

He chuckled. "What a pair we are." He pressed a kiss to hand.

"We're a team," she corrected. She reached out with her bandaged hand and touched his hair. "We'll raise horses and babies together. Create a new Hunt legacy for future generations."

He smiled at her, clearly enjoying her touch. "What did I ever do to deserve a woman like you?"

She smiled. "You rode out of the darkness and saved me."

"No," he corrected with a tender smile. He

gazed at her for a long moment, his heart in his eyes. "You saved me. Thank you, love."

She cupped his face with her bandaged hand, her lips curving in loving gentleness. "You're welcome."